SPARKS

SPARKS

AN ANTHOLOGY OF ELECTRICAL HORROR
COMPILED AND EDITED BY
MATTHEW CASH AND EM DEHANEY

BURDIZZO BOOKS 2017

Copyright Matthew Cash Burdizzo Books 2017
Edited by Matthew Cash, Burdizzo Books
All rights reserved. No part of this book may be reproduced in any form or by any means, except by inclusion of brief quotations in a review, without permission in writing from the publisher. Each author retains copyright of their own individual story.
This book is a work of fiction. The characters and situations in this book are imaginary. No resemblance is intended between these characters and any persons, living, dead, or undead.
This book is sold subject to the condition that it shall not, by way of trade or otherwise, be lent, resold, hired out or otherwise circulated without the publisher's prior consent in any form or binding or cover other than that in which it is published and without similar condition including this condition being imposed on the subsequent purchaser
Published in Great Britain in 2017 by Matthew Cash, Burdizzo Books, Walsall, UK

COMPONENTS

FOREWORD   9

ELECTROPHORUS ELECTRICUS
CALUM CHALMERS   15

IN FOR A SHOCK
PIPPA BAILEY   47

THE RAPE OF IVY HOUSE
EM DEHANEY   71

OFF THE HOOK
BETTY BREEN   89

THE FINAL CHARGE
PETER GERMANY   117

THERE'S NO LIGHTS ON THE CHRISTMAS TREE MOTHER, THEY'RE BURNING BIG LOUIE TONIGHT
MATTHEW CASH   129

KAYLA
LEX H. JONES   145

POWER CUT
CHRISTOPHER LAW   181

I'M YOUR ELECTRIC MAN
DANI BROWN   197

POWER TRIP
DAVID COURT   215

IN LOVING MEMORY
MARK CASSELL   235

WOLPERTINGER
G. H. FINN   251

THE REEL TOO REAL
SAMANTHA HILL   277

THE CONVERSION OF ANDREW CURRANT
C. H. BAUM   283

PURKINJE FIBERS
ASH HARTWELL   305
AUTHOR BIOGRAPHIES   317

FOREWORD

I was very young when I first learned about autism. I was the last sibling born of a branch of five children. I had three sisters who ranged between twenty and twenty-five years my senior. The middle one of the three was autistic and as a child growing up in the eighties she was the only autistic person I knew. Although that's a bit of a lie, back in the day, we did have something called The Special Class. They don't have these anymore thank God, at least not at my kid's school. But I knew from the word go that there was something about Mary (which made us laugh when years later the film came out), that she was special.

I always saw Mary as a child, very limited where the learning process was concerned, but with an adult's body. My brother came along when she was in her late teens and me her early twenties, and as she was used to a mainly female environment, she didn't like the change at all. Violent tantrums, physical attacks and even self-harm were unfortunately common in those early years, before my brother and I grew to be big enough to calm our boisterous essences. They always varied her medications which sometimes made things better, sometimes worse but the bad times are not what I remember about her. I remember her excitement over photographs, random fixations over completely obscure objects such as chimneys, pianos and this little lever that train drivers used a long time ago when you could actually watch the driver drive. She would draw endless detailed sketches of these objects until another took its place. Her artistry was amazing. She would sing along to the radio, to songs that she and our sisters had listened to growing up in the sixties and seventies, filling in the lyrics she didn't know with her own special gibberish language.

Sadly, we all got older and our mother died and father, who was older than our mum by fifteen years, became frail with dementia. My brother heroically put his life on hold and cared for him in his last days whilst I was living a hundred-odd miles away in the West Midlands. Mary was put into sheltered living where she had a wonderful life until they discovered she had multiple sclerosis and she rapidly declined after that. I never had a great relationship with her whilst she was alive. I grew up watching stuff I shouldn't, and I was convinced she was the next Michael Myers. Throwing my brother down the stairs and head first through the front door didn't help to extinguish that. She had the tantrums of a four year old but had the body of a physically fit woman. But we all understood that.

When my son Mortimer, who many of you may have heard about on my Facebook, was queried autistic during his second year my blood froze. This thing from my past had come back to haunt me, my penance for not being patient or understanding enough with my sister, for being embarrassed by not only the fact I had old parents and old siblings but also that one of them was special. It scared me, it still does. But as I now sit beside him, cuddled up on our big leather settee, I know that I love him with all my heart and soul and wouldn't change him for the world. He's one of the most frustrating dudes I've ever had the fortune of knowing but also one of the friendliest, loving little men and I am proud to call him my son. He is now five and although I do see traits of Mary in him, I see a lot more of Mortimer. He has similar random fixations, mostly of the kind children a few years younger than him grow out of, and an obsession for numbers and buttons.

He has come on leaps and bounds over the last year and is currently at a regular primary school working with a teaching assistant. He is awesome and has a lot more manners and love in him than I've seen in a lot of older children.

So autism has always been a part of my life and I have learnt it's a vast and varied spectrum in which I have found one major similarity. Autism is just a variation of normality and no matter how severe one is on that spectrum, once you tune into their wavelength magic happens.

We've all heard terms like "he's got a loose wire" or "wired differently" and to some they can offend but it's generally how I see Mortimer and my own experience with autism. It was with this in mind that I chose the theme for this anthology to be electrical. And with help from my right-hand lady Em Dehaney we are bringing you the very best electronically charged horror and sci-fi stories we could tap into.

So untune your TV so there's just snowy static, and enjoy our little collection. All proceeds will be going to Resources for Autism, a charity that provides practical services for children and adults with an autistic spectrum condition and for those who love and care for them. Thanks for your support.

Matty-Bob

Xxx

In the time that I have got to know Matthew Cash, the one thing that shines through above all else is how much he loves his kids. Being a parent is hard. It is thankless, demanding, the hours are relentless and the pay is terrible. So why do we do it? Because those rewarding moments are worth everything. This is all magnified when you are the parent of a child who is on the autistic spectrum. The battles are tougher, the tantrums are apocalyptic, and the everyday becomes epic. Just a trip to the shops can be an emotionally draining, meticulously planned expedition.

But when you get those moments, those small magic moments, they too are magnified. A smile. A hug. Finding the exact right food at the exact right time. Seeing their face light up when they have their favourite toy back after thinking it was lost.

When Matty-Bob said he wanted to put out an anthology to raise money for autism, it was an instant YES from me. This is a cause so close to his heart and I hope the sales from this book can help to support other kids like Mortimer and other parents like Matty-B.

I want Sparks to be the best Burdizzo charity anthology yet. We have gathered together some Burdizzo Family favourites as well as welcoming some exciting new authors into the fold. They have done us proud, writing shockers, shivers and electric nightmare givers. Add stunning cover art by our in-house designer Matt Hill into the mix and I think we have created something special. We hope you love Sparks as much as we do.

It's electrifying!
Em.

ELECTROPHORUS ELECTRICUS
CALUM CHALMERS

"It's raining..." Blake stretched his arm out into the sheet rainfall, as if to confirm his suspicions

"You sure about that buddy?" Morgan sniped back.

"Fuck you man, I mean it's like proper raining, not just a drizzle." Blake wiped the water from his arm onto his already sweat dampened shirt.

"You do know what monsoon means right?" Edward's voice arose from the rear of the minibus as he struggled to load everyone's luggage. Blake turned towards the voice but quickly became distracted by small dog that was sheltering from the rain.

"And you do know what rabies is?" Morgan snatched back Blake like a toddler before dragging him into a vacant seat.

"Now I want you to sit down like a good little boy and not talk to strangers." Morgan patted Blake's head.

"We're in a foreign country dumbass, everyone's a stranger." Satisfied he had beaten Morgan in a game of wits; Blake shifted to the far side and stared out of the window. With the Brazilian skyline illuminated in neon he quickly zoned out.

"Right, that's the lot. We make a good team you and I." Edward shot a dirty look towards the driver who had spent the whole time propped up against the wall, cigarette in hand.

"A ajuda extra sempre vem com custo extra." The driver flicked his cigarette into a nearby bush before making his way to his seat.

"What he say?" Edward looked back at Morgan who seemed equally confused. "Fuck it, as long as he takes us where we need to go he can say whatever he likes".

Morgan took a quick snap of their minibus before uploading it onto his Facebook page; Watch out Brazil, The Wet Boys are in town.

"Dude, you better not be posting some shit online about 'The Wet Boys'. I've told you before; it is in no way as cool as you think it sounds."

Edward slid the door shut, instantly raising the temperature inside. "This fucking heap better have AC," he complained. As if on cue, the fans erupted with an ice cool breeze.

"We are male right?" Morgan gestured to the group. "And we are scuba divers?" His hand now gesturing over their luggage. "I challenge you to come up with a better name."

"Scuba Bros."

"Divers Who Are Male."

"Scuba Explorers."

"Wet Cave Divers."

"Ricos mergulhadores," the driver added.

"Yeah man, Big Balled Divers!" Blake shouted over the group.

The driver sneered in the mirror.

"So Edward, come on then, what's the big surprise? Why are you so desperate to go diving in Brazil?"

Edward's eyes lit up like a teenage boy getting his first glimpse of a real live boob.

"Ok guys, get this. We are heading down into the Amazon, there's a small village and a tiny tribe with an unpronounceable name. This tribe has been sending people out into the rivers as sacrifices every few years. Well, the village deny any sacrifices are taking place but there's supposed to be a cave filled with skeletons."

Morgan shifted uneasily, the idea of intruding on a place of sacrifice; a place filled with religious importance just didn't sit right with him. He knew Edward was just in it to eyeball a few bones and would treat the site like a theme park.

"But the best part," Edward continued. "Is that the cave doesn't exist out of monsoon season, no one can find it. People have tried in the dry seasons but...nothing!'

"It's probably just really dense jungle out there and when it floods you can float over it all," Morgan interjected.

"Dude! Seriously, just give me this one OK?" Edward looked pained. Holding Morgan's stare he willed him into submission, the silence marking Edward's victory. "Thank you. Right, where was I? Oh yeah, the cave....no one can find it in dry season, only when it's flooded. But!" He held a finger up to mark his exclamation. "When it floods it becomes accessible through diving."

Edward paused as if pre-empting the shocked gasps or maybe even a small applause, when it was evident he was to get neither he begrudgingly continued with far less enthusiasm.

"And yeah, that's why we are here. We're going to find the cave, dive in and, yeah, see some skeletons and stuff."

"I'm in!" barked Blake.

"We are already in Brazil, in a minibus, on the way to the village that houses this mysterious cave. Guess I'll have to be in." Edward either failed to spot Morgan's sarcasm or just chose to ignore it.

"Guys, I promise this will be awesome. So few people even know this cave exists let alone dived to it. You're not going to regret this."

Morgan began to warm to the idea; it would be worth huge bragging points to say that he had done it. Being able to go back home, upload some pictures of this amazing, life defining dive, in a cave that none of the other divers would have even heard of. Yes, this was going to be the dive that would finally put him on the map. The guys from Reckless Diverz would have to pay attention to him now.

By the time Blake awoke the city lights had long disappeared, in fact all signs of civilisation had been replaced with trees and the occasional shack. With one hand picking the grit from his eyes, he blindly rummaged through his rucksack and with a satisfied grunt retrieved a can of energy drink emblazoned with exclamation marks and explosions.

"You still drinking that shit man?"

Edward was stretched out across the back seat, his beard littered with crumbs. Blake paused for a minute, all those crumbs but he couldn't see any evidence of what he had been snacking on.

"I tell you dude, this is like 100% more powerful than what we can get back at home, you can feel it setting fire to your veins."

"That's what I mean, that stuff can't be good for you."

Blake flicked up a finger before knocking back the whole can. A deep and resounding burp confirmation of his accomplishment.

"Your funeral dude." Edward tilted his cap to shield his eyes from the early morning light. Scratching his beard, his fingertips lost in the dark fuzz, he growled like a small bear readying for a nap. "Not far now, may as well wake Morgan so that he can try and kick start his brain before we arrive"

Taking his orders, Blake bounced his empty can off Morgan's head. "Morning sweetheart!"

Morgan hardly reacted as he slowly sat himself upright. "We here?"

"Nearly man, about half an hour out. The rain's died off a bit so hopefully tomorrow's boat ride won't be too bad."

Edward pulled out a notebook from his back pocket. Every trip was issued with a new notebook, containing flight times, taxi numbers, hotel reservations and even local hospitals were carefully detailed throughout. This holiday was different however; there were no reservations, no restaurants, not even local pick-up lines. This time the book was eerily empty, details only of the minibus operator and a crudely drawn map to point at when confronting the locals. "By my estimates we are really close".

Five minutes later the minibus came to a screeching halt.

"You here." The driver pointed to a small village no more than half a mile ahead.

Edward leaned across the seats arching himself to get a clearer view through the windshield. "Right boys, looks like we made it!"

Turning towards the driver he was surprised by how close he had inadvertently got to his face, unperturbed he ordered, "Vamos."

"No, you walk, road…" The driver twisted his hand as if it aided his thinking "…Inundado"

Edward looked back at Morgan silently urging translation.

"What the fuck you looking at me for?"

"You took Spanish at school."

Morgan and the driver scoffed in unison. "Firstly they speak Portuguese in Brazil, secondly I took it for my GCSEs nearly ten years ago, and I failed, badly"

Edward, undefeated, turned back to the driver who was now pointing at the road ahead of them. "Inundado," he repeated. Following the driver's finger, Edward could make out a river now flowing where a road should have been. A small wooden raft was already being launched from the opposite side, the locals clustered on the riverbank.

Morgan had already gathered his rucksack and was making his way out of the minibus; opening the back he began to load himself up for the short walk.

"You're lucky this isn't Uber otherwise I'd be giving you the shittest review right now." The driver flicked a finger behind Edward before lighting up a cigarette.

"Right then gents, each one takes his own gear, I'm not being loaded up with all of your scuba stuff while you walk off with something light." Morgan and Blake, each already carrying their own gear, nodded in agreement before heading off towards the river.

"You ok buddy?" Blake was much more heavily built than Morgan, every weekday evening he could be found either down the gym or undergoing some hideous regime in the name of good health. "I don't mind taking some of your gear if it helps?" Morgan thanked him but being so close there really was no point. In less than a minute they had reached the raft and were mobbed by locals all eager to help them unload.

"Gentlemen! I trust your journey was adequate?"

Before either Blake or Morgan could answer Edward had pushed past and offered an open palm to the young man. "You must be Hugo?"

"That I am good Sir, I am to believe you are Mr Edward?" The young man's accent was thick but he put a lot of effort into his pronunciation.

Morgan sat patiently in the raft, eyeing the lapping water beneath him he longed to climb overboard and swim across. As he ran the cool water through his fingers an elderly man smacked a large stick on the side of the raft startling him.

"Nāo!" The old man's voice was stern and commanding, on his cry a nearby young woman ushered Morgan's hand back onto his lap. They shared a brief and uncomfortable smile before she sat back on the raft, turning back the old man had his eyes fixed sharply on him. "Nāo" he repeated.

"I think he doesn't want you to do something Morgan, what did you do? Did you do something Morgan? Morgan, did you?" Blake was lying in the middle of the raft, a sly grin across his face as he shielded his eyes from the burning sun.

Before he could answer Edward's raised voice cut through the small crowd.

"You have to be fucking kidding me! I told you that is the sole reason we are here, I don't want to fish, I don't want to see the fucking nature and I sure as shit won't be taking no as an answer."

The English-speaking local had both his hands up in an attempt to calm Edward. They both headed to the far end of the raft to finish their conversation. Edward was soon smiling.

"You reckon they don't want us here?" Blake was now leaning on his side to face Morgan. "You think they are hostile to outsiders?"

"Nah mate, if they were hostile they wouldn't have sent this raft over to bring us into their village. My bet is that guy is trying to get more money off of us some way or another. Nah, we're fine, just leave Edward to sort it all out."

The short journey across the river came to a jolting end as the wooden raft moored itself on the bank. Before either of them could stand up, their luggage was carried off into awaiting huts with Edward and his new friend wandering off in a separate direction, still deep in conversation.

"And with that, I'm off to sleep."

Leaving Blake on the raft, Morgan followed his luggage and made his way into his waiting hut. The air was stiff, not a breeze to be felt. Morgan knew he was going to be in for a long night. His luggage had been placed beside a small and notably stained mattress. Tonight, despite the heat, he would be sleeping clothed. He gave the mattress a sturdy kick before placing himself on it. The last thing he wanted was to be tucking up next to some ginormous tarantula.

"We're on our own." Edward stood against the doorframe; he massaged his temples before sliding down to the floor.

"They say that the rain has been heavier than usual and that the waters are becoming more treacherous. Not even a crocodile would brave the cave now." Edward's voice was softer, all the previous bravado drained away.

"I got so excited about the cave I didn't even think about what was in the water. Crocodiles, piranha, fucking big ass snakes. They say that the waters are full of Enguia Morta, that the heavy rainfall and the heat have made it perfect mating season for them. I don't even know what that is but I'm scared of it."

"We don't have to…"

"Of course we have to! I've told everyone what we're doing, we can't back out now." Edward rose to his feet his fingers still pushing on his temples. "We can and we will, they are prepared to give us a boat to head out on but they won't come with us. I paid for someone to come with us and somehow they've managed to get me to pay more to go it alone. FUCK!"

Morgan joined Edward by the door placing a hand on his shoulder. He could feel Edward's shoulders trembling as if he was fighting back tears.

"So we do it. If it was that dangerous, they wouldn't let us go."

"Of course! They had no intention of coming with us; they just made all this bullshit up to get me to pay out more for the boat. What a fucking idiot. And I fell for it.

You're right, we can do this. Hell we could swim to it if we had to."

"Maybe not the whole way, just a quick off the boat and into the cave. Seriously mate, the waters in the Amazon can be pretty treacherous"

"Crocodiles are a problem but if what they say is true, that the crocs don't go near the cave at this time of year, then we have nothing to worry about. Maybe there is too much foliage in the water and they just don't like going that way."

Edward joined Morgan on his mattress; Morgan could now see that he had been crying.

"Snakes don't like water, I read that somewhere I'm sure of it, and Piranha aren't as dangerous as the movies make out. Remember Steve's brother?"

Edward nodded.

"He used to have a shoal of them in his front room; he used to put his hand in all the time. It was only if he starved them that they got aggressive."

"I remember." Edward wiped his nose on his sleeve

What started as a pep talk for Edward was quickly becoming reassurance for Morgan too. He didn't know if he believed one hundred percent in what he was saying but it certainly gave him comfort.

"And these Enguia Morta, I saw a show about these fish that go into your dick and get stuck in there because of little spines. I bet that's what they are talking about."

"Erm...I don't want fish in my dick dude.

Morgan laughed. "Me neither but what I mean is we can plan against them. They only swim up if you get your dick out and piss in the water; they follow the warmth of the stream. All we have to do is keep our dicks under wraps and don't pee in the water"

The pair sniggered. It was brief but enough to ease Edward's mind.

"We can do this bro, we're The Wet..."

"Don't you dare."

Blake stood in the doorway, his hand buried in a pack of crisps before moving at an incredible speed into his waiting mouth. "We're The Big Balled Divers and don't you dare say otherwise. Anyways, these Engigia Moota sound pretty kinky."

The trio laughed, for a split-second Morgan felt like he was back in his parent's sauna, stoned and desperate to sober up. One of them recommended sweating it out but it only made them high and hot.

"Enguia Morta. If you're going to fuck a fish, at least get its name right."

"Ahh your mum never complained when I called her Tony."

Again the group broke into laughter, all fears of man-eating crocs and piranhas forgotten. At least for now.

The rumble of distant thunder broke Morgan from his sleep. They had drunk too much and laughed too hard, passing out on the floor. It was apparent that Morgan's plan to sleep fully clothed was little more than a fuzzy memory. He lay face down on the mattress, one hand still holding an empty bottle of local cachaça, the other tucked into the front of his underpants. Opting to drop the bottle first he scratched his neck, a rash of some sort was spreading down into his armpit. Giving it a quick sniff he hoped it was nothing more than heat rash.

Blake was seated against the furthest wall, fast asleep, a trickle of vomit tiptoeing down his front. Edward was already awake and sitting in the doorway, a faint trail of smoke emerging from the corner of his mouth, his now depleted cigarette hanging listlessly on his lips. Brushing the ash from his beard he stood up and made his way back towards Morgan.

"Now or never bro...." His voice seemed ragged and somewhat distant, like the spirit of a man twice his age and ten times more of a smoker "...the boat is ready and our gear is loaded."

Morgan looked about his hut; everything except from his overnight bag was gone. Somehow, despite their intoxication last night, they had managed to pull their kit together.

"We did all the checks last night dude..." Blake was swiping the tendrils of vomit from his mouth. "You were being a bitch about it and made us double check each other's work."

Grabbing a half-eaten cereal bar Morgan trundled after his friend. Shielding his eyes from the sun he was taken aback to how well his body was adjusting to this early morning start. Blake wasn't far behind; he had already downed a can of his energy drink and was quickly polishing off a second.

Morgan could see their contact Hugo with his feet resting on the side of the boat. He looked smug, insanely smug. It was at that point Morgan knew Edward was right; this whole thing was a scam to extort more money from rich white kids. There was no plan to take them out, fuck, there was probably no cave. They were going to spend the rest of the day bobbing about in the rain whilst these inbred fuckwits planned how to snare their next victim.

Morgan wanted to slap the guy, and he would have if he wasn't so sure that that slap would result in them all being beaten and fed to the crocodiles.

"Caiman…" Blake was now standing to Morgan's side funnelling Oreos into his mouth.

"What?"

"There are no crocodiles in the Amazon. Black Caiman rule these waters. They are a cousin to the alligator but they certainly aren't crocodiles."

"How did you? I didn't say…"

"You look terrified mate, reasoned it was because of the Caiman that are undoubtedly in the water. Why else do you reckon the villagers are all living in the centre of this…village…is it a village?"

Morgan looked about. Blake was right; all the inhabited huts were in the centre. Those about the shoreline seemed dilapidated and vacant. He shook the idea of 8ft reptiles bursting from the water and tearing through someone's home.

"You thought I was scared, so to comfort me you correct what I assumed were crocodiles to in fact be caiman. And then you point out that the villagers are scared of the water because of the caiman. Way to reassure me, dude."

Blake finished making a six filled Oreo sandwich before waving it in front of Morgan's face.

"Education my friend, know thy enemy."

"Morgan, stop fucking about and let's go!" Edward shouted.

Hugo meanwhile was quietly scurrying off, money firmly wedged in his pockets. The snake had retreated to his hole, no doubt already planning to fleece the next gap year idiot with too much money that comes along.

The boat wasn't the best in the world, it probably wasn't even the best in the village, but the water stayed on the outside, and to be honest what more do you need from a boat? Faint blue paint flakes peeled from the sides. Morgan couldn't quite make out if the colour was deliberate or whether it was a darker colour now lightened through years out in the sun or a lighter colour darkened by years of abuse.

As the boat gently rocked, it was clear Edward was unnerved. A slight ripple to his side and he was instantly tightening his grip on the oar, knuckles white with tension. Blake was pretty relaxed; a little too relaxed in some instances. Morgan would have to repeatedly remind him to keep his hands inside the boat; a few times he had caught him running his hand through the waters. It was only a matter of time until Edward caught him at it, then it was a pretty sure thing that he would break down completely.

"Should be about an hour downstream." Edward's eyes were fixed fast on the river ahead. "Hugo said it's opposite a beach"

"Nice! We can get a bit of a tan on." Blake's excitement made it difficult for Morgan to discern whether he was joking or not. Knowing Blake he was probably a little bit serious.

"No...No, I think it would be best if we stayed in the boat until we reach the cave. We can get in the water then but for now let's stay in the boat."

"Yes Captain," said Blake, signing off with a salute.

Something splashed on the opposite bank, causing Edward to leap up from his seat, nearly dropping his oars. The short distinctive splash soon exploded into something more. Water shot skywards as whatever was underneath fought for its survival.

Morgan could see the fear in his companion's eyes

"Guys it's OK, this is nature. Remember when we saw that brown bear take down a deer in Alaska? You didn't worry then and we don't need to worry now."

Blake chuckled to himself.

"And what the fuck do you think is so funny?" Edward pointed, childlike, at the accused.

"That deer, the bear ate its arse first. He literally ate out the deer's arse."

Morgan stifled a laugh. Edward was clearly upset and right now he felt laughter may not be the best medicine. The splashing had subsided and with it the threat seemed to dwindle. Silently, Edward continued to row.

Out of sight, the last few bubbles broke the surface. The rigid body of an oversized caiman emerged, its eyes washed white. Whatever fought the caiman had won.

Three hours later they laid eyes on the beach. Morgan assumed finding it took so long because Hugo lied about the distance, but a little something in the back of his mind blamed Blake. His constant distractions meant Edward did the majority of the rowing.

"OK fellas, listen up, the beach is just over there. Hugo said the cave is directly opposite. Despite the trees there is a stream noticeably cutting through them."

Sure enough the stream opposite the beach stood out amongst the deep jungle, wide enough to fit their boat. Just. Edward instructed Morgan to act as guide; he repeated the need to keep the boat away from any debris five times. Morgan tutted louder each time.

"OK, dude. I get it."

Breaking through the sunken trees Morgan snapped a few arty shots, tilting his camera and arching his back to make sure he got the ultimate picture of what was effectively branches in a river.

"Hey Morgan, when you're done making out with Instagram filters you reckon you could at least GUIDE THE FUCKING BOAT SO THAT WE DON'T FUCKING SINK!"

Morgan knew better than to answer back when Edward became this flustered. Using a broken branch he pushed against a tree, forcing the boat through an easier path. He wasn't about to make matters worse with Edward. He was afraid but would never admit it.

"Hugo said to watch out for some shitty totems that we should still be able to see the tops of. He said something about fish and snakes."

"Wow, really? Thousands of years of heritage whittled down to 'something about fish and snakes'."

Morgan was about to educate him in how the local tribes would use totems as connections to the spirit world but was cut short by a sickening thump. The boat rocked heavily before a large splash silenced their bickering.

"You fucking idiot! You broke it!" Blake pointed to a large wooden pole protruding from the waters. The totem which would have easily reached 15-foot ground to top now sat a few feet shorter as some sort of fish head drifted into the treetops.

"Shit, that can't be a good thing, can it?" Morgan tried in vain to hook the emblem with his stick yet only succeeded in pushing it deeper into the undergrowth.

"Don't worry about it, no one will know and if they do find out we will be long out of the country before then.

Besides, if that's the totem then the cave will only be a few more metres ahead of us." Commanding the situation, Edward pushed on forcing the boat towards their destination.

A red rock face erupted from the water, towering above their heads the obstruction finalising their journey. Morgan held his camera in anticipation. This deep into the trees there should have been plenty of life, lizards, birds, even insects. But there was nothing. He looked skyward. Grey clouds hung like a watercolour painting. He waited for birds to litter his vision but again he was faced with nothing.

"Bit quiet ain't it guys?" Blake's deep voice broke through the stillness, it was only then that Morgan realised the air had dropped, the once breeze-filled trees remained lifeless as their boat pitched softly against the never ceasing lapping of the water below.

Prrrrbbbtttt....ffftttt
"Guys, you hear that? It's a rare butt frog!"
Blake's constant flatulence never failed to break the tension, the man had quite a talent. They all roared with laughter, the din of the three friends' glee punctuated by a stormy rumble overhead.
"And with that, I guess the only way is down."
"That's what she said..." Edward's first joke of the day. It was amazing how much tension a fart could break.

Tying the boat off on a sturdy tree the trio prepared their gear for the dive. Rain was beginning to fall and in the short time it had taken to get their suits on the hull of the boat was soon obscured by a layer of water.

"Right guys, no fucking about, this rain is coming down pretty hard now. I'd say we have thirty minutes in there before things start to get silly. Let's get in and get out sharpish."

Morgan strapped on a locator beacon, a small LED light which flashes underwater to help divers locate one another. Blake quickly turned it off.

"If there are things in there, caimans and the like, let's not advertise our presence," Blake winked before tossing the beacon back into his rucksack.

The flood waters from the mountains had carried with them a plethora of dirt and detritus, thick brown clouds swirled before Morgan's already limited view. Pushing it aside he swam deeper into the murky waters, Edward had spoken of underwater streams that fed clean water into the river keeping the depths almost crystal clear. Surely a few more feet and he would reach these mythical waters. Something heavy smacked his thigh, turning towards the impact his view was limited by the brown snowflakes that drifted through the water. Shadows danced around him, their frequency and speed spun through his mind and within seconds he was lost. Struggling to decipher his location, bubbles seemed to drift in multiple directions making focusing impossible. The shadows continued to spiral, smaller impacts now glancing off his body from all angles. He began to panic, his breathing becoming quick and shallow as he felt his mind cloud with the static of pins and needles. He resisted the incoming dread, biting his tongue as he tried to remain conscious but each millisecond his brain pushed itself further and further from this world.

An unknown force gripped his leg, something strong, and something that did little to defend against his flailing attacks. It began to pull at him, pull him down, deeper into the depths. He could do little to resist as his body felt like it turned to lead.

Coughing, Morgan spilled a mixture of water mixed with mucus which splashed back over his face before he was quickly spun to his side. Vomiting the brown liquid, he spluttered as his fingers gripped onto whatever he was now lying on. It was solid and dry and very welcome.

"He's back." Blake's voice sounded as if he was riding a rollercoaster, it shifted and pitched along the tracks as each word corkscrewed towards Morgan's ears. A heavy smack on his back reminding him that this hellish ride was now over.

As his eyes began to refocus the illuminated faces of his friends bared down over him, each one encased in the darkness of the surrounding cave.

"It's ok dude, you had a bit of a panic attack, we've gotcha covered though." Edward wrapped his arm over Morgan's shoulder as he helped him sit up. He had been diving for twelve years now and had never experienced anything like that. Despite his weakened state, he only felt embarrassment.

"You swam into the middle of a shoal of fish you muppet, bloody things went mental."

Morgan managed a laugh. It was a freak event, so at least he could say that that would never happen again. This gave him little comfort.

"Where are we?"

"The cave, we must have swum right into the mouth when we were in all that shit." Drawn towards Blake's voice, Morgan could see he was hunched over gripping his lower leg.

"Blake, you ok?" Suddenly, Morgan's near drowning seemed insignificant.

"Oh yeah man, just a friction burn, must have got my leg caught in something. Hurt like crazy but it's dying down now." As if to prove his theory Blake gave his leg a gentle slap and tried to conceal a pained wince.

"Guys, he's fine, you're fine, and I'm fine. You're missing the point, we're here, and we've done it."

Edward shone his flashlight about the cave. Human remains littered each rocky shelf. Skeletal grins peeked out from every crevice, the occasional gold tooth flickering against the light.

"How many are there?" Blake was now standing; any pain that he may have felt was numbed with awe.

"Last count I read about was three years back, they estimated thirty four." Edward stared in wonder at the remains closest to him. "All male, all healthy. It's as if the locals give up their fittest men as sacrifice."

Morgan said a silent prayer. He wasn't at all religious but seeing the remains of those who clearly were, he saw it as the correct thing to do.

Each of the remains looked surprisingly clean. The bones were bleached white, not a single piece of flesh remained. Every sinew, every tendon was gone. Morgan began to have his doubts.

"Sorry Edward, I should have asked sooner, but where did you hear about this place?"

Edward, still aimlessly wondering about the cave a single answer, "Reddit."

"Ah shit! You serious? This is all a big hoax guys."

Blake and Edward turned to face Morgan the non-believer, fixing their lights directly onto his face. The beams blinded him. Stumbling back he caught his ankle, sending him reeling into the water.

The cool darkness quickly embraced him, and without his torch he struggled to make sense of his surroundings. Once more the dread began to flow through his mind. Once more something took hold of his leg. The searing pain rocketed through his every muscle. His limbs contorted uncontrollably as if hundreds of hands were bending him into ungodly spasms.

Blake dropped to his knees, thrusting his hand into the water as he searched for his friend. Edward, now wielding both torches, scoured the murky water for any movement. Blake fell back clutching his wet hand. A scream like Edward had never heard before echoed amongst the walls. Each softer bellow hit him with unreasonable force, his stomach bruised from the beatings ushered up vomit in return.

Blake wriggled on his back like a stranded beetle, the pain evident on his tortured face. His hand was still attached, so at least it wasn't a crocodile thought Edward.

"MOTHER FUCKER FUCK FUCK FUCK." Blake, now on all fours, was slapping the ground beneath him, his pained hand curled up by his gut. Through the torchlight Edward could see the skin flaking from Blake's hand, chunks of flesh dripping from his knuckles. Arm outstretched, he moved towards Blake before a volcanic gurgling erupted behind him. The water bubbled as thick black things wrapped and writhed around one another. Their glossy flesh entwined a ball of grotesque proportions. Edward could see a hand encased within. Morgan's hand. It shuddered, twisted, the clear sounds of bones breaking as fingers were bent over knuckles. Then, as soon as it had started, the water returned to its oppressive calm.

Blake had fallen silent; he was staring at the water in disbelief, at their friend pulled down into the depths.

"What was that?" Edward was shaking, the torch light dancing erratically across the cave. He withdrew to a far corner, tripping over bones before sinking to the floor. His fingers wrapped around the remains, picking what he could only assume was a thigh bone he tossed it at the water, screaming as it spun through the air. As the bone tumbled into the water, it once more burst into life. Slime covered creatures gurgled against one another before a single face became evident. These weren't tentacles from some hideous hell beast, these were eels. Hundreds upon hundreds of eels all intertwined with one another.

"Electric eels," Blake's voice trembled, gripping his hand tight he grimaced in pain.
"Electric eels? Are those even real? I thought they were like unicorns or vampire bats." Edward flung a skull against the wall showering Blake with bone fragments. Sobbing he balled up on the floor, tucking his knees under his chin he began to wail.
"Vampire bats are...oh never mind." Blake brushed splinters of skull from his shoulder. Edward continued to cry, his sniffles echoing into an endless torrent of misery.
"My Mum told me not to come, she said I wouldn't like it here, she was right. I want to go home." Edward's pitiful whining failed to tug at Blake's heart. He was never a huge fan of Edward, their relationship only sustained by their affection for Morgan. With his passing, Blake could

think of nothing better than never seeing the spoilt, stuck up brat ever again.

Struggling to open his first aid pouch, Blake pulled out a strip of gauze to bandage his hand, pus instantly seeping through the material leaving a dark brown stain. "Why did you come then? What did you have to prove?"

"Fuck you! I didn't need to prove anything. We go on these holidays every year. We get pissed, get laid and then come home. Don't you want more than that?"

"Sure, but I didn't want to die looking for it."

Edward sat up wiping his nose on his wrist. "Do you really think we're going to die?"

Blake looked at Edward, his eyes red and puffy. His friend had died right in front of him and it still hadn't even crossed his mind that his life was in danger. Selfish prick.

"We're in the middle of the jungle, in a place the locals won't even go near. It's the middle of the monsoon season, we're trapped in a cave surrounded by electric eels which have already killed Morgan, and now the cave is flooding. So yeah, I think we're fucked."

Edward looked down to see the floor of the cave was now completely covered in a thin layer of water which was quickly spreading. Blake shifted himself onto a rock furthest from the water. He lifted his scuba gear to a ledge and began to inspect it.

"You can't be thinking about going in the water?" Edward's accusing tone washed over Blake. Right now he had more important things to worry about.

"I just want to make sure I can get in quickly if needs be. Oh and get yourself off the water. I don't know how many times I have to tell you that those eels are electric."

Edward splashed a puddle with his foot before realising as long as he was touching the water he was at risk. Scurrying to a highpoint he shoved the remains of some poor sap aside sending them bouncing to the ground. Amongst the shattered bones sat a cracked and damaged satellite phone. Blake picked it up, twisting the remains through his fingers before launching it into the water below.

"We could have used that to call for help!" Edward's cry echoed around the ever-shrinking cave.

"Seriously? A broken satellite phone that has been submerged for at least a year? Not to mention we are completely encased in rock. You think THAT was of any fucking use?"

"I just...I just" Edward's voice shuddered, he was clearly about to cry again.

"Look," Blake sighed. "No one is coming to save us. If we are going to get out of here we need to save ourselves. Crying isn't helping either of us. Check your gear and prepare to go under."

"I'm sorry," Edward sniffed. "I'm sorry for everything. I'm sorry for being a jerk, I'm sorry for pushing you about, I'm...I'm just fucking sorry."

Blake couldn't tell if Edward was talking to him or to the remains of Morgan, either way he nodded in agreement. "Don't apologise, just make sure he didn't die for no reason."

The water bubbled in response. The eels, growing in number, made their presence known. With the water now edging ever closer to Blake's feet he knew it was time to either dive in or climb up. Using his good hand he palmed the rocks above him, solid flat rock greeted every touch. To his right there was a ledge, a good seven feet away. Normally, with the water to break his fall he would have jumped without hesitation. But now, in full scuba gear and with a hand that felt as if it was dropping off, he wasn't too sure.

It was now or never.

He unstrapped his oxygen tank and tossed to across to the ledge. He wasn't quite ready to brave the water, just a few more minutes and maybe. Just not now. Getting to his feet he steadied himself before eyeing up the distance one last time. Knees bent, one arm swinging at his side to gain momentum, he prepared himself.
"Dude wait!"
Edward's words knocked Blake off balance, his foot slipped as he pushed himself forward, arms now flailing he reached out in a vain attempt to grab the ledge missing it by a clear foot. His body twisted, pain split down his side as his ribcage smashed against the rock face. Exhaling a silent scream, his body plunged into the waters.

Reaching his hand into the darkness, water filling his lungs as he grappled for something to right himself. His hand settled on something smooth, slime slipping his fingers from making proper contact. He knew what he had grabbed, he knew what it meant.

Blake's body disappeared into the murky waters. Before the erupting water had a chance to settle, a thick fizzing foam covered the pool. There was no scream. There was no fight.

Edward began to cry. Not because he was the reason behind Blake's death, that idea never entered his head. As far as he was aware Blake died failing a jump. All he knew now was that he was alone.

No matter what, he was alone.

Water lapped just below his ledge, above him the cave ceiling stretched into darkness. If there was a way to get higher he couldn't see it. Taking his torch, he leaned out aiming it skywards, desperate for just a few more minutes before the water enveloped him. Twisting his wrist, he slipped; pushing his outstretched hand against the wall he steadied himself enough to watch his grip on the torch falter.

The small black device dropped silently into the water. Tumbling, the light spiralled illuminating the almost green depths, the beams reflecting off hundreds of eyes, each one watching, waiting. The light pulsed before plunging Edward into darkness.

The absence of light only made his cries more pitiful, pathetic whimpering now emphasising his destiny. Water reached his ledge, cold and thick it crept to his knees. Edward thought back to a better time, a time where the three friends laughed and cheered. A time when booze flowed with no limit. A time where they were together, safe.

His feet began to tingle, pins and needles tickling under the surface. The minor irritation trickled up his body, growing, swelling in intensity. Hairs on the back of his neck stood, reaching to escape the inevitable. Edward brushed the goose bumps on his arm, his fingers gently caressing each mound before the water rose to his armpits.

Everything felt heavy, his breaths now deep and shallow. Saliva filled his mouth saturating him with the taste of blood. The sound of each heartbeat now a booming orchestra in his ears, he focused on the sound. His chest tightened, invisible fingers wrapped around his beating heart, stifling its rhythm. He could feel his eyes moving, each twitch scratching against bone, and grating as they throbbed from their sockets.

Water now reached his chin.

His teeth shuddered, biting down they cracked and jostled from his jaw, warm blood filling his mouth. He inhaled sharply, choking. Skin began to slide from muscle and muscle from bone, blisters ruptured as soon as they formed. Searing pain jolted up his spine as if a fuse burned through each vertebrae, pops and cracks punctuating each new bone as it rocketed towards his skull.

Water now submerged his eyes.

Edward's skull began to split, boiling fluid rushing to fill every crevice as his brain pushed to escape. He held his eyes shut as they trembled, the vicious movement now forcing them to the back of his skull. Still, he sat, and waited for the end to surely come.

Water now encased him.

SPARKS

IN FOR A SHOCK
PIPPA BAILEY

Blood streamed from Hannah's broken jaw, soaking her shirt. Her effort to remain upright now impossible. The buzzing electrical giants dragged her between two rows of similar glowing creatures, all assembled on transparent pews. Everything glinted, everything seemed made of glass. Her feet slipped in blood.

A bitter sulphurous stench issued from the creatures, but she could still smell her burnt and blistered skin. It was worse than the sunburn from that holiday in Greece, which seemed like a billion years ago.

She had to do something, anything.

Her arms shot out to the side, reaching for the nearest surface.

The monstrous creatures that held her jerked to a standstill. Blue lightning fired beneath their translucent skin and crackled across their featureless faces. Electrical tendrils whipped under their immense bodies, struggling to hold her. She clawed at the nearest pew, her stinging fingertips snatching at the glass.

Gasps echoed around the courtroom, and many electrical creatures leapt to their feet. They shot backwards, hurdling benches, and clambered over one another. Twists of lightning struck the floor, trailing ash.

She ignored the chaos and screeches that sliced the air, and clutched a smooth armrest. Her blistered hands slipped and her face whacked the floor. Blood bubbled between her teeth with each rattling breath. The creatures lashed more tendrils around her arms, and buzzing coils burned through remnants of her clothes to leave her naked. They yanked her limp body towards the gigantic doors at the end of the room, her feet squeaking across the glass.

The onlookers twisted for a better view, their gangly bodies contorted around each other in a sea of electric blue.

They slammed her into a frosty metal chair. Her head swam and she struggled to regain focus. Wishing the pain away, her entire body throbbed. They wrenched her arms onto the rests, ice crumbled away in a shower of crystal filaments.

The chamber was sparse, devoid of the courtroom chatter. Two glowing creatures skittered around the electric chair which stood in the centre of the room.

One monstrous creature pulled a hide glove over its spindly fingers. Flexing, it ran its hand down the length of her face, and squeezed her shattered jaw. She howled and kicked out. It slopped a wet sponge atop her matted hair. Icy trickles ran down her face, stung her eyes and seeped into her open mouth. A familiar sting of pool water from years of lessons, but this reeked like a stagnant pond.

She wrenched her head sideways, her neck crunched. A worn chin-strap cinched and pulled a large rusted dome against her scalp, forcing shut her misshapen mouth. She screamed through gritted teeth, choking on the residual water and blood.

The creature nodded to a second one behind the chair. It rested its hands atop a colossal glass orb on an elegant metal podium behind the chair. At its touch the orb pulsed, glowed, and emitted a mechanical screech.

Hannah's laptop buzzed its dusty fan not so efficient anymore. Her phone's familiar alarm punctured the drone and roused her: it was one o'clock. As a night-owl, she often went to sleep at peculiar hours only to wake having lost half the day.

She unstuck her tongue from the roof of her mouth, and scratched crusty drool from the corners of her downturned lips.

The alarm sounded again. She rubbed her eyes with sweaty hands, threw off the covers, and yanked her phone free from its worn charger cable. Being a slave to social media, she caught up with an array of messages on Facebook before leaving her bed. A loud ping drew her attention to the noisy laptop. She tapped the stiff spacebar.

Your battery is charged above 70%. If you continue to charge the battery above this level for extended periods, it can cause permanent damage.

Despite the warning, her laptop was continually plugged into the overfilled extension lead beside her bed. Not the most organised of people, various cables lay knotted, creeping from under her bed. She closed the PC window, and left her laptop to continue its extensive download list.

She headed downstairs, though the cluttered lounge and to the kitchen – which wasn't much better. Fragrant coffee leaked from a cracked mug, pooling on the counter. She shrugged, threw a dishtowel over it and made a fresh one.

Cold struck her bare legs and left a line of goose bumps. The fridge was open. Dropping to her knees, she peered inside. Not sure if she'd caught the door in her pre-caffeinated haze or left it open all night, she grabbed the milk. A guarded sniff, followed by a bout of retching, told her this was an all-night job. Clots of white coated the inside of the bottle. She booted the door shut and poured the pungent chunks down the sink,

Sipping the black coffee, she headed for the lounge to collapse onto the sofa. She thumbed the TV remote.

A newsreader's voice burst from the huge TV's speakers: "Detective Pascal gives updates on the attacks in the Alnwick area. Live at four. How long until we have a real answer to what's happened?" asked the frowning newsreader.

He slammed his fist down on a small pile of paperwork that littered the neon-lit desk, and scattered the sheets.

A female reporter paced in front of a vast brick building. "Well, John, this seems to tie in with the large number of freak occurrences across The Midlands over the past year. Can we talk spontaneous human combustion for a minute?"

John shook his head. "Despite the strange goings on, I think we can agree to disagree this is a hoax."

"Three bodies in the last year John, three." The reporter pouted, and waved her microphone at the camera.

"Yes, well..." He fiddled with the clip on his tie, and straightened himself in his chair. "Are they investigating these events? No, they've kept it all hushed. It seems pretty suspect to me," she shook her flabby arm at the building behind her. The cameraman panned to the police station logo above the front door.

"Suzie, I think we'll have to see how Pascal's investigation progresses." With a nod, he signalled the station to cut her feed. "Now over to Heather with the Weather." He shook his head and grimaced.

Cameras flipped to a bouncy young woman with waist-length dreadlocks, gesturing to a map of the British Isles.

"Hey, John, it's going to be a balmy twenty-five degrees tomorrow, so avoid that Sunday sun and—"

More weird happenings.

She'd noticed an increase in strange reports on the news: Men found comatose on their beds and entire towns with clocks frozen at the same hour. And now they were talking about spontaneous human combustion. Freaky.

Bounding into the kitchen, she poured out dregs of cold coffee and swilled residual chunks of milk down the drain.

Upstairs, scrambling around the bed for her hairdryer, she shifted a grey cloud of dust bunnies. She coughed and sneezed a few times, and pulled on a pair of jeans and a baggy shirt while she continued her search. This was the usual arrangement, given that she was forever losing electrical appliances. Some were left in sockets around the house; others simply chucked into empty draws, or discarded under her bed. Alas, this time her hairdryer evaded her.

She forced her damp, lilac-scented hair into a loose knot above her head. Residual auburn dye stained the collar of her shirt. She shrugged; it always came out in the wash.

Ping. Her laptop announced its download was complete.

She swiped her finger across the pockmarked screen and selected the next movie in her list. The buzzing machine concurred and got to work. She loved having a large collection of films to watch. TV content had taken a turn for the worse recently: shitty shows about couples on islands, and far too much sport. She had switched to illegally downloading movies to satisfy her needs. Horror was her genre of choice.

She plopped onto the soft double-bed and scrolled through notifications on her phone. Several from her mother reminded her that they had arrangements for lunch. Punctuality was never her strong point, and repeatedly got her into trouble at her last job. Now working from home as a reviewer, it was too easy to ignore the clock.

Texting a quick apology to her mother who was determined to go out for food, she agreed to meet her at a local café. At least they made good coffee at Café Nerd, as she called it.

Downstairs, the TV still mumbled in the lounge. She rarely turned it off, nor the lights. The house was, as her dad would say, "Constantly lit up like Christmas." She grabbed her bag from the wobbly rack beside the front door, and stuffed her phone and keys inside. They tumbled and chimed against her purse. The walk was only ten minutes, so she didn't bother with a jacket.

She set off down the road.

It had been yonks since she'd ventured out. Preferring to avoid raucous crowds, and being far from her beloved internet, drove her slightly crazy.

The café was quiet. A few groups of teenagers milled about drinking tall iced coffees, slurping cream and chocolate sauce from their straws. At twenty-nine, and wiser than a few years ago, years filled with banana milkshake, cakes, and candy. She now avoided sugary drinks. She'd even quit putting sweetener in her coffee. "Clean eating for a better body," her friend had said.

Her squat mother's chatter was punctuated by the staccato tap of fork against plate. Hannah added the occasional yes, no and hmm into the conversational mix, and stabbed at her chicken salad. Tepid pieces of mayonnaise-soaked meat skidded around, and kept her entertained for a while.

The door opened a few times: an elderly couple, a woman with bouffant blonde hair, and lastly a rugged guy in combat trousers, his arms covered in intricate tattoos.

She found herself admiring the swirls and symbols on the guy's arms. It was nice to see body art more often now. People covered it up less, the old stigma was gone. She thought about her unfinished back tattoo. Her mother had paid for it when she was twenty-one, but she couldn't bring herself to get anymore done, couldn't handle the pain. Like her, it remained a work-in-progress.

A young barista shuffled through a door behind the marble counter, and shot a huge grin at the guy.

"On your own again, Liam?" The barista rolled up her coffee-stained sleeves, and began to press grounds into one of the handles.

"Yeah, it's all good. I'll just take this one to go, today," he said, mirroring her smile.

"Oh, that's no fun." The barista looked up at him, and ran her fingers through a tangle of hair.

Hannah fought back a snigger. Watching the barista try to flirt was far more entertaining than listening to her mother's list of issues with the dog's anal glands.

Tattoo guy lifted his baseball cap, and ran his hand over the back of his head before replacing it again. "Rhea's been busy at work. You've seen the news?"

She could see the barista nodding, but couldn't hear her response over the whirr of milk being foamed in a large metal jug. BANG.

The jug caught the counter top and splashed steaming foam across the baristas hand. She shrieked, dropped it on the counter, and ran through a door to the rear.

Raising an eyebrow, Hannah looked back to her mother, who hadn't noticed nor stopped talking. It was worrying that her mother was oblivious to the world outside of her own conversation. They only met up for lunch a couple times a month, but it was more than Hannah could handle, preferring online conversation to the real thing.

Tattoo guy peered through a small round window in the door, no barista. He shrugged, turned, and rested his back against the counter.

He grabbed his phone from a pocket and punched in a few digits that clicked loudly. Phone to his ear, he headed towards the door. "Rhea, Rhea Pascal please."

She watched the door snap shut behind him, thinking of that surname. Pascal, the detective's name they mentioned earlier on the news.

The barista rushed through the door. She looked around for the tattooed guy, her hand now wrapped in soggy kitchen roll. She huffed, and ran a cloth over the mess of foamed milk that coated the counter.

Her mother waved a hand in front of her face. "Hello, I was talking to you."

"Huh?" She snatched her gaze away from the counter and back to her mother. "What's up?"

"I've got to go soon," she said, and drained the dregs from her mug sliding it to the centre of the table. It scraped through loose sugar granules.

"Oh, sure. Sorry, I got distracted." Hannah offered a weak smile.

Her mother rolled her eyes. "That doesn't surprise me."

She pushed her bowl and mug to the centre. "Well I'm good to go."

"Okay, sweetie." Her mother grabbed her in a bear hug, and slipped folded banknote into her hand. "I'll see you for lunch next weekend?"

Hannah nodded. "Yeah, sure. I'll try to be on time."

She knew she wouldn't be.

The sun had set by the time she reached home. It was dark and quiet inside the house, she slapped around for the light switch. Maybe there was a power cut? The lights clicked on, she squinted. Odd. She hadn't turned them off before she left, nor the TV. Placing her palm against the screen it gave off no heat. When her parents complained about the extortionate electricity bills, she claimed living alone as an excuse. The constant light and sound made her feel safe.

Perplexed, she grabbed the remote and hammered the standby button. Nothing. Peering behind the TV unit, mired by cobwebs. The wall sockets were off. She couldn't reach them without moving the unit. This was starting to creep her out.

The stiff unused switches fought her as she turned them on. Static hummed and the babble of TV voices filled the room.

A quick tour of the house revealed nothing. She pressed her face against the cold glass of the lounge window and peered outside. Breathing heavily, her nostrils flared and spread condensation over the glossy pane. She tripped over loose wires, and plodded through to the kitchen to make a cup of tea.

The TV died with a loud snap.

Irritated, she ran back to the lounge.

The sockets were off, again. An unusual sulphurous odour hung near the TV. She wondered if there was an electrical fault. Maybe it was a safety feature, things get too hot and the power cuts out. Melted plastic couldn't smell this bad. She remembered the stench of her overheating hairdryer after it ate a chunk of her hair.

Thump. She yanked the plugs from their sockets and inspected them. No obvious damage. The TV powered on without issue. Stupid fucking technology.

Crashing on the sofa, she forgot about the tea stewing in her mug. Alien was on. She grinned and curled up under a blanket.

She managed twenty minutes of the film before she nodded off.

Blood spurted from the man's chest. He screamed and shook. A pasty, throbbing creature tore through his ribcage.

A dark spot rippled at the centre of the TV screen. It smothered the lurid image, and killed the sound. Globules of smoking plasma dripped and converged on the outer frame. Fingers of blue light stuttered on spindly arms of static, which pierced the gloom. A mire of ozone and sulphur saturated the air, penetrating her nostrils. She retched, the foul odour jerking her awake.

She focused on the intense light. Like a blowtorch flame, it hurt to look directly at it. At them.

Monstrous creatures, their gigantic bodies made of lightning that writhed below a transparent skin. They had no faces, only voids where their eyes should be. Sparks of energy hissed and danced between them. Their elongated bodies travelled on glowing tentacles, which scoured the room. Hunting.

Clamping hands over her mouth muted a guttural scream. The stench tore through her clasped fingers. She vomited, and choked on the chunks of acidic meat.

Struggling to her feet, she dodged the electrical giants and leapt into the kitchen. She swung her arms blindly, reaching for the knife block and striking a pile of washing up. Porcelain cups fragmented and clattered on the tiled floor. She grabbed a carving knife. The other blades unsheathed and skidded across the mucky surface.

Years of watching horror films, promising she'd never be the idiot who backed herself into a corner, and there she was: no escape.

The doorway to the kitchen grew brighter. Electrified fronds cascaded across the walls and ceiling, illuminating the room. Coils of energy snapped and tore at metal. Hooks gave way to molten ooze that popped, and dribbled from holes. Taps warped and sealed themselves into shapeless silver lumps that clung to the sink.

She trembled, and backed away from the buzzing light. Her shallow rasping breaths punctuated the hum of electricity. Ridges from the oven bore into her side, her body pressed hard against it. She knew metal and electricity was a bad idea, but still flailed the knife towards the open door.

The noxious creatures ducked the doorframe, lightning skittering over broken porcelain.

Raising its arm, one of the creatures fired a hot electrical coil. It crackled through the air, and struck her neck hard, snapping it backwards. The coil constricted her throat. She dropped the knife, and strained to release the burning noose, it gripped tighter. Her flesh bubbled and leaked acrid fluid from sizzling wounds on her hands and neck.

The reek of burning flesh urged her to fight harder against the noose; the pain was too intense for words. She'd had an accident working in a restaurant many years ago. A hob left on overnight and touched for a second. She'd lost the palm of her left hand. That pain, the pain of skin sloughed from her hand was nothing compared to this. Her vision faded to black.

The creatures lifted her limp body. Parts of her jeans and shirt smoldered and fell away in smoky clumps, leaving a trail of ash through the lounge.

They skittered through the blackened portal that scarred the TV. The portal hissed and shrank, until it was only a blemish on the screen.

Awake, Hannah lay contorted on the floor. Sparks flew from rusted metal poles that stood in the corners of the glass room.

Her eyes crossed as she looked through the ceiling. Layers of distorted people filled the cells above her. She raised her hands to her face; each finger was red and blistered. The wounds wept where tight skin had split. Her hands shook as she lowered them again, wincing.

Waves of static pulsed like bass music and made her body throb. She knew she was in a cell, a glass prison cell.

A creature approached, its blue hue warped by the thick walls. Vines of electricity twisted into the room, peeling layers of molten glass, like a zipper on a pair of jeans. Its stench saturated the room.

She gagged and rolled onto her side. Her empty stomach contracted, and forced her knees to her chest. Hot tears streamed down her face and struck the floor sending streaks of lightning snaking across the floor. If she closed her eyes tight, she could pretend this wasn't real. Monsters weren't real, she knew that. But the pain from her neck, and stench of her burned flesh, that was real.

A series of clicks and whistles issued from the mouthless creature, repeating until they formed words: "Time. To. Go." Its voice hurt her ears.

She remained foetal, squeezing her eyes shut.

It slithered towards her. "So. Be. It."

A twist of blue energy crackled from its hand and crept across the floor. It snared her ankle, blistered her skin and wrenched her closer. She twisted and clawed at the ground, her fingers leaving red streaks.

"Walk," it hissed, and threatened her with another coiled tendril.

She acknowledged its request, and scrambled to her feet.

A creature fired lightning at her heels, ushering her through a buzzing glass corridor. It was full of cells like her own. People cowered in corners, sweaty, naked, and hammering on walls. At the end of the corridor was a bright, square room. Its walls covered with thousands of small TV screens like some 1990s MTV display. Each TV exhibited a different location.

Horrified, she understood. These were people's homes. This was how they'd watched her, how they knew where she was. A creature approached one of the TVs and it touched the screen. A portal appeared and it stepped inside.

"Holding. Cell," the creature behind her hissed, and forced her through a door at the end of the room. The door slammed, she was alone again.

Hannah's shaking legs gave out, and she collapsed to the floor. Time stood still, or moved too quickly, she couldn't tell anymore. It could have been hours or days since they brought her here. Closing her eyes, she drifted into an exhausted sleep. Rings of steam escaped her sore lips.

She didn't hear the wall open, or the creature pass through.

"Do. You. Know. Why. You're. Here?" it boomed.

Startled, she crawled towards a corner. "I'm not here. This isn't real," she shouted, and smacked her forehead against the wall in the hope that it would wake her from this nightmare.

A tiny crack appeared. She watched it grow and mar the pristine surface.

The monstrous creature released a sequence of clicks which formed an unmistakable laugh. "You. Are. To. Stand. Trial," it said.

A crystalline chair and table erupted from the floor and clattered towards the centre of the room. Standing, she flattened herself against the wall. The creature gestured to the seat. She didn't obey. It fired a warning shot of lightning at her feet. She jumped forward to avoid it. The frozen chair veered behind her and slammed into her calves, forcing her to sit. It escorted her to the table.

She couldn't understand why they wanted her, what she'd done. It made no sense. They couldn't keep her here much longer, could they? Then the questioning began…

"I've not abused anyone," she stated again, and again. After hours of interrogation her eyes were still trained on the growing crack in the wall, "I shouldn't be here!"

She edged her glass chair back from the table.

"You. Abused. Power."

"What do you mean, I abused power?" She demanded.

Sparks fired rapidly beneath its translucent skin. Ignoring her, it tapped its fingers against the table. Strands of lightning danced across its surface towards her.

"Wasted. Used. Too. Much." The creature's voice grew more menacing with every crackled syllable. "Not. Long. Now."

She had to make a move. Her only option was the crack in the wall.

Gripping the edge of the table, she slammed into the body of the creature. The glass warped on contact, melted, slowed the creature's movements. She wrenched her chair from the ground and swung hard at the cracked glass wall. The chair crumbled.

Jagged lines splintered the wall's fragile beauty. It crunched, creaked, and began to fragment. Chunks fell from the shattered wall and smashed at her feet. A ragged hole opened in front of her but it was too small to climb through.

The creature struggled to untangle itself from the molten table.

It was going to hurt more than her burns, but she knew she had no choice. Running, she slammed her shoulder against the hole, forcing it to widen. Splinters pierced her upper-arm and fragmented. She howled, fighting her way through the broken glass. Blood seeped down her arms. Tatters of her flesh clung to the jagged hole.

Free from the room, she ran.

The creature thrashed at the wall. Its tendrils whipped and tore through the glass.

It wasn't far behind her.

She bolted into the gigantic room of TVs.

A deafening shriek filled the air. More creatures gouged clefts in the slippery floor as they sped after her. With her heart screaming in her ears, she dove for one of the screens. It split with a strident crack and she disappeared through.

Fuzzy carpet broke her fall. She rolled and smashed into a liquor cabinet. Colourful bottles rattled and tumbled over each other.

Ignoring the pain from her bloody shoulder, she raced to the front door and wrenched the handle. It didn't budge. Grabbing coats from a wrack she hunted through the pockets for keys. There was nothing. No keys, no knives, not even a lighter.

That familiar stench poured into room and stung her nostrils. Bursting through another door, she spotted the stairs and scrambled up.

A bedroom door hung open revealing a varnished wooden floor, illuminated by sunlight. She spotted the window and tried to force it. Resisting her attempts, it creaked and stuck partially open. She struggled and pounded her fists into the panel. It didn't budge. A loud crackle came from the open door. There was no option left but to fight. If she could get to another room maybe there was a way out. She hunted for a weapon.

Blue coils scorched the doorframe, and licked towards her. It was here.

She grabbed the first item: a cup of water. She flung it towards the creature in the doorway. It exploded on impact. China and water flew in all directions. Screaming, its grotesque body contorted and fragile skin buckled. Tentacles flailed and struck nearby furniture. Giant spurs of lightning smothered the bed with flames.

Hannah gasped. She couldn't believe one cup of water could do so much damage.

Hiding behind the door, she watched the creature begin to disintegrate. Flimsy sections of translucent membrane sloughed from its torso. Its broad chest tore open, and released the crackling energy beneath. The creature was reduced to a glowing pile of gore.

She crept round the door.

It was too late...There was another.

CRACK. An electrified vine whipped through the air, and hurled her against a wall. She smashed through a bookcase, wedged between its splintered wooden shelves and fell onto the ream of books below. Deep electrical burns smoldered on her misshapen cheek. Blood poured from her mouth and soaked into the pages.

"Wake. Up," a voice echoed.

It was hard to move, her stiff back crunched as she straightened it.

Every inch ached. She remembered destroying one of the creatures. Beyond that it was a blur.

She stood in a vast courtroom, hunched over a crystal podium. Seated on frosted glass pews encircling her, hundreds of glowing creatures bobbed and weaved with nervous energy. Her heart drummed in the crisp silence of the room.

Sat at the colossal raised bench was a grotesque electrical creature that dwarfed the others. Its body quivered like jelly, flabby arms undulating. Its tendrils, thick like tentacles, slapped against the bench as it spoke.

"You. Wasted...You. Killed," the creature boomed.

She attempted to answer, but her mouth wouldn't move. A strand of crimson drool spattered the clear stand in front. Her face numb, she raised a hand and ran it along her slack jaw. A chunk had pierced through her cheek. No energy left to panic, tears streamed down her face. The salt stung her wounds.

"There. Is. No. Choice," it hissed, leaning over the bench.

She tongued her cracked lips and tried to speak. "I ..."

It interrupted and pointed at her. "Words. Do. Not. Matter."

She spluttered more blood across the podium, and lifted her swollen head. The creature's vacant face, a swirl of pulsating green, morphed with every word.

The crowds shuffled and chattered, their angry cries echoing. A charged frond of electricity soared from within the surge of movement and struck the back of her head. The shock slammed her face into the congealed gore that coated the glass, and plumes of smoke spiralled from scorched hair.

"Take. Her. Spark," it commanded.

She trembled, unable to answer.

"Extraction. Chamber. Immediately."

She was dragged from the courtroom, a quivering, bloody mess. Sparks hissed and flew in her direction from the chanting crowd. The room was a blur of light as she skidded in her own blood.

She didn't understand what he meant by, "Take her spark." She didn't have any sparks. Exhausted and broken, she tried to free herself from their grip. Scorching fronds tore at her body, burning through the remains of her tattered clothes, and left her naked. The pain crippled her further. Collapsed on the floor, they yanked her through huge doors at the end of the room.

The dark extraction chamber held a solitary metal chair, filling the centre of the room. Hannah had seen one of these before. An electric chair. But she'd never seen one entirely made of metal. Worn straps hung from the arms, tarnished buckles scraped the floor. A rusty dome hovered above the backrest. Behind the chair a transparent sphere, its bulk dwarfed elegant glass podium it balanced on.

A creature hovered nearby.

She struggled as they slammed her into the seat and strapped her down.

It was too late. The creature touched the orb. It pulsed, glowed, and emitted a mechanical screech.

Every muscle tensed, contorting her limbs. Agony tore through her chest.

SNAP. A bone in her twisted leg fractured, a large fragment piercing her skin. Hot blood spurted down her quivering thighs. She howled. Her body convulsed.

No more thoughts, no more feelings.

She vomited thick red clots onto her thrashing lap.

The glass orb crackled beneath the creature's hands. Bolts of lightning swirled inside. The creatures watched the spark of life siphon from her crippled body.

Her fingertips blackened, like a gangrenous progression. The darkness crawled up her limbs, reducing them to charcoal. There was no more pain, no more blood. Her body slumped in the chair; the darkness clawed its way up her mutilated neck, and smothered her scarred face. Char and ash rained from her open mouth.

A small light flicked within the sphere, gravitating towards the creature's hands. In an instant, it was gone.

BANG.

"Hello?" a man's voice called from outside the front door to Hannah's house.

BANG.

The policeman pulled a torch from his back pocket, and shone it through the front window. No movement. He scurried back to the door and knelt. Peering into the lock, his light wouldn't penetrate the mechanism. The key was evidently still inside.

He booted the door. It shot open and splintered the frame.

He wrinkled his nose.

"Hello?"

Torch in his teeth, he steadied himself and found the light switch. No power.

"This is Constable Jefferies. Is there anyone there?" he called into the darkness.

Entering the lounge, Hannah's scorched body lay hunched on the sofa. Black, cracked skin covered her naked body. Her limbs hung awkwardly giving the appearance of a disfigured marionette. Eyes now lumps of coal, wide open. Her face contorted into a terrified scream. A breeze from the open door stroked her body, her face crumbled.

He forced his hands over his mouth, and tripped as he lurched from the room. A stench of burned flesh followed him through the house, knocking books across the floor as he ran. The door slammed behind him, and he collapsed on the wet grass.

"Jones. Jones!" he shouted into his radio.

"What's up Brian?" a voice returned.

"Its...It's..." Brian stumbled over his words. He struggled with every breath still hunched on the grass.

"Spit it out, man," said the sharp radio voice.

"There's been another attack. Get detective Pascal on the line."

THE RAPE OF IVY HOUSE
EM DEHANEY

'Mr. Gonputh? Mr. Gonputh, are you there?'

Anita Sparrowhawk rapped her knuckles on the door, dusting her fingers with splinters of ancient paint.

'I'm from the council. You've been awarded a grant, Mr. Gonputh. It's part of our Clean Green Energy drive. We are modernising nominated houses in the local area. Bring you into the 21st Century, eh?'

This one's not even made it to the 20th century yet, she thought to herself as she stepped back and stared up. Thickets of ivy completely obscured the upstairs windows. Not that anyone would be able to see through them. The single paned sashes were thick with grime and framed in rotten wood. The house was built in 1875 as testified by the stone plaque above the door, which sat in the middle of the square brick frontage with two windows either side at the top and bottom. It was just like a child's drawing of a cottage, if that drawing had been crumpled up and left in the bottom of a bin for a hundred and forty years.

'I've got a few leaflets here explaining everything. I'll pop them through the letterbox. It's very exciting and it won't cost you a penny.'

Anita paused, certain she saw a twitch of yellowed net curtain.

That always gets 'em, tight old buggers. I bet he's got fifty grand in out of date bank notes stuffed under his mattress.

'I will be back on Monday with the workmen so we can get started. Yes, it's all very, very exciting.'

'I don't want no electrickery,' the old man shouted through the crack in the door.

'You can't fight progress, Mr. Gonputh, and this is all for your benefit.'

'And I told you, I don't want no electrickery, now sling yer 'ook.'

He slammed the door and a large branch of ivy dislodged, showering Anita with dusty spores.

'If you could just let us inside Mr. Gonputh,' she spluttered, brushing dead leaves off her not inconsiderable bosom. 'Then we can assess what needs to be done.'

She turned to the two workmen, who were eyeing the house with trepidation.

'If he won't let us in, we'll just have to find another way.'

She hoisted her handbag defiantly over her shoulder and fought her way through the overgrown front garden.

Sat at his kitchen table he could hear her rustling and bustling, trying to find another door. Good luck wi' that, he thought. The back door hadn't been opened since The War. His memory got hazy when he tried to remember which one. The kettle on the coal range started to whistle. Stan Gonputh hoisted himself out of his chair and shuffled over, taking the threadbare linen from the front of the stove to protect his hand. As he was pouring water into his well-seasoned teapot (some would say dirty, he would disagree), Stan heard a muffled 'Shit!' from the rear of the cottage, and he chuckled to himself. That'll be the coal bunker.

Anita Sparrowhawk rubbed her bruised hip and leaned back in her fully adjustable lumbar-supporting ergonomic office chair. She had a migraine coming, and when she closed her eyes the black and white zig-zag patterns at the edge of her vision danced and jerked. Pinching the bridge of her nose, she shouted across the open plan office.

'Anyone got any ideas how to get a stubborn old git out of his house long enough so we can get in and do the necessary?'

'Has he got any family?' someone called back.

'No. He was married once. She died.'

'Perfect.'

Stan Gonputh turned up the wick of his handheld oil lamp and stared into the eyes of the only woman he ever loved. His Mary. His golden morning. His pretty petal. He didn't come up to see her as often as he used to. He found it hard to get around now his knees were shot. His joints screamed in pain, his legs were bandy and bent. But today he climbed those stairs. He needed to see her. To talk to her, like he used to.

'I'm keeping my promise, petal.'

She didn't answer. She never answered. Her mouth was a thin, grey slash.

'They're trying to get in, but I won't let 'em. It's just us here, eh petal? We don't need no-one else.'

Silence.

'And we don't need no electrickery, right?'

The flame inside the lamp flickered, causing a shadow to jump over Mary's cheeks. That was all Stan needed. She heard him. She knew he was keeping his promise.

The promise he had made before her light snuffed out forever.

The following week, Anita Sparrowhawk trotted up the path to Ivy House using a lever-arch folder like a machete, slashing away at the overgrown grass and weeds. The bruising from her collision with the coal shed had faded, but her indignant need to get this man out of his house had not. *Why won't these silly old fools just let me do what's best for them?*

'Mr. Gonputh? Mr. Gonputh, I really wish you would open the door. I just want to talk. No harm in a little chat, hmm?'

She was not taking no for an answer today and continued to bang her fist on the door. Her wide-brimmed summer hat had gathered some strange looks from the neighbours, but it now protected her from the shower of dead leaves and wasp carcasses that fell as she hammered on the wood. Eventually, the door shuddered open and a pair of eyes magnified behind thick glasses peered out.

'You again? I thought I told you...'

'And I told you Mr. Gonputh, this is for your own good.'

Two thick-necked thugs in white uniforms appeared from behind her and barged their way into the house, almost pushing Stan to the floor. A muscular arm scooped him up and two hands gripped his shoulders. He attempted to twist out of their hold, but the hands clamped down so hard he thought his collar bone might snap.

'Don't try to fight, Mr. Gonputh, you'll only make it worse. I have a court order here allowing me to enter your home and assess your health and wellbeing.'

She brandished a piece of paper in front of his face. It could have been her shopping list for all he knew.

'These two gentlemen are fully qualified carers, they will sit with you while I take a tour of the premises and complete a twenty-one point checklist of health and safety requirements before the workmen can move in.'

Anita took a cursory glance around the dim kitchen.

'Of course, you won't be able to live here while the renovations are being completed.'

'But this is my 'ouse! It's always been my 'ouse. I was born 'ere and I'll die 'ere.'

The bouncer in ill-fitting whites who held Stan in his chair glared down at him. The message was clear. That can be arranged.

'Now, now. Don't be silly Mr. Gonputh. Just think of it as a nice holiday. I've got a brochure here. You will be staying at The Pleasant Rest Care Home.'

'Peasant's Rest? That's where they send poor folk to die. You go in there, you never come out again.' Stan tried to stand and follow Anita, who was now squeezing her buttocks past a pile of newspapers and into the dark hallway. A hand the size of a bunch of bananas pushed him back down.

'You'll stay there, Gramps, if you know what's good for you.'

He doesn't know what's good for him, thought Anita as she felt her way through the gloom, that's the problem. Her fingers brushed against a door and she reached down for the handle. This would be the room known as the parlour, used in Victorian times for entertaining and high tea. The stiffness of the door in the frame suggested it had not been visited for some time. She gave it a shove and a gust of stale air puffed out. The room was in black, with only a slit of light coming from edges of the thickly curtained window. Anita took four paces across the room and ripped the drapes open in a flurry of dust. She coughed, her eyes tight shut, tears streaming down her cheeks. When the wheezing and spluttering subsided she opened her eyes, expecting to see a room crammed full of worthless trash. Instead, she was staring into the eyes of a young child. She fell back, colliding with a dresser causing the china within to rattle. She clutched her hand to her chest, her heart thudding hard against her fist. A life-size portrait of a golden haired boy hung above a fireplace black with decades of soot. A teary-eyed cherub, his lips were thick and pouty as if he had just been scolded. Anita rubbed grit from her own watering eyes, and looked around the room. It was filled with portraits of the same sad, strange child. They were hung on faded William Morris wallpaper and propped up against walls. Small canvases were stacked on shelves and a series of cameos in silhouette were lined up on a mantel inch-thick with grey ash. Peering closer at the three oval frames, Anita saw only one was of the boy, the other two were a man and a woman. A mother and father. Parents and child. The eternal triangle.

A commotion in the hallway caused Anita to turn just as one side of the triangle came bursting through the door.

'You get out of 'ere! This ain't for youse, so get out!'

Stan snatched up an ancient chenille cloth from the table in the corner and tried to cover up the biggest of the portraits, but his efforts were cut off by a solid fist to his jaw.

'Don't do that you animal! You'll kill him,' Anita yelled as the old man's eyes rolled back in his head and he crumpled to the floor with a thud and a puff of dust. The last thing he saw was the blue-eyed boy that never was.

He always came to Stan in dreams, but the older he got the harder he found it to sleep. The punch had knocked him out cold, and for that he was grateful. She was there too, looking as beautiful as the day he met her, before she became a living ghost. It started with the painting. Mary was such a talented artist. She used to paint portraits of their friends. Just for fun, she never took any money. Painting is my pastime, she used to say, not my profession. Stan would ask her, what you passing the time 'til, petal? And she would always reply, 'til I become a mother.

But the time passed. And still she painted.

Soon the friends stopped coming to visit. They had families of their own. Friends went off to war, friends died; friends came back with pieces missing. Some of those pieces were obvious in their absence, others not so much.

And still she painted. She painted Stan. She painted herself. But most of all she painted him. The perfect golden-haired angel, who never cried, never spat out his milk, never broke his toys, never kicked his mother, and never woke in the night.

The perfect child who never existed. Not at first anyway.

The two workmen, Darren and Terry, took up residency that very afternoon. Now Stan was out of the way, they could get to clearing the years of accumulated shit out of this dump and make it habitable for human life again. Thick insulation boards to cover the original walls, loft lagging, a telephone line and Wi-Fi, rip out the fire places and replace them with eco-friendly faux log burners, and of course fully wiring the house up to the mains. Electric lights, electric heating, electric oven, microwave, dishwasher and fridge-freezer.

'Lucky old bastard,' Terry said as they filled the newly delivered skip with junk. 'I wish someone would come to my house and give me a load of free stuff.'

The kitchen was easy. Everything had to go. Floors were ripped up, holes smashed in walls, ceilings yanked down. The rape of Ivy House had begun. When they got to the parlour, the face of the flax-haired boy shone down upon them. Without knowing if the paintings were worth anything or not, Darren moved them out of the room and piled them unceremoniously at the bottom of the stairs. Battery operated clip lamps were soon attached to the woodworm ridden bannisters and around the tops of doorframes. The corners of rooms were now shadowed in dark relief to the harsh artificial light. Spiders scuttled under skirting boards and mice cowered in tiny gaps in the walls. Darren shone a torch upstairs, but thought better of venturing up there. The risers were covered in threadbare carpet and the wood underneath probably rotten. Plus he had heard stories about this house. Stories that got passed around the village when he was a kid, embellished each time so that truth was lost long ago. All he knew was he didn't want to be the first one to find out what was waiting at the top of those stairs.

Stan Gonputh lay with starchy sheets over his head, not moving, barely breathing. If he stayed motionless long enough, one of two things was bound to happen. Either she would bugger off and leave him in peace, or she would think he had finally carked it and set off some bloody alarm sending every nurse and his dog running into the room.

'It's no use pretending I'm not here Mr. Gonputh. The sooner you sign these papers, the sooner you can get back to your home. That'll be nice, won't it?'

Anita Sparrowhawk's voice was as sweet as a Diet Coke enema, and just as unpleasant. She was sick of his games. Sick of his stubbornness. Sick of the sheer bloody-minded pointlessness of his objections. She had decided weeks ago that he was just being obstructive for the sake of it. There could be no other explanation. The renovations to his house were not only free, but the solar panels would save him money on his future electricity bills and might even make him some money, allowing him to sell energy back to the National Grid. You'd think the tight-fisted old grunion would be grateful. But no, each time she argued with him, he came back with the same old line.

'I don't want no electrickery.'

So in the end, she lied.

'Mr. Gonputh.'

She laid a hand on top of the bedcovers where she imagined his shoulder to be.

'Stan. The council has listened to your concerns and has agreed that wiring the house up to mains electricity will no longer form part of the planned eco-upgrade. They're going to put in a wind-powered generator instead.'

She heard a soft rustle underneath the sheet. I've got him.

'Yes, they are going to install a small wind-turbine on your roof. You won't even be able to see it. But it will be enough to power the appliances that we are putting in. Appliances that will make your life easier, Stan. All of this will make life better for you, I promise.'

A tuft of white hair emerged at the top of the bed, followed by the thick black rim of Stan's glasses.

'But it won't be electrickery, right? We won't be hooked up to nothing? It'll just be the wind making my 'pliances work?'

'Of course. Now sign here, there's a love, and you'll be back home in no time.'

Stan thought back to the promise he made. The promise Mary begged him to make with her dying breath. He told me Stan, she had croaked in his ear. He told me not to let them hook us up to the electric lights. He said Mother, you mustn't...

He remembered cutting her off, even as sick as she was, angry that she was keeping up this stupid charade. There 'ain't no one to call you Mother. There is no boy.

There never was. The guilt he had at shouting her down, of yelling at his dying wife in her final hours never left him. But he had long since had enough of hearing about the boy. Had enough of looking at his face in those paintings. Had enough of feeling the child brush past him when he was in bed at night, sending prickles over his skin and freezing the very breath in his throat. Promise me, she hissed through gritted teeth speckled with blood. Promise him. Promise your son that you won't ever get the electrickery.

I promise, petal. I promise.

Work on Ivy House increased in pace. The council had an allocated fund per nominated house, but the quicker and cheaper they could get the job done, the more of the money they could funnel back into the council coffers. Although the workmen were on a day rate, they didn't realise their foreman had signed a contract meaning they would only get paid if the work was completed on time. For every day over the deadline, they would have money deducted. So the time had come for work to begin upstairs.

'You know what they say about this house?' Darren shouted up at Terry, who was clipping lamps at the top of the stairs.

'I know what I say about this house,' Terry yelled back down. 'I'm sick of the sight of it. Sooner we get done the better. I wanna get paid.'

'They say the old boy who lived here...'

'Lives here,' Terry interrupted. 'He ain't dead yet.'

He flicked a switch, flooding the landing with light. Darren peered up the stairs, his face pale.

'When I was a kid, they used to say he kept his dead wife up there.'

'Bullshit,' Terry laughed. 'Now get your arse up here and bring that loft lagging.'

Darren started to heave a large roll of insulation up the stairs with a grunt, pausing on each step.

'We used to hear him up there, talking to her. In the summer, when the windows were open.'

Step.

'It used to be a dare. Who could get closest to the house.'

Step.

'My mate Trev climbed up on that old coal shed round the back once.'

Step.

'I watched him pull himself up on the window sill. He was always a strong one, Trev. He pulled himself up just enough to see in.'

Step.

'He saw her, Terry. He saw the wife. I've never seen anyone so scared in my life. He screamed and dropped down on the coal bunker. Twisted his bloody ankle, but he didn't care. He just kept saying he saw her. The dead wife, Terry, she's here.'

Terry leaned down to take the lagging from his younger, and more gullible, workmate.

'He was having you on, Daz. There is no dead wife. Now stop being a pillock, I'll bring up the tool bags and you find the loft hatch.'

Alone on the landing, the light should have been a comfort to Darren, but instead it threw sinister shapes and created giant shadow cobwebs. He looked up, hoping he would see the small square door cut in the ceiling above him, but no. He would have to go into the bedrooms and check. He waited for Terry to come back up, but could hear he was now deep in conversation on the phone. Picking up one of the clip lamps, Darren peered into the nearest room. A pale death mask shone back at him. A woman long dead, her skin grey and peeling. He yelped and dropped the lamp on his foot.

'What are you squealing about, you big fanny?' Terry had arrived at the top of the stairs to see Darren cowering in the corner.

'Dead wife! In there...she's...in there.'

Darren pointed a shaking finger towards the bedroom where he had seen the ghost of Mary Gonputh. Terry pushed the door open and shook his head in laughter. A half-finished portrait of a woman in dried-up oils stared accusingly out at them both.

'Turn her round will you Daz? I can't work with her looking at me.'

The day Stan Gonputh returned to Ivy House, nothing much looked different from the outside. He squinted up at the eaves and chimney to see any sign of the windmill, but that Sparrowhawk woman did say it would be discreet. Once inside, however, Stan didn't recognise the rooms he had lived in his whole life. Gone were the cool, gently worn flagstone floors, covered over with springy oak laminate. Gone were the blackened glass oil lamps, replaced with energy saving light bulbs. Gone was the coal fired range that his own mother used to heat his bath water when he was a small child, splashing in the tin tub in front of the fire. All his memories, all the physical landmarks of his life in Ivy House were gone. The walls had been painted magnolia in a slapdash manner that left splatters on the door frames and floors. He could see the dotted and dabbed plasterboard underneath where the walls had come down to make room for the cables. Cables that, Stan Gonputh had been assured, were not hooked up to the National Grid. He stared at the new microwave. It stared back expressionless, a blank faced robot. A futuristic intruder in his home. He wanted a brew, but the pristine white electric kettle looked too delicate for his gnarled old hands. Tired only the way a nearly ninety-year old man could be, he wanted to be back in his own bed after the hard institutional slab he had been sleeping on at Pleasant Rest. He trudged through to the hallway, reaching for the oil lamp that wasn't there anymore. He stood at the foot of the stairs and flicked the light switch. The bulb at the top instantly illuminated the shady corners of Ivy House with a pIng. Maybe this electric thing might not be so bad after all.

Electrical current flowed through the newly fitted consumer unit and into the maze of cables that now circuited the house like a network of nerves. Anita Sparrowhawk had lied. A white lie. No harm could come of telling some old codger a fib. She slept happily in her bed, her conscience clear, as flames licked out from inside the metal box in Stan Gonputh's basement. The unit had been installed in a rush, and a single screw had not been correctly fastened, causing faulty connections inside the distributor box. The fire quickly spread to a pile of old papers that had been chucked into the basement during the renovation. Landmark news stories from as far back as the 1930s went up like dry tinder and burned a path all the way up the cellar stairs to the ground floor. The plastic underlay between the original floor and the laminate quickly melted and the newly painted doors began to bubble and warp in the heat.

'Father! Father! Wake up!'

The boy's voice came to him in his dream. He even felt the familiar tug at his arm in the moment between sleeping and waking.

You ain't real, Stan Gonputh said sternly inside his head. You ain't real so leave me alone.

Smoke soon tickled its way under his bedroom door. The fumes filled Stan's sleeping lungs, and he was dead before the flames ripped through the top floor leaving nothing but a blackened shell.

When the firemen combed through the burned wreckage of Ivy House, the only thing untouched by the fire was a portrait of a handsome young couple and their smiling, golden-haired son.

SPARKS

OFF THE HOOK
BETTY BREEN

Ernie and Sue Smith
August 20th

"I told you Ern, I don't want one of those things. I have a pair of legs don't I?" Sue stood over her husband as she picked at some loose thread on her latest knitting project. Ernie rolled his eyes, muttering to himself. Ignoring his wife was a skill he had learnt many years ago.

"Are you sure it won't go into my brain? What did Rosie say again?" Sue started pacing. "Waves...that's it. She said they go into your brain and give you tumours!"

Ernie took a deep, calming breath.

"It's the Devil's work you know. Father Michael..."

"Sue, please, unless you want me to electrocute myself, will you keep the ideas of your preacher to yourself." Ernie exhaled.

"Worse than those talking boxes he says. Straight through the ear into your brain. Oh I pray our Lord takes me from this wicked place." Sue held the cross that hung from her neck and closed her eyes.

Ernie continued in silence, he knew better than to get into a conversation about God. He was never one to believe in all that mumbo jumbo. If there was a God then why would he make women and men so different?

"Done. Now don't touch it. I'm gonna go down to the phone box and call you to see if it works." Ernie packed his tools away and placed the telephone on the table.

"I'm not touching it...can't you answer it?" Sue dropped to the sofa.

"How can I ring it from down the road and then bloody answer it in here woman?" Ernie said, now getting annoyed.

"Maybe...well...I don't know Ern, I just don't like it."

"Look, all you have to do is pick it up and when you hear me saying hello just put it straight down, okay? You don't even need to put it against your ear if you don't want to. I'll speak loudly so you can hear me." Ernie, now feeling bad that he had got frustrated, sat down and held his wife's hands and spoke gently.

"Okay." Sue suddenly felt very silly.

"Right, I won't be long, so stay close to the phone and when you hear it ring do as I said." Ernie gave her a gentle kiss on her head and before heading to the door he grabbed his opened bottle of beer.

Sue waited anxiously. She looked down at her knitting. "Oh damn."

She ran out to the kitchen and grabbed a pair of knitting needles when the phone rang. Her heart began to race as the ringing filled the empty house. She stood over the telephone and waited before she lifted the receiver. She didn't hear anything. She waited a few seconds.

"Hello," she called out. There was nothing. She placed the receiver slightly closer to her ear. "Ern are you there?" slowly she lifted it closely thinking she heard a faint whisper. "Ern say something?" Annoyed at her husband's lack of conscience for keeping his promise she placed the receiver right next to her ear. "Hello?"

A quiet whisper wormed its way into her ear; she stood frozen for a moment. She placed the phone back and turned towards the kitchen.

"I forgot to bring money for the payphone," Ernie walked through the front door and started to look for change. "Sue?" He peered into the empty front room. He turned and saw his wife was standing by the kitchen sink.

"Sue, did you hear what I said? I forgot change. Do you have any?" Getting no answer, he moved forward and reached out his hand.

Detective Barker
August 25th

"Hello everyone, so what do we know?" Detective Barker placed his shoe covers on and put an unlit cigarette between his lips. He knew he couldn't light it yet, but habit made him do it. The smell told him that he would need the nicotine.

"Not sure on all the details yet Sir, but looks like a domestic case. No sign of a break in, nothing seems to have been taken. No other rooms in the house have been disturbed."

Barker pulled out his handkerchief and placed it over his nose, moving his cigarette to behind his ear. "Jesus Jones, who's who?"

Barker stepped over an arm and what looked to be half a left foot. Images of the two victims came into his mind.

"It looks like the wife was the perpetrator, Sir. Mr. Smith has been chopped up, then his torso flayed." The Sergeant pointed to what looked like a pair of dark curtains hanging from a door frame. "His head has been removed and then," moving towards the cooker he gestured to a large ceramic cooking pot, "...boiled Sir..."

"Holy shit."

"The wife has slices across each wrist."

"What's that?" Barker looked closer at the corpse that wore only a nightgown.

"Knitting needles, Sir. Through both ears. Most likely what killed her. The cuts here are deep but the needles would have done it." Jones walked away, holding a hand over his mouth.

Barker had also seen enough, he needed that cigarette. He followed the Sergeant out of the house. "Any history of mental illness with the wife?"

"Not sure yet Sir. Waiting to get all the reports. Neighbours statements say they were happy. Married for over 40 years but no children. He worked as a builder and she was a housewife. She was extremely religious but he never attended church." Jones flicked through his note pad.

"Any history of domestic violence?" Barker pulled out a second cigarette, lighting it without a thought.

"None reported by neighbours. Some did mention he liked his drink." Sergeant Jones said. "Sorry Sir, best get this sorted quickly. Don't want the papers getting any pictures."

"Thank you, Sergeant." Detective Barker made his way to his car and pulled out his notepad: clear cut case. Won't be much need for a Detective. Wife finally gone mad after years of living with an alcoholic/abusive husband. Couldn't talk about it, most don't. Might not have even been physical. Why no kids? Emotional abuse maybe?

Underlining the last sentence, he lit another cigarette and drove away.

ANON
January 1st

New Year, new me. I am putting an end to all this belittling, shame. I can't put up with it. God I am so pathetic, such a coward. Mummy is right. Why do I even exist? What have I even done to make a difference in this world? Other than burden her and take away her freedom.
I hate her. I hate everyone.
No more. This year is going to be different, this year is my year.

Detective Barker

August 25th

Barker pulled into his parking space at the station and pulled out some nicotine gum. Placing two pieces in his mouth he made his way into the dull grey building that had long felt like home. The doorman gave him a nod, letting him pass freely without the obligatory search. Barker had been working there too long now; he was known and respected by all. Stepping into the lift he hit the button and reached for his note pad. Under his notes he added: case closed. As the doors opened, he saw the Superintendent waiting in his office.

"So Barker, details on the case?" he said not looking up from his seat.

"Clear case of domestic bliss gone Pete Tong," Barker said. He sat down and brought out his pad. "No sign of a break in. Wife killed the alcoholic husband. No kids. She probably just had enough."

"Good. When will you get the file to me?" The Superintendent stood up and headed for the door.

"Just waiting for a few more reports. Tomorrow morning I'd say."

"I expect it tonight. Oh and Barker, your room stinks of cigarettes. Sort it out."

The Superintendent left and Barker gave a large sigh. God he hated him. Only got the badge because his daddy was on the board. Wouldn't know a day's work if it slapped him square in the face. Barker moved over to the opened window and lit a cigarette. After what he had seen this morning he needed it before he could begin the report. He wasn't half way through it when the phone rang.

"Barker." He carefully stubbed out the cigarette before placing it behind his ear. "Who am I speaking to?"

Barker wrote down what the voice on the telephone was saying; an address, a quick detail, then hung up.

"Jesus. Another one?"

"You alright boss?" A familiar face peered in through the door.

"Another homicide. God this world is shit." Barker stood up. Realising he hadn't even taken his coat off, he headed straight for the door. "If you see the Super, tell him I'm out on a call."

"Will do boss."

Barker ran down the stairs, and back to his car.

Sammy Worthing
August 24th

Sammy sat in his room and turned up the volume. His parents had been arguing for nearly an hour now. This was nothing unusual. However today was Sammy's birthday and he had thought that perhaps his mother and father would be able to be friends for at least 24 hours, for his sake. His mother, barely sixteen years older than Sammy, wasn't exactly the motherly type. Got knocked up way too young, then forced to marry the man who did it too her. She made Sammy know that he wasn't wanted and a huge inconvenience for her. His dad on the other hand stepped up to the mark. He made him feel wanted. Sammy loved his dad.

Tonight, they were arguing about Sammy's party. His dad had been flirting with one of his friends. Sammy wouldn't put it past him, but then the way she treated him, Sammy couldn't really blame him. Plus, his mum was a slut. Every weekend she went out clubbing, wearing practically nothing, coming home in the early hours. Sometimes not at all. Anger was bubbling up inside of Sammy. It wasn't fair, today was meant to be his day and his selfish mother couldn't even give him that.

Sammy snapped off his headphones threw them across the room.

"Will you shut the fuck up?" Sammy shouted through the comforting four walls of his bedroom.

The shouting stopped momentarily. Suddenly his door swung open to reveal his mother holding a kitchen knife.

"What the fuck did you just say?" Her eyes pierced through him.

"I said to shut up," Sammy replied, "come on mum it's my birthday for Christ sake. Can't you and dad just quit it for tonight?" Sammy was angry but he had his father's passive nature. He didn't want to argue, not with her, not with anyone.

"How dare you speak to me like that?" She stepped forward into Sammy's room. He stood up, aware that his mother wasn't in the mood for bargaining.

"Dee, the kid is right." Sammy's dad appeared in the doorway and grabbed at his wife's arm. "Let's just cool it for now. For his sake, yeah?"

Muttering under her breath Sammy's mum turned and pushed past Mike. "Fucking men."

"Alright kiddo?" Mike winked at his son. "Sorry about all that."

Just then the phone rang. The sound echoed through the house before they heard Sammy's mum shouting, "Who the fuck is this? Say something you piece of shit."

The receiver was slammed down and Mike reached out for his son. "Just stay in here okay. I'll make this up to you I promise." He turned and left. Sammy kicked his controller across the floor and dropped onto his bed.

It was dark when Sammy woke. He headed out to the bathroom where he splashed some water on his face and brushed his teeth. As Sammy walked back out into the hall he noticed all the lights were still on.

"Mum? Dad?" Sammy called out across the landing. There was no reply. He looked in his parents' room, the bed was untouched. The time from his dad's clock flashed 01:34am. "Hey where are you guys?"

He started to make his way down stairs. The TV was off, but there was a noise coming from the kitchen. Sammy suddenly felt strange. He wasn't scared but something wasn't right. He crept into the kitchen. His mother was there by the stove.

"Jesus mum, you gave me a bloody fright. What are you doing? Where's dad?" Sammy walked in and opened the fridge. "Holy fuck."

In the middle of the fridge was his father's head. Placed on a plate, surrounded with chopped veg. In his mouth was a red apple.

"Sit down dear; I'm making you a special birthday treat." Sammy's mum turned from the stove. In her hands were what looked like a line of unseparated sausages. Sammy turned and threw up. Then he saw the headless body of his father lying lifeless on the floor. The intestines slipped out of the slashed torso as his mother continued to pull on them.

"Can you be a gem and get me a large pan. This doesn't want to fit on the frying pan." Sammy began to scream.

Detective Barker
August 25th
By the time Barker arrived at the quiet, middle class estate, the place was swarming with police cars, several ambulances and a fire engine. He was greeted by Jones, who quickly filled him in.

"Mr. and Mrs. Worthing, both in the kitchen. I've got to warn you boss, it isn't pretty in there." Jones handed Barker some notes and walked away. Barker took out a cigarette and held it delicately in his hands. A man dressed all in white ran out of the house and started throwing up.

"Jesus, pull yourself together," Barker said moving aside to avoid the splash of vomit.

"Sorry sir."

"First time?"

"First day sir. Talk about getting thrown in at the deep end."

"There's never a good day for this shit. Go clean yourself up. Then get back to work."

"Yes sir," the man said stumbling away.

Barker carefully placed the cigarette behind his ear before putting on a face mask. Following the sounds from inside the house he made his way into the crime scene. Blood splattered the ceilings, the walls, a pot on the stove stained red. A mutilated body lay on the floor, its insides leading their way carelessly to the kitchen counter, previously used to prepare the family meals. The body had no feet, no hands, and no head. A woman sat at the table wearing an apron that once displayed a floral detail, but now told a picture of the night's events. A plate in front of her held the remains of her last meal. The woman, late thirties Barker thought, was missing a nose and an eye. Protruding from one ear was the handle of what Barker assumed was a kitchen knife.

"Afternoon Sir, what a day right?"

"Yeah."

"Same as this morning. No sign of forced entry, nothing obviously taken. Seems like another domestic. Must be something in the water." The officer chuckled at his joke.

"Do you think this is funny?" Barker clenched his fist.

"Sorry Sir, no. I just..."

"Get on with your job. Play Joker in your own time."

Barker moved closer to study her face, trying to see if he could see any rage, anger, bitterness. Anything to give a reason as to why she did it. Seeing enough, he started to walk around the house, looking for any clues into the family life. On the mantel were the photos of a mother, father, and their son. Frozen images of what looked to be a happy family.

"Where is the son?" Barker shouted.

"No sign of anyone else in the house Sir."

"Doesn't mean he isn't here. And if he's not then we need to find him before he finds this."

Barker walked upstairs to search the bedrooms. In all the years he had been doing this he always felt like an intruder. Sneaking into people's personal lives, the ones we all keep perfectly hidden from the world. He moved into the teenager's room. No sign of a disturbance, just the typical chaos a teenager lives in. Barker sat on the edge of the single bed and took out a cigarette. From across the room came a noise.

"Hello? Don't be afraid I'm here to help."

Barker heard the gentle tap again coming from a trunk at the end of the boy's bed. It was locked with a padlock.

"I need help up here." Barker shouted.

Two officers came running in. "There's someone in there. Get a hammer, anything, quickly."

Barker smashed the hammer over the lock breaking it open. Inside was the young boy he had seen in the photographs. Curled up and covered in blood, the boy was barely conscious, but alive. "Get the medical team up here. NOW!"

"He's sedated. No major injuries, only a few minor scratches to his hands and back. But he's upset," said the Doctor. Barker followed him into the boys' room. Barker sat down smoothing a cigarette longingly through his fingers.

```
ANON
January 23rd
     I thought she'd appreciate it. I made it
for her. To help her. She is always moaning
about the house work. That's it that was the
last time I try and help her. Hours I spent,
wasted. You would have thought a thank you,
or well done. But no, nothing so kind could
ever come from something so evil. It's time
someone taught her some manners.

     She had it coming the whore. She
deserved it. Every fucking blow. She
thought she could rule me forever, that she
was cleverer than me. Well I proved that
bitch wrong. God the freedom feels
exhilarating. She was holding me back. You
were right, she was jealous of me, of my
greatness. She was nothing more than a
stupid little housewife. And now she is
nothing more than worm food.

     Nothing can stop us now. We can be
together. She tried to keep us apart. She
```

knew how great we could become. Well she is gone now. It's just us.

Detective Barker
August 26th

"Sir the doctor says he's awake," Jones said handing Barker a paper cup filled with coffee.

Barker felt a warm hand on his shoulder as he stood out in the summer storm. Putting out his smoke he took the coffee and made his way to the boy's room. As he entered he could no longer see the cheerful, carefree boy from those photos, instead he saw a thin, pale, scared little boy.

"Hey Sammy, I'm Detective Barker." Barker sat down next to the boy and gave a smile that he hoped would help him feel safe. "I'm sorry, but I need to ask you a few questions, about what happened the other night. Would that be okay?"

Sammy stared across the room, a tear rolled down his cheek. For a while neither of them spoke. Barker didn't want to put any pressure on the boy, he knew he would talk, but he also didn't want him to know that as the only survivor he was their number one suspect.

"Can you tell me what happened the other night? Did someone come into the house?" Barker knew not to ask leading questions but he needed answers to close the case.

Sammy shook his head.

"Were your parents arguing?"

"Arguing? They were always arguing. I never thought she…" Sammy started to cry.

"It's okay, take your time." Barker handed him a tissue then sat down on a chair.

"It was my birthday. It's all my fault…"

"What do you mean?"

"I told her to fuck off. I was sick of her treating my dad like shit. I just wanted to have a normal family."

"What happened next?"

"My mum left and my dad said he would sort it out. I fell asleep. If I'd known I would never have…" Sammy started shaking.

"It's okay," Barker said reaching out for the boy's hand, "do you want a drink? Something to eat?" He felt the boy was beginning to trust him.

"No, I'm okay thanks." Sammy blew his nose. "I woke up and noticed that all the lights were still on. I walked down stairs and…and…oh god, she was eating him…she had his insides in her hands…she asked me for a…for a…"

"Okay Sammy, that's enough for now." Barker looked through the glass door at the doctor and gave him a nod.

"I've given him some more sedatives. What that boy has seen is enough to give anyone nightmares."

"That's okay Doctor. I'll come back later and see how he is doing." Barker dropped his coffee cup into the bin and left.

Barker sat in his car and pulled out his notepad; domestic … woman goes mad, kills husband, boy manages to escape. How?? Why not kill him too? Throwing the pad onto the passenger seat he made his way back to the office.

ANON
Feb 11th
It's her fault. She made us this way. If she had only let me be free. Who's the stupid little boy now eh? Dumb bitch.

We are so close now. Only a few more adjustments and we shall be the most powerful, feared people in the world. People will worship us, they will bow to us and admire the talent and power we have.

We are God.

We are greater than God.

I told you not to question me. I know what I am doing. It is easy to control them. All of them. Why discriminate. Old, young, male, female? We can control them all. All from here. Mummy would be so proud. She didn't want me going out, making friends, leeching into their minds she would say. Well I don't need to go out. I'll do it from her four walls. For 25 years she locked me up here in this filthy place she called home. She couldn't even cook a meal without burning it. Well we don't need her. We've proved that. We don't need any woman telling us what to do. We are going to be telling them what to do.

It's going to be beautiful. I can already smell the chaos. Taste the anarchy. We will have so much power.

No, I told you, not yet. A few alterations and checks. We need some lab

rats to test on first. Make sure it's perfect. Mummy would never allow anything less than perfection.

Dr Willow
September 1st

It was 7:30am; Dr Willow made his way to work, whistling loudly with the birds. Today was his last day. Thirty years he had been at this surgery and today he was finally retiring, handing it over to his son, also a partner in his practice. He loved his job, helping people, making people better. However, the quiet villa in France was calling him. In a month's time, he and his wife would be moving across the sea where he could live out the rest of his days in peace, doing his second passion, fishing.

"Morning Dr Willow, how are you today?" Claire, the young receptionist he had recently hired peered over the desk and gave him the warm, welcoming smile that had landed her the job.

"Morning Claire. I am fine and dandy. Last day today," he said smiling back, "many patients today?"

"No one this morning. Just a telephone appointment at eleven then the drop-in clinic until one o'clock."

"Great. I've got lots of paperwork to do." Dr Willow poured himself a mug of coffee and made his way down the hall, feeling elated that this would be the last day he would have to drink the awful stuff.

At 10:45am Dr Willow called through to ask for the patient's file. He was old fashioned and refused to work from the computer. Something his son would be changing as soon as he was in charge.

"We don't seem to have one for him I'm afraid. I'll check the out tray and bring it in."

A few minutes later the smell of fresh coffee filtered up the hallway.

"Come in."

Claire walked in carrying a mug and a small file. "Doesn't look like we've seen him before."

"I know the family. Seen the mother for years. Haven't heard from her in a few months. Thank you Claire." Dr Willow placed the file on his desk and picked up the phone.

"Hello, Dr Willow here, I was wondering if I could speak to Mr..." he paused for a moment, then pressed the receiver closer to his ear, "Hello, are you saying something?" Dr Willow stopped as the whispers spread through his mind like a fire. A heat raced through him like electricity, attacking the synapses. He replaced receiver and started to make his way down the hall into the waiting area.

"Everything alright doctor?"

Dr Willow stood frozen; he was seeing the world differently. Colours changed, the caring feeling he felt when looking at his patients was gone. He could see their souls. Their hatred, their filth poured out of them and danced beautifully, inviting him to dance with them. He turned at hearing his name. The once young, pure secretary looked old, her skin oiled with the evil that was in her soul. The whispers in his ear became louder.

Kill her

He didn't ask why. Electricity raced through his brain. The whore didn't deserve to live. He could smell the evil. He walked around to the other side of the desk, searching.

Use the scissors

He reached over, a tingle spread through him, down to his fingers. He clasped the scissors and sliced them across her throat. The demons fled her body. Dr Willow smiled as he turned to face the waiting patients.

They all need to die

He pressed his lips together and started to whistle.

Twisted Nerve. Our favourite.

Children clung to their parents' legs as they pleaded with him. Cocking his head, he looked down at them.

Let them be. They are innocent.

Pushing the children aside he slashed the others one by one as the sweet sound of harmony echoed through his mind. Blood poured from them, black and heavy. One went for the door. He grabbed her then bit down on her nose. Using his teeth, he severed it from her face. Rage made him move him quicker than he had for years. Until finally he was the only one standing.

You're work here is done. You are done.

Looking down at the scissors his muscles ached, he wanted death, a release from the selfishness of this world. The whispers grew inside, louder and louder they commanded him.

ANON
May 22nd

Of course it works.

I know you thought it would, but I needed to see it with my own eyes. It's beautiful though, it truly is. Complete mind control. No questions. And how you knew the correct code to use, brilliant. She ripped that dog apart. It was like she was consumed. Oh, I can feel her rage, the power. God it was glorious to watch.

However, we must do it again. We can't risk taking it out there until we know for sure that it works, 100%. We need more test subjects.

Don't argue with me. You are nothing without me, remember that. I'll get them don't worry. I know the place. A place where no one cares if you go missing.

Misty

June 14th

Misty waited at her corner. It had only taken a few months before she got command of the best spot. She was beautiful, slim, and fresh meat for the punters. The others had been working there much longer and their appearances showed it. Years of drug abuse and thousands of sexual encounters takes its toll. Misty however had only been on the streets a short while. Her addict ex-boyfriend had got her hooked. Then after taking everything she owned he screwed her for the last time before moving on to the next unsuspecting girl.

Misty saw headlights coming towards her so she made her move.

"Hey there stranger, looking for some company?" Misty leaned in through the window, filling the car with her sweet scent.

"Hi gorgeous. Get in," the guy said opening the door.

He had a cute smile Misty thought. He looked young, someone who would happily pay for not a lot of her time. She climbed into the car. "I'm all yours," she said placing her hand gently on his crotch.

"Would you mind if we drove a little first. I'm a bit nervous."

"First time eh? Well don't worry, Misty will look after you." She leaned over and pushed her tongue deep into his ear.

"Um yeah." He pushed her away.

"You wanna just talk first? That's okay but you will have to pay for that. My time isn't free."

Driving for a while, he didn't say much, muttering sometimes then smiling across to her. They drove away from the streets.

"Would you mind if we parked up and got in the back?"

Misty never felt nervous, she was tall and strong, and it didn't take long on the streets to learn how to take care of yourself.

"Sure baby."

He parked up and they got out.

"You know we don't have to do it in the car. It's dark out here. It would give us some more space."

She walked slowly over to him; sliding her hands over his torso she felt his muscles through the thin cotton shirt. He smiled at her and for a second Misty thought she saw something in that smile which told her to run.

Misty woke up. Consumed not with the groggy feeling she had got used to from waking up from a high, but with confusion. Looking around, not recognising where she was she tried to remember the night before. As flashes of headlights and a young man came to her, she felt the cut on her forehead.

"The bastard nutted me," she said aloud. "Hey, sicko where the fuck are you? Coward!"

"No one calls us a coward," a voice boomed out across the tiny room, "I think you'll find you are the coward. Selling your body for money. Whore."

"You wanted a piece of it last night. Pervert."

"It's people like you that make this world a sick place."

"Whatever you freak. Look if you're going to kill me then just get it over with." Misty didn't really care if she lived or died. She knew her life was pointless, and painful. Death would be a sweet release.

"Kill you? Oh no, it's you that's going to have that pleasure." The voice started to laugh as a phone began to ring.

"Fuck you!" Misty shouted. The phone continued to ring. After several minutes, Misty picked it up. "I said fuck you, freak."

Dirty whore, you know you don't deserve to live.

"I don't deserve to live," Misty repeated.

`Look over there across the room. See the knife. Go pick it up.`

Scarcely audible, the whispers snaked through, consuming her.

`Take it. Hold it in your hands. Look at yourself in the mirror.`

Staring at herself, she looked closely at a reflection she barely recognised as hers. She looked old. Withered. Her teeth were rotted, her eyes soulless.

`Cut your face.`

Her hand twitched as she felt a warm tingle run down her arm. It flexed, she slid the blade down her cheek.

`Slowly.`

A thick black liquid oozed from the wound.

`Now pull out those disgusting teeth.`

Misty couldn't stop the voice in her mind. She didn't want to stop it. She was a soulless whore. As each tooth dropped to the floor her mind buzzed, the colours of the room danced before her eyes. Was this really happening? It felt like a dream, a nightmare. One that she didn't want to wake from.

`Cut off your tits. Eat them. Enjoy it.`

Smiling, she gorged on the fatty breasts. Unable to chew she swallowed whole lumps as a warmth filled her belly.

`I'm bored now. Finish it.`

Looking once again at her maimed reflection, she smiled one last time.

Detective Barker

September 2nd

Barker sat and stared out at the bleak morning. Images of the people at the doctor's surgery filled his mind. He badly wanted a cigarette. The woman with her face half eaten made his stomach tighten. This can't be a coincidence. Three separate incidents in two weeks, all with such brutality. The only link: the murderer committing suicide by sticking something in their ear. There was no other connection between them. He had to be missing something.

The board that hung across from him held pictures, notes and all the minor details from each case. The only witness statement, from Sammy, lay on his desk. He had re-visited Sammy trying to get a clearer version of events. Something felt wrong to Barker. He had read the statement dozens of times. Nothing stood out.

"Sorry Sir, I thought you should know that we have managed to get the telephone number of the patient Dr Willow called just before his rampage," said Jones.

"Thanks Jones." Barker sat up. "Hang on Jones, telephone call?"

"Yeah, we found a paper file on his desk. He had a telephone appointment at eleven. We traced the phone records and he did make that call, to a Mr...um..."

Barker, only half aware that Jones was still talking, flicked through Sammy's statement. "Ah! The telephone rang; his mum went to answer it." Barker then started to look through the details of the first incident. "Mr. Smith had installed a telephone that night. That's the fucking link..." Barker jumped from his seat grabbing the piece of paper from a silent Jones before running out the room.

"Sir, I think I have a possible link. I don't fully know how. I just need to get the phone records from the Smith and Worthing case."

Barker paced. Opening a new pack, he took out a cigarette.

"Sir, we got the records."

Tossing the unlit cigarette onto the floor he ran inside. The Smiths only had one number on the received list. The Worthings had two on the night of their deaths. But one matched the Smiths and the one Dr Willow had called.

"Holy fuck, I think we have a lead. Get the Superintendent and all the officers together now."

```
ANON
July 18th
```
I think we are ready. It works. It's bloody genius. I wish mummy was here. I'd love to have controlled her. To get her grovelling at our feet.

Soon the entire world will be begging for our mercy. Ultimate control over their minds. The world is ours. We are their masters. All those spineless pieces of soulless shit will be gone. They don't deserve life, judging everyone they deem to be less worthy than them. Our world will be perfect. No more shutting people away in their homes. No more cowering in the corner waiting for the next beating, being told how hated they are.

We will be loved. We have the perfect weapon.

What does anyone do when they hear the phone ring…they answer it. It's perfect. It's genius. No one will ever suspect. It's the perfect crime. We'll leave no evidence. We won't need to get our hands dirty.

We just need to get into their minds, control them, and then we are free. Our minds, our thoughts, all electrical impulses, just passing through the innocent telephone wire.

Detective Barker

September 2nd

"I don't know how, but right now it's our only lead so unless you want more dead bodies on your hands I'm thinking let's just bloody go with it."

Barker was driving, talking through his hands free. His superintendent hadn't seen the link that Barker could so clearly see. He didn't understand it, but then neither did Barker. He didn't really know much about technology, but if you could send viruses through the internet then why shouldn't you be able to through the telephone line. However, trying to convince his technophobe boss you could transmit a virus that would make someone kill was impossible. Saying it out loud he knew it sounded ridiculous, but it was a lead. All he could think about was poor Sammy. He had killed himself three days after Barker last saw him. Left a note on his bed saying he couldn't shut his eyes and see his mother eating his father any more. He wanted to be with his dad. He knew it was far-fetched. But he had to do it for Sammy, and all those kids who made it out of the doctor's surgery. Poor little fuckers Barker thought.

"Look Sir, if this turns out to be a load of bullshit it's my mistake, I'll take the rap for it. I'm doing this on my own time." Barker hit the end button on his phone and pulled up outside an old empty looking house. Getting to the front door he knocked and waited.

"Police, open the door please." He saw the curtain twitch, so he tried to get a view inside. He couldn't see anything through the dirty net curtains. "God these old houses give me the creeps."

"Hello, can you please open the door." He looked down at the notes Jones gave him about the occupants; one female, aged 65, one male, 25. Maybe she can't get to the door he thought. Maybe her son is out.

"I just need to ask you a few questions Mrs..." his mobile began to ring. Without a thought, he picked it up.

"Barker here."

Hello Detective.

SPARKS

THE FINAL CHARGE
PETER GERMANY

67%

His heads-up display said 67%, and it wasn't going to go up. The only change would be the free-fall as he began to move.

"You ready for this, Sean?" Janel said.

"No, you?"

She shook her head. "Not even close. 71%."

"That's 4% more juice than I'm packing."

"Considering we've had three days of rain, I think we're better off than we could have been. Oh, and don't forget the firefights and bombardment by hi-explosive shells and cluster bombs."

"Incendiary," Sean added.

"We can't forget that."

"Shit," Cole said. She was hitting the frame around her leg with a club hammer. She flexed and it began to move freely.

Sean Banner looked down at his leg, wrapped in the same exoskeleton that encased his whole body. It hadn't had a proper service for almost eight months, and it had repeatedly gone wrong over the last few days as they'd waited for the inevitable attack, and then the order to counter-attack. Almost three hundred years after the Great War and they had reverted to that same old suicidal strategy. One group of troops dug in a hundred yards away from the enemy's trench. One side would go first, then the other.

Death would have a busy day.

66%

The drone footage being transmitted to his heads-up display showed the objective: a nuclear power plant, the last one in Europe - maybe even the world. It was enough to power eighty percent of the survivors but what was left of the European Government didn't want to share with the British.

The last war had seen Europe caught in the crossfire of a biological, chemical and nuclear onslaught. Now everyone was rushing to grab what was left of the resources after war had bled it dry, and the politicians were sending troops to fight each other instead of finding ways for everyone to survive.

Sean thought they should use their limited munitions to shoot all the politicians. Once they were out of the way, the survivors would just get on with it and share this power plant. Those politicians were secure in bunkers with their own generators and solar cells while everyone else had to fight for any form of electricity they could find.

Sean could see a lot of movement in the footage, meaning they were surely outnumbered. The Europeans were dug in deep with infantry, armour and artillery, but most of all they could keep their weapons charged.

58%

"Why haven't we gone over?" Janel said.

"I don't know." Sean's muscles ached. They'd been in their exos for almost three hours. All of them had their suits on standby, not wanting to use up too much of the power.

"What the fuck is command playing at? We can't be on standby this long, it's draining the cells, and our bodies can't take the pressure. We're going to be exhausted by the time they send us over."

"Since when has command cared about us, down here in the shit? They're back at base eating steak and patting each other on the back."

"You two, shut up," Company Sergeant-Major Bird said. "We're going over in five minutes, five minutes people."

50%

Whistles blew and everyone rushed over the edge of the trenches to begin their kamikaze charge for the enemy lines.

Sean and Janel were side by side as they launched themselves into no-man's land. Bullets from both sides flew passed them. Disruptor mortars erupted all around. One caught Bird, his exoskeleton convulsed, breaking both his arms and legs. His body bent backwards, spine shattering. Sean didn't stop moving. To stop was to be a stationary target and that meant death.

Janel took a hi-ex round to the body and blew up, covering Sean in blood, bone, and intestines but he kept running. The enemy lines were less than fifty yards away when he stood on a mine.

36%

Sean could taste copper when he woke up, but it took a moment for his brain to fully process what it meant. He lay in mud where he had fallen. No-man's land all looked the same: mud and bodies. He tried to get up but couldn't, so lifted his head and looked down the length of his body. His left foot was a bloodied mess. The exoskeleton's boot had taken the brunt of the mine's force but not all of it. His right ankle had an unnatural twist in it. He couldn't move his right arm and his back felt strange. His heads-up display was cracked, but still working. It showed his exo's power cell capacity, and a technical image of the exoskeleton against the cracked screen. The parts of the suit that weren't working were illuminated in red. The whole suit was pretty much in red, with a few sections in amber. The only part of the exo that still shone a healthy green was the control panel on his left arm, but as he couldn't move his right arm, he had no way to operate it. What troubled him most was there was no static in his ears. He couldn't hear the sound of war.

They had lost.

Sean looked at his right hand and tried to flex it, but nothing happened. Looking down to his legs he wondered just how much pain stoppers his exo had pumped into him.

An explosion shook the ground. He flinched and turned his head to where he thought it had come from but couldn't see anything, except the corpses of his friends. He strained to see if any of them were alive but it was obvious that none were. You don't spend three years at war without knowing a dead body when you see one. His eyes welled up as he remembered what had happened to Janel. Sean had been fighting alongside Janel for a little over two years, and they had been through all levels of hell together. Now he was covered in her. Tears streaked down his face, carrying away dirt, grime and blood.

28%

Artillery rounds tore apart the lines where his side of this pointless, bloody war had been held up. Sean wondered who had survived long enough to get back to their lines, and if any of them would be alive after the ferocious bombardment they were going through now.

Did it matter if any of them were alive? None of them would be coming to get him. Even if his comms were working, he doubted anyone would come. He was in the middle of no-man's land and any attempt to rescue him would be deemed suicidal. The enemy wouldn't come for him; they wouldn't even come out to attack. They were well fortified and not stupid enough to risk their numbers. Even if they did come out they wouldn't help him. To them, Sean would be just another corpse. If he wasn't a corpse when they found him he would be soon after. Prisoners of war was a phrase for a time when integrity meant something. Even if the troops on the ground aided him, their commanders wouldn't, and punishment would be swift on those who had helped. His side wasn't any better. Their orders had been clear: if they're not on our side, they never will be and don't deserve to live.

Sean licked his lips and tried to forget about where he was. He reached for his canteen and struggled as he undid the cap. He wasn't feeling light-headed, so he knew he wasn't losing blood. His display flickered and he saw that his exo's power cell was down to 35%. The exo had a first-aid unit built into the back, but it wasn't a medical kit in the traditional sense. It was connected to smaller kits that were built into other areas of the exo and would communicate with the other devices and regulate treatment. Treatment meant pumping the wearer full of painkillers, adrenaline and military grade amphetamines. It wasn't designed to save the life of the wearer, just to keep them fighting.

But when the exo's power cell died, so would the pain relief.

23%

Sean's vomit splattered onto his torso, and clung to his chin. He'd been feeling nauseous for a while and hadn't been able to stop himself from being sick when it had finally come. He sipped his water slowly, not wanting to take too much in case it caused him to vomit again, but he needed to take away the acidic taste he had in his mouth. At least the artillery had knocked their bombardment on the head.

He froze as he heard someone cough. Despite the pain it caused he looked over his left shoulder. He hadn't noticed but he was up against one of the metal crosses placed on the battlefield to prevent armour from moving easily across no-man's land, not that they had any armour but the enemy hadn't known that.

Straining, he could just see a woman in an exoskeleton trying to get up. She was on her hands and knees and looked like she was swaying a little. She didn't have her helmet on and he could see her shaved head and knew it was Bren Wood. Bren was good people and someone who he had a lot of time for. He wished she'd keep her head down. She was a good soldier so she had to be suffering from shell-shock. There was no way she'd be exposing herself like that for any other reason.

Sean tried to call out, but all his vocal folds gave him was a scratchy gasp. He tried again as Bren fiddled with the release of her exoskeleton. It clanked as it opened and she fought her way free of it. He watched in horror as she got to her feet and began to stumble around the body-strewn battlefield.

"..en...get...own."

Bren looked his way and locked eyes with him just before she took a bullet to the chest. It didn't knock her off her feet like he'd seen a hundred times before, but instead made her stumble back. She looked down at her chest in confusion before collapsing to her knees. Another shot and her head snapped back. Her body fell to the blood-soaked ground, leaving a red mist where her head had been. Machine gun fire tore up the ground around him as the enemy gunners honed in. In his effort to help Bren he'd brought the eyes of the enemy straight to him.

Each time a string of bullets dug into the ground, Sean flinched. The gun crew didn't know exactly where he was and he tried his best not to give himself away any more than he had done. After a few more bursts, the machine gun fell silent. Sean braced himself for the next round but it didn't come. For the first time in hours there was no gunfire, no explosions, no sounds of pain and agony. It was just quiet and that freaked him out more than the cacophony of war.

As his ears got used to the silence, he could now hear the hum coming from the power plant behind enemy lines. He glanced over his shoulder and saw the complex just a few hundred metres away. A few lights shone in the windows but he couldn't see much more beyond the fortifications. Nine weeks of fighting for an inch at a time and this was as close as he'd got. This was as close as they would ever get. The enemy had been digging in for months before Sean's regiment had been dropped in a mile out from the power plant. They had begun fighting as soon as they had touched down. Their drop ship had gone down before all of the troops could get out, its power cell taking a direct hit and tearing the mammoth aircraft to shrapnel and those in it to bones covered in charred flesh. Drop craft had re-supplied them from high-altitude but the last one had been four days ago. They had to take this power plant. If they didn't then their loved ones would be living in the dark ages once again.

5%

Sean woke slowly as rain fell on his face. He'd passed out. The first thing he saw was his exo's display flashing deep red numbers across the cracked screen, but it then changed to a radiation symbol. He wet himself. This either meant there had been a leak from the power station, or that his side had launched a nuke and he was right in the blast zone.

He shook his head. Maybe it was a malfunction with the exoskeleton - he knew it was damaged. Panic filled him and he tried to move again but all this did was bring pain. He cried out, and machine gun fire tore the sodden ground up around him once more.

His people wouldn't nuke it, it was the last power station known to man. There weren't the resources in the ground to burn, or the ability to make another one. That's not to say they hadn't tried. A whole swathe of northern Europe was a nuclear wasteland because of it. The smog blocked out too much of the sun's light to make solar viable. Without this station, what was left of mankind would have to rely on wind turbines, which the wealthy controlled and charged excessive fees for the electricity. His people wouldn't nuke it, but their leaders would. Sean knew if those who ruled from their fortified bunkers couldn't have something then they wouldn't let anyone else have it either.

Sirens sounded from the power planet. Anti-aircraft guns pumped flack into the twilight sky. He smiled at the beauty of it, like fireworks that he'd seen videos of when he was a kid, before electricity and food and water were rationed. He thought back to celebrating his wedding with the recycled water that his now dead father had been saving for a special occasion. The two families had all chipped in with their rations of electricity to have a party with music and flashing coloured lights.

The rain hid his tears from the dead that lay around him, but it didn't hide the weak smile on his face at the thought of his wedding to Sarah. He wondered if war or nature had buried her yet. He didn't like the thought she was out there waiting for the scavengers to come. He knew she was dead, even if he hadn't been officially been told. She'd been deployed on the other side of the power plant. Their drop-ship had dropped them half-a-mile closer to the power plant than it was meant to, and into a minefield that had become a shooting range. He'd seen drone footage of the fight, and of the bodies scattered after the shooting had stopped. They never stood a chance.

The display over his eyes stopped showing the remaining charge. Now it just urgently flashed the nuclear alert. Sean closed his eyes as humanity came to an end.

SPARKS

THERE'S NO LIGHTS ON THE CHRISTMAS TREE MOTHER, THEY'RE BURNING BIG LOUIE TONIGHT

MATTHEW CASH

The Nice Lady said that if I told you about what happened she would let me see Saffy, my sister.

Me and Saffy don't like Louie.
Even Frankie doesn't like Louie, and he likes everyone.
I hate him I do, hate him loads, more than mash potato.

Louie is a naughty, evil, wicked man. "A devil in disguise," that's what Nanna said one day near my birthday before she left on the 57 bus. On Sundays Nanna would come round really early and wake us up. Me and Saffy was ever so excited every time Sunday came. Nanna used to bring breakfast, sometimes donuts but not the yucky ones with custard in or jam that squirts on you like fly guts and brains. She would bring the round ones with a hole in the middle. Me and Saffy would scoff 'em down, sometimes cuz I'm a big boy she'd let me have two.

Afterwards she would bring stuff out of her wheelie bag and put it in the oven. "Every family deserves a good Sunday dinner," Nanna always said.

Mummy and Louie would always get up really, really late, sometimes after twelve o'clock in the day! Mummy would always look tired and sometimes she had purple stuff around her eyes. Saffy used to think that was funny cuz it made Mummy look like a panda. "Panda-Mummy," Saffy would shout jumping up and down when Mummy came downstairs for her drink. "Mummy juice" is what Mummy called it but I know it is called COFFEE cuz I'm good at reading and writing and Miss Farr at school says I'm the best in the class. COFFEE tastes yucky, but I like the smell it does cuz it makes me think of Mummy.

Nanna would always look at Mummy funny, her eyes gone all slitty and her mouth screwed up really little, but she never said nothing. When Louie came down the stairs it was like an elephant. Nanna always looked at him funny too, the same face she made when I stood on dog poo in my trainers once and walked it on her carpet.

Louie would always wind us up like, he would snatch a donut out of our hands and ruffle our hairs like he was joking but he never gave the stuff he took back.

On that day Saffy was really happy cuz Mummy had got panda eyes again, she danced round and around and around the kitchen singing a song about Panda-Mummy having her Mummy Juice. When Louie laughed it sounded like he had a bad cough, like Jimmy Morgan in my class gets after P.E when he has the asma. He did that laugh and said, "Mummy had plenty of Mummy juice last night, and loads of daddy juice." He did the laugh again but I don't think his joke was funny or maybe Mummy and Nanna didn't get it cuz no one laughed.

Louie wasn't our real Daddy and we didn't have to call him it either, but he told us off like he was our Daddy which wasn't fair if he wasn't.

Me and Saffy were told to go and play in the garden by Mummy cuz Nanna had started shouting at Louie cuz of his joke that wasn't funny. It was cold outside and all the ground was wet.

Outside we could hear all the shouting, it was very loud. I held Saffy's hand cuz she didn't like the shouting, it made her cry and put her hands over her ears. Cuz it was fireworks three weeks before I talked to her about fireworks and bonfire night and how we would get sparklies and hotdogs and toffee apples and sweets next year when Mummy took us, and how we would have to wrap up warm cuz in the autumn it gets colder and colder and when you do fireworks it's at night time so it's even colder. Cheered her right up that did, talking about fireworks. And we talked about Christmas coming and what things we wanted. We chased each other around and around and around the garden pretending we was fireworks for ages until I needed a wee and we went back to the house.

The kitchen was a right mess when we came back in, the table was on the floor and there was washing up everywhere, some of it brokened. I told Saffy not to touch it cuz broken stuff could give you a poorly and she'd probably get told off if she got a poorly.

I called Mummy but she didn't answer.

The door to the base...thingy under the kitchen was opened. No one was allowed down there or "they'd be in for it" that's what Louie said. He said it was his man-cave, but I remember when I was really little and before Saffy was borned Mummy used to have the washing machine and tumble dryer down there and it wasn't a cave, just a dark dusty room full of boxes and tools. Caves were all dark and drippy and spiky and trolls lived in 'em. There weren't any trolls down there when I went down that time.

But when Louie came to live with us it was then called his man-cave. He sometimes had his friend Steve round to play and they'd go down and play loud music and drink beer. Beer is also yucky, once I tried some of Louie's beer he had in a can which said SPECIAL BREW and it made me pull a face and go yuck. Louie saw me do it and I thought I was going to be in for it but he did that laugh of his and then told me to drink it all. I cried cuz it tasted yuck but he did his angry face and told me he'd turn me into a panda too if I didn't. So I dranked it all and soon as I dranked it I puked everywhere. All over the floor. It was brown with Rice Krispies in it. Louie laughed and then Frankie came in from digging outside and started to lick the floor which was really really yucky. Frankie is my best dog and I tried to stop him but slipped on the sick and felled on my bottom. It made me cry some more but when Frankie had licked all my puke up he licked my cry away too. I love Frankie. Every time Louie went near Frankie he used to woof and make a thunder noise in his mouth. Once, just after Louie came to live he kicked Frankie in the tummy for knocking over one of his beers. He didn't do it on purpose cuz dogs don't do things like that on purpose.

When we walked to the man-cave door Louie came out really quickly like he was running.

Louie couldn't run he was big and fat. Once him and Mummy took us to the park and me and Saffy ran after the ice cream van as it was getting late and he tried to catch up with us but couldn't. His big tummy was wobbling all over the place. It was funny, like Daddy Pig in Peppa. But he shouted at us for running off and then at Mummy who said "Don't you shout at my children." And when the ice cream man leant out of the window to ask us what we would like Louie said, "Fuck off you dirty, Paki cunt!"

I don't know what any of those words mean apart from 'off', 'you' and 'dirty', but he seemed like a nice friendly man, not dirty or smelly at all, and the other words must've been nasty as Louie's face went all red when he shouted 'em and the nice ice cream man looked like he was going to be crying. Saffy cried when the van drove out the park, I just felt upset.

Louie banged the man-cave door shut and locked it with the key he kept in his pocket. "Mummy and Nanna have gone to the shops. Go to your room," He said before walking to the fridge and getting a SPECIAL BREW out. His boots went crunch on the broken washing up.

We did as we was told cuz we had to be extra good when Mummy was out or Louie might lose his rag. I'd had never even seen him with it so don't know how he could lose it. I sawed Nanny's wheelie bag and thought, blige me, why ain't she taken that to the shops? She always took it to the shops. Then I remembered it was Sunday and how Mummy told us the shops shut early on Sundays cuz of God and thought maybe they would be back soon and had just gone out to get one thing.

We played upstairs for ages and ages until it got dark and Louie shouted us to come down. Mummy and Nanna still weren't home and Louie had tidied up all the mess in the kitchen and got the red plates out that we had Christmas dinner on. Nanna's meat she put in the oven was on the table but instead of all the gravy and vegetables that we had to eat or no pudding, there was just meat and a pack of bread. Louie cutted the meat up all messy, not how Nanna does it and made us red sauce and meat sandwiches. Me and Saffy couldn't eat our sandwiches cuz the meat was too hard and hurt our teeth, it was always nice when Nanna made it with gravy and roasted potatoes. Louie shouted at us and said we would eat it or starve. I didn't know what starve was but we had been learning about opposites at school with Miss Farr and I thought that if starve was an opposite to eat it meant we would be hungry. I was clever though cuz I tooked the meat out of our sandwiches and gave it to Frankie when Louie went to the fridge. Louie caught me though and kicked his foot up Frankie's bum and he made a squeaky noise and ran upstairs. Louie growled in my face but he talked at the same time and said, "Eat your fucking dinner."

We had red sauce sandwiches.

Mummy still hadn't come home the next morning which was weird cuz she never was out overnight. Louie was sat in the armchair asleep; all around him was cans and cans of SPECIAL BREW. He smelled bad. I tried to wake him up cuz of breakfast and school but he was snoring too loud. I felt really upset and worried cuz I know it's naughty to miss school if you're not ill and I like school, especially Miss Farr. She's my favourite teacher ever in the world and I think I love her. Saffy was upset lots cuz Mummy not being there still and she wanted Rice Krispies for breakfast but she couldn't have 'em cuz I couldn't reach 'em on top of the cupboard above the microwave. There was still bread on the kitchen table and even though it was a bit stiff it was alright with red sauce on.

After breakfast we went into the lounge and put CBeebies on, it was cool cuz we didn't get to watch it that much cuz of school and even though I'm nearly seven I still like watching the programmes on there. I let Saffy have the buttons cuz it always cheered her right up but she put it up too loud and Louie woke up really really angry and threw a can of beer at her head. Even though it was empty it still smacked her one and made her cry, and when Louie picked her up by her clothes and shouted, "shut the fuck up you little cunt," right in her face she did a massive wee right down his t-shirt. Louie's face went all red like a great big tomato and he threwed Saffy against the TV on the wall. She hit it with a loud bang and it went off just as Mr. Tumble came on which was good cuz I don't like him, he's a right weirdo.

Saffy laid on the floor and Louie looked at me all funny like Billy Coleman in Mrs. Cameron's class in assembly once when he was messing about with Danny Williams and accidentally knocked the fire extinguisher off the wall. He put his hands on his big fat red face and looked at me really scared, Louie did. He moved towards me but I was frightened he was going to hurt me too so I stepped back. Then Saffy started crying louder than I'd ever ever heard her cry in my whole life and Louie didn't look so frightened. He all of a sudden smiled and picked Saffy up and said sorry lots and lots and cuddled her even though she had weed herself.

Louie was really nice to us afterwards and even said we could put the Christmas decorations up for a surprise for Mummy and Nanna. It was like someone had swapped Louie for a Nice Louie. He even went out to McDonald's to get us a Happy Meal each at lunchtime. I was a bit scared at being at home without an adult but he told me not to answer the door to anyone or touch the phone and that I was a big brave boy for looking after my sister.

Saffy was happy she was getting McDonald's but she kept moaning about her arm being poorly.

When Louie went out to get the McDonald's I thought I would surprise him and show him how much of a big boy I was by getting the Christmas decorations out from the basement. I remembered the word now. BASEMENT. I knew Mummy used to keep 'em down there cuz before Louie came there was a big box behind the tumble dryer with 'XMAS' written on it.

Louie always locked the door but I knew there was a key in the knives and forks drawer which we wasn't allowed to touch and cuz he knew I was a big boy now I thought it would be okay to go down and get 'em.

So I told Saffy to stay and watch CBeebies cuz the telly was on again even though the picture was a bit squiggly or else she'd be in for it. She was a good girl and sat watching Balamory and hugging her poorly arm.

I got the key from the knives and forks drawer and was careful not to touch any of the big sharp knives that Mummy used to cut stuff with and went to the basement door.

I undid the door and it was all black down there. I was a bit scared but I knew there was nothing down there that could scare me really, apart from maybe a spider but I don't mind spiders.

Spiders catch flies and I hate flies.

There was a really nasty smell, worse than farts, that came from Louie's man cave and I'm positive I could hear flies buzzing.

I couldn't find the light switch, it might have been too high up but last time I went down here when Mummy had the washing machine and tumble dryer in there it was a string that turned the light on but I couldn't find it. I checked the other side of the door and all of a sudden I heard Louie shout at me really, really angry, so angry Frankie came running in the kitchen woofing. "DAVID!" He shouted and I turned round and saw the two Happy Meal boxes on the floor. Louie's face was all red again and he stomped across the kitchen at me. Frankie started woofing around his feet and Louie did something really evil then. He kicked Frankie so hard he flew through the air and down into the black basement. I turned to run down the steps to get my dog, he's a sausage dog, and Louie grabbed his hand around my neck and pulled me backwards. He slammed the basement door shut and made a fist like people fighting do and hit me in the eye. I fell on the floor and went to sleep for a bit.

When I woke up my eye and face really hurt, my face was all big and felt sore and funny. Saffy was sat on the sofa still watching CBeebies with an empty Happy Meal box beside her and a purple Fruit Shoot. She looked at me and laughed and said, "Panda, panda!"

Now I knew how Mummy got her panda eyes.

Louie sat in his chair with another beer, and beside him was the box of Christmas decorations, Saffy had dobbed us in. All he said was, "you don't go in my man-cave."

I ate my McDonald's cold only cuz I was hungry. I missed Frankie. I wanted to know where he was and if he was okay.

Louie started being nice again and said that whilst I was asleep he fetched the decorations and made sure Frankie was alright and that he had made Frankie a nice big dog bed in the man-cave so he could be warm and cosy.

After that Louie climbed up into the loft and got down our Christmas tree and told me and Saffy we could decorate it ourselves whilst he did something in the man-cave.

I don't know what he was doing but he must have gone in the garden as well cuz he was all dirty and sweaty afterwards. His white tracksuit trousers were disgusting; they had all kinds of yucky stuff on 'em. We showed him the Christmas tree and asked him if he would help us with the lights. He said we had done a good job but wanted to have a bath as he was tired after all the work he had being doing in the man-cave, and that he would probably have even more work to do when we were asleep. He must've seen I was sad cuz he sighed and said he would help us stick the lights on after his bath. Then he took two beers from the fridge and went into the bathroom.

I couldn't wait to see the lights on and last year Mummy always plugged 'em in before putting 'em on the tree to test they worked as they had been Nanny's lights when Mummy was a little girl so they was really old. They are little lanterns that light up in all the colours you can think of.

While Louie was in the bath, cuz CBeebies had ended I thought it would be cool to show Saffy the pretty lights and tell her about Mummy having 'em at Nanna's house when she was a little girl. I made sure she was very very careful, that they weren't a toy, but she wanted to see 'em turned on. I said no she couldn't as it was dangerous messing with lecktrics and that only adults were allowed. But she kept going on and on and on and on and on so I put the plug in the plughole by Louie's chair. They came on after two seconds and they were really pretty. Saffy said that she loved 'em and picked up a blue lantern to look at it closelier. Then one of the red uns made a fizzy noise and popped and went out.

I was upset and didn't want to get told off so did what Mummy always said. "If you break something, it is better to come clean about it."

So, even though I was frightened Louie would hit us again I knew that I had to tell him.

I lugged all the lights up the stairs and was careful not to stand on any in case I broked em. In the hallway opposite the bathroom was a plughole so I plugged 'em in so I could show Louie the light wasn't working. I switched 'em on and a green un went fizzle too. I knocked on the door and told Louie I needed to show him something. He moaned at me and said, "If it's not fucking important then it'll wait till after me bath." I heard him open another can of SPECIAL BREW.

I said to him that it was very, very important and that he needed to see it right now. He said more bad words, I said earlier I didn't know the words but I had heard 'em before just don't know what they mean. He said, "Oh for fuck's sake, get in here."

So I bundled up the lights in my arms and walked in. Louie had been really naughty cuz Mummy said that whenever she got us ready for our baths to put a towel down in case we slid on the wet floor. My Transformers sock slipped on the floor where some of the bath water had spilt and I chucked the bunch of lights into Louie's bath with him.

They made lots of funny noises and did funny sparkly things, it was really pretty and I have never seen 'em do that before. Louie shouted out and I ran out of the bathroom and fell on my bottom in the hallway. For some reason Louie did a really strange laying down dance in the bath, the water went everywhere, nearly on the hallway carpet. He crunched the SPECIAL BREW can in his hand and stopped moving.

The lights in the whole house went out and I heard Saffy moan from downstairs.

It was dark everywhere, even the light in the fridge was not working. I held Saffy's hand and cuddled her on the sofa and told her it was going to be okay and that Mummy and Nanna would be home soon and would turn the lecktrics back on so she could have her moon nightlight at bedtime.
We sat there for a long time, until we went to sleep.

I woked up the next morning when it was light and went to see where Louie was. I thought it was funny that he was still in the bath and thought he was asleep but saw his eyes were open. Then I knew he had had a poorly, a bad one. That he might even be dead like Grandpa and Danny Williams's Daddy. I was very frightened but last month a policeman called PC Andrews came into our class to explain STRANGER DANGER to us and how we should always tell an adult and dial nine nine nine in an emergency. I went and picked the phone up but they weren't working cuz the lecktrics had broked and our phones plugged into the plugholes.
So I got Saffy and gave her a carton of juice and her favourite My Little Pony and we went round to Charlotte's next door but one to tell her as Mummy always said that Aunty Charlotte was her "best friend."
Aunty Charlotte called the nine nine nines on her mobile phone and when the ambulance came and even the police they went down into the basement to look in

Louie's man-cave and found the floor all dug up like the garden with two great big holes that somebody could fall in if they weren't careful. Don't know what he was digging for, maybe buried treasure.

    Then you took us and we saw the Nice Lady and she gave me an orange squash and a cheese sandwich and I ate it all up even though I don't really like cheese.
Can I see my sister now?
When will Mummy come and get us?

SPARKS

KAYLA
LEX H. JONES

How do you start a story that doesn't make sense? The standard answer is 'at the beginning', but that would suggest a sense of logic that might be lacking in the words that follow. I suppose the first thing I want to say, and it's important that you take this on-board, is that I'm not crazy. Yes, I'm telling you this from inside the walls of my cell in a women's psychiatric ward, and yes many of my ward-mates would probably make similar claims if you spoke to them. But for me, it's true. I'm just the victim of circumstances which now find me sat here, judged delusional when I'm not, merely because the people I told my story to couldn't accept it as truth.

I've told my story to police, to doctors, and even to a couple of lawyers. My therapist asks me to tell it repeatedly, which I've done. It's my own fault really for refusing to lie. I have no criminal record, no history of violent or unstable behaviour. I think they're willing to accept that I had a mental breakdown after the death of my boyfriend. If I played along with that, started to say that I accepted I was delusional, that everything I told them wasn't real, and then maybe I'd get out of here. But I can't. Because she needs me to believe in her. It's what keeps her alive, and I don't want to be the thing that kills her. She's here now; she has been since the day I arrived here. They just don't realise it. Kayla's real. She's as real as you or me.

My name is Melissa Jane, and I first met Jason Stringfellow nearly ten years ago, whilst we were both at university. I had seen him a few times but never actually spoken to him. He was shy, a typical science nerd, I guess. His friends used his surname as something of a mockery, given that Stringfellows is a strip club and Jason could not be further from that kind of razzmatazz. Our first meeting was when I bumped into him at a party. Literally, I bumped into him, and spilled my drink, dropping my cup in the process.

"Oh my God, I'm so sorry," he'd stammered, looking everywhere but my eyes as he frantically picked the plastic cup from the floor.

"My fault, I wasn't watching where I was going." I said, and meant it.

It was my fault. And yet he acted as though I was about to yell in his face for daring to be stood where I was currently, blindly walking through. This made me feel sorry for him, wondering what kind of formative years he must have experienced to make him feel as though he were always the one at fault, always the one that needed to apologise.

High School can be hell for people like Jason. The smart ones, the shy ones, and the ones that aren't content to play sports and flirt with girls. I'd never been one of them, but wasn't quite the popular type either. I guess I was pretty enough that I wasn't completely excluded from that crowd, and I sort of hovered near enough that I could avoid being the target of their hostility. I doubted the same could be said for Jason.

I know pity isn't the best way to start a connection with someone, but it made me notice him. And made him notice me. We got talking about everything and nothing, and before I knew it we'd been sat on a couch all night. Jason told me he was studying string theory and other concepts I'd heard of but didn't fully understand. I was studying sports science and application. I'd always wanted to be a fitness coach; physical health had always been something of an interest of mine.

The first time Jason told me about his favourite area of physics, I thought he was joking. He started talking about the theory of multiple dimensions. That a billion universes were all lined up, separated only by dimensional walls. It sounded like something I'd seen on TV shows, where people hop from one world to another, and each one is like ours but slightly different. How in one world, Hitler won the war, and in another there's still dinosaurs, that kind of thing. But Jason laughed it off.

"It's not like that," he'd explained. "You're talking about different realities, as in different versions of our own world. As in, if I'm sat here talking to you then there must be a world out there where I'm not. That's a different theory, and it's definitely interesting, but that's not what I mean. I'm talking about different dimensions, as in other universes that bear no resemblance to our own."

He'd gone on to explain how things would be so different in every one of these places, governed by their own laws of physics and biology. He'd even said there might be forces that we don't have a name for in these places. It was all pretty interesting, but I think I insulted him when I said it was fun but pointless. He'd asked what I meant, and I said it was like talking about time travel. It might be fun to theorise, but that's all you were ever going to do. Nobody was ever actually going to time travel, and we were never going to get proof for the kind of theories he was talking about.

The first time Jason spoke about Kayla, we were lying on a patch of grass beneath a tree. I remember it well. We'd talked about past relationships we'd each had, me more than him (much to my shame at the time.) The only one he had to speak of was a girl named Kayla. He told me how when he was fifteen, he'd met her and she'd just been exactly what he'd wanted at the time. She was kind of a Goth chick, based on his description. Into the same music as him, cute, pale, liked the same horror films. It all sounded quite sweet and full of youthful joy, and I'd assumed there must be some tragic 'great romance' ending to it all. Turns out there wasn't; they merely drifted apart after he'd started university. I'd said at least that worked out for me and we'd both laughed and then spent a fair amount of time kissing.

The second time she came up wasn't quite so cute. I'd bumped into an old boyfriend of mine, Ben, on campus. I hadn't even realised Ben had been studying at the same college, it was just pure coincidence really, and more so that I'd crossed paths with him, given the size of the place. Jason had been threatened by the encounter, and as much as it annoyed me at the time, I do understand why. Ben was the sort of guy I typically hung around with when I was younger. If you used the word 'jock' then you wouldn't be far wrong, I suppose. Ben wasn't really as bad as he had been; he'd grown out of a lot of the worse traits he'd exhibited at high school, and to talk to him now he was a fairly decent guy. But I understand how he would have seemed to Jason. Like the sort of person who'd made his teen years hell.

We got into a bit of an argument about it; he said I still missed being around guys like that. I shot back that he probably still thought about his old teenage Goth girl. And then he said something I had not been expecting;

"Kayla isn't even real."

Now I'm not going to act like this was a moment in a Hollywood movie. The world didn't stop and fall to silence or anything quite so dramatic. But I was taken aback, I won't lie. When things settled back down and I'd convinced him I wasn't going to run back to my old boyfriend, we talked about what he'd meant.

"I made her up," he confessed, looking down and fiddling with his hands as he spoke.

"You made up a girlfriend so I didn't think you'd never had one? Why would you think I cared? I kind of like being the first," I'd assured him, backing up my words with a kiss on his cheek, my nose bumping his glasses as it always did.

"No, I didn't make her up just now. I made her up when I was fifteen."

"Ok you're going to have to explain that."

"I will, but I'm now at risk of you thinking I'm pathetic."

"I'm not going to change my opinion of you based on something you did when you were a teenager, Jason."

"Alright, well, I guess you know I was pretty lonely as a teenager, right? But I haven't even told you the extent of it. It wasn't bullying, as such. You say that word and people think of physical or verbal abuse. Direct, targeted derision of a person. I had some of that, but it was more about isolation. For whatever reason it seemed a universal decision at my school that I didn't exist. Unless I was being targeted for mockery, I wasn't even acknowledged. That sat pretty much alright with me for the most part. It was better than being attacked. But of course it did mean that when my hormones got to the stage where I actually wanted companionship; there was zero chance of it happening."

"Kids can be dicks. So is that when you made Kayla up? Started telling people you had a girlfriend?"

"Actually, I never told anyone about her. I didn't create her for anybody else's benefit."

"Just your own?" I asked, finding myself a little confused.

"Yeah. It wasn't about impressing anyone, or fitting in with the crowd. It was to combat the loneliness. I imagined what the perfect girl….well, the perfect girl for fifteen year old me… would be like. How she'd look, how she'd sound, what films and music she'd like. Everything, every detail. And when I would go places, alone of course, I'd imagine she was there with me. Holding my hand, looking at stuff in shops, sharing an ear from my headphones. It wasn't really sexual, although obviously she'd creep into my thoughts when I was…well, you know."

"How long did this go on?"

"About seven minutes usually," Jason joked, earning him a punch in the arm.

"You know what I mean, how long did you imagine her for?"

"I guess I stopped when I got comfortable at university. It was like I didn't need her anymore. I wasn't the person that high school had forced me to become."

"I understand all of that, so why tell me about her as though she was real when I first asked about your past relationships?" I asked.

"Ok now that was embarrassment. I just thought I'd seem less of a risk for you to date me if there'd already been someone else."

After we spent some time laughing at the level of 'risk' involved with dating him, he seemed relaxed to have confessed all of this to me without me judging him. As far as I was concerned there was no damage, so there was nothing else to say.

Jason didn't take long to find a job after university. He more or less walked straight into one, working at the university's own experimental physics laboratory. In his last couple of years at Uni he'd taken on an engineering qualification too, because he wanted to be able to get a better understanding of some of the stuff he'd be working with. I followed his reasoning behind that, but the fact he could learn both at once made me very aware once again of the gulf between our intelligences. He always assured me there was no such thing, that we had skills in different areas and that he understood my fields of interest as little as I understood his.

The area Jason and his colleagues were experimenting with was connected with the multiple dimensions theory he'd told me about. They were building machines that could send signals out to what they believed to be other dimensions. I asked if it was like the one they sent into space, and he tried to explain it to me.

"Not really," he'd said, scratching the back of his head as he no doubt struggled to find a way to make me understand. "If we send a signal to space, we know space is there, and the signal will just go for as long and far as it can. But with what we're doing, we don't actually know where it's going, if it's going anywhere at all. It's like standing blindfolded in a building, and then shouting 'hello'. You can't see how big the building is, how many rooms there are, how far it all goes. So you have no idea if there might be anyone to respond, or if you're actually just stood in a broom cupboard shouting to yourself."

"So if you get a response, any kind of response, that proves something?"

"It proves everything," he'd said excitedly. "But we're not hopeful."

Jason took me to the lab a few times and showed me the machines. Lots of metal coils and switches and lights but no obvious purpose. You see a machine at a factory and at the other end there's a car door being made or some other obvious output. To a layperson like me there was no discernible output from this thing, but Jason said it was like a phone or a fax machine, sending out the same message over and over again. And if one came back, it would know.

I remember the day he came back with a bad burn on his hand, covered by a bandage and with some antibiotics to prevent it getting infected. We'd moved into a small terraced house together shortly beforehand and there was still a lot of unpacking to do, which was now slowed down somewhat by his injury.

"If that's going to keep happening then we may need to hire some people to make the rest of the flat pack furniture," I'd suggested, pointing at his wounded hand.

"Hopefully it was a one-off," he'd replied, forcing a smile. He couldn't fake it with me, though. I could always see through him.

"Ok, what's wrong?" I asked, putting down the box I was holding and folding my arms.

"The signal creator gave off an electrical surge when I was using it, hence the burn. But we've checked the circuit breakers, the fuses, everything. We even contacted the power company to make sure nothing happened at their end. All came back with nothing. Simply put, there is no reason that surge should have happened."

"But you're working with an entirely new piece of technology, aren't you? And whenever someone does that for the first time, stuff will happen that you couldn't have predicted."

"You're right, unknown variables. But at the end of it all, this machine is powered by electricity. We know how that works. You don't get a sudden surge without it originating from the power grid."

"You know what I'm going to say to you, right?"

"That it's not safe." Jason shrugged, not exactly rushing to disagree with me.

"I also know you're not going to quit working on it, so can you at least start wearing rubber gloves or something?"

He'd agreed that safety gear in the lab was now a priority, which made me feel a little better but not entirely. I did ask why it hadn't been from the very beginning, and he'd started ranting about how things like that can often hamper the ability to work. I'd pointed out that no work would get done at all if he got seriously injured. Something had gone wrong with their machine

SPARKS

and they didn't understand how it happened. That meant it, or something worse, could happen again at any time. I lost a lot of nights' sleep to that thought.

It was on one such night, lying only half-asleep with worried thoughts about Jason getting seriously injured or even killed, that I heard him talking to somebody. I rolled over in bed to find I was alone, and his voice was coming from out in the hall. My first thought was that he was probably on the phone, or failing that, sleepwalking. I'd heard it was bad to wake sleepwalkers with a shock, so I crept quietly out into the hallway to make sure he was alright.

I found Jason standing with his back to me, his hands gesturing in the manner of a conversation. The hallway was lit by an electrical blue light, as though someone had a television on, except there wasn't one upstairs. The light flickered slightly as I approached, and the air was so charged with static that my hair stood on end. Jason was talking but his words seemed muffled, there was a humming in the air that made it hard to hear properly. He didn't even realise I was there until I touched the wall and got a static shock, making me yelp.

"Hmm? Melissa, are you OK?" asked Jason as he turned around.

I wasn't sure if he was awake or not. To be honest I could say the same about myself. The whole situation seemed dreamlike. The flickering blue light disappeared the moment Jason turned to speak with me.

"I'm fine, are you OK? Who are you talking to?"

"Hmm? Oh, nobody. Sleepwalking, I guess."

I nodded and led him back to bed, glancing over my shoulder at the spot he'd been staring at when I found him. There was nothing there, but as I turned back I could swear, just from the corner of my eye, that I saw a figure stood there watching us walk away. I couldn't sleep the remainder of that night; I just lay staring at the bedroom door expecting someone to come in at any moment. I even dialled 9-1-1 on my phone and had my thumb hovering over the 'call' button, just in case.

Things got weirder after that. Jason became increasingly stressed at work. They couldn't replicate whatever had gone wrong with the machine, which sounds like it would be a good thing, but the university health and safety guys said the machine wasn't to be used until they figured out what had caused the power surge. It was a sensible decision, and I actually agreed with them, but I never shared that opinion with Jason. He was devastated; all that work now amounted to a machine they weren't even allowed to switch on.

Constantly trying to justify his work to men in suits made him tired and even started affecting his eating habits. I assumed this was why he kept sleepwalking, why I'd find him talking to himself in the middle of the night. This was partly a lie to myself, I know that now. Jason being tired couldn't account for the electric blue lights I kept seeing around him, the static shocks that became a regular occurrence in the house, or the fact that light bulbs would blow out more or less daily. It may seem odd to be so casual about it, but it's amazing what you start to think of as normal. Once you've convinced yourself of a mundane explanation, like faulty wiring in the house, the brain tends to comfortably accept that rather than admit the possibility that something unnatural might be occurring.

Jason was sleepwalking on the night we finally had the conversation. I'd found him downstairs, sat on the armchair facing the couch. There was nobody there, of course, but I swear to God when I walked in that room I could almost see a shape in the corner of my vision. A human shape, lying on that couch facing Jason. It's so easy to dismiss things when you're half asleep but the fear I felt was real. Fear because I knew that if I turned around, the figure in the corner of my eye wouldn't be there anymore. Whoever she was....and I could see enough to know it was a girl....would be gone if I looked directly at her.

I shook Jason by the shoulders to wake him, and discovered that he wasn't even asleep. His eyes were red raw, his entire manner was slowed and strained, but he was awake. I wondered if he'd actually been sleepwalking all this time, or if something had been calling to him in the middle of the night. He met my eyes and I asked him who he'd been talking to.

"Kayla."

We went back to bed and I watched him until he fell asleep. I couldn't really sleep myself, I was too on edge. As we left the living room I'd seen...or thought I'd seen...something sit up on the couch behind us and turn to watch us leave. I daren't turn to look, but I could feel my hair rising up as though I was touching one of those electrical balls they have at gadget shops.

The following morning we sat across from each other at the kitchen table. Jason wouldn't meet my eye.

"You said you were talking to Kayla."

"I know. I think I..."

"Don't tell me you were dreaming," I interrupted him. "There's something weird going on, it's too much now to just push me away. Talk to me. What do you mean you were talking to Kayla?"

"OK," said Jason, followed by a deep sigh: "I keep seeing her. More and more often. Hearing her, smelling her. Sometimes she can even touch." Jason leaned forward and put his head in his hands.

"But you said that you'd made her up."

"I did."

"This doesn't make any sense."

"You're telling me," said Jason, forcing a smile. "Do you know what it's like, seeing something that your brain tells you can't be there?"

"The obvious answer would be that you're having some kind of breakdown....except I've seen her too."

"You have?" Jason raised his head, his eyes suddenly wide with hope.

"Not fully. But I've seen her a couple of times now, in the corner of my eye. And then there's all the weird stuff with the electricity."

"I'm sure that's her, I just don't know how. I can't explain any of this."

"You're a scientist," I reminded him.

"This falls a little outside of that."

"OK, but how do scientists solve anything? You ask questions, right? So the first thing I'd ask, when did this start? When did you start seeing her?"

"It was after the machine broke when we ...oh shit."

"What?"

"When we had the electrical surge."

"Bit of a coincidence, don't you think?"

"I had thought about that, but I assumed the shock I took messed me up, started me hallucinating. I've kept waiting for it to go away, but if you've been seeing the same things or at least some of them..."

"I don't think it's going away, Jason."

"So it's real. She's real."

"What do you say when you talk to her at night?"

"I'm not talking to her. Not really. I just keep saying 'you're not real', 'please go away', stuff like that. Mantras to try and hold onto my sanity."

"But if she is real....how is that going to feel to her?"

"You're actually feeling sorry for... a ghost or whatever the hell she is?"

"How can you have a ghost of someone who never lived?"

"Well what else would you call it?"

"I don't know, and maybe I am feeling sorry for her. You just said you have no idea what she is. Maybe she doesn't either. We should try and talk to her."

So that night we sat cross-legged on the living room floor with a few candles placed in front of us. We held hands and I told Jason we should close our eyes.

"This is stupid."

"I know it feels stupid, but I'm not exactly an expert in contacting spirits or disembodied whatevers. This is what I've seen in movies, so this is what we're trying. Unless you have any other suggestions?"

"So if this doesn't work we go and buy a Ouija board?"

"Shut up. Let's just try this. Talk to her."

"Alright…um…Kayla? If you're here, can you give us a sign?" He paused and there was nothing, so he continued. "I'm sorry I didn't believe you were real. That's probably upsetting. I didn't meant to be that way with you. It's just that I thought it was my imagination. I couldn't see how you might have become real, and to be honest I still don't. But if this is real, if you're here and you can show us, then I want to help."

There was a hum in the air, which sounded as though somebody had turned on a fridge. A shudder travelled the length of my spine.

"I'm here, Jay," said a soft, female voice. She sounded distant, like speaking to us through a Skype call that was suffering from a poor connection. "I can't stay, not yet. But I'm getting stronger."

"Kayla, I have so many questions, I don't know where to start," said Jason. I don't know if he'd opened his eyes at that point but mine were still tightly shut. Whoever was talking, I didn't see them.

"You can ask me anything, you know that."

"Who are you?"

"It's me, Kayla, silly."

"But how? Where do you come from?"

"I don't know," the voice had a tone of concern to it, as though she really couldn't find an answer to the question and this bothered her. "Who's the girl?" she asked, and despite my eyes being shut, I suddenly knew that she was stood in the room staring at me.

"This is Melissa, you'd like her."

"If you like her then I do too. Three can be fun."

"Can you show yourself to us?" asked Jason. "If we open our eyes, can you make it so we can see you?"

"I'm trying, Jay. I'm not strong enough. I'll try again later, OK? I need to rest for a little while."

Nothing else was said after that. We called out a couple of times to see if she was still there, but whether she was or not she didn't (or couldn't) speak to us.

"I kind of wish I'd opened my eyes. I was scared, though," I admitted.

"I know what you mean. It's the brain trying to protect itself from something it can't cope with. But I'm not even sure we'd have seen her. She said she was trying to make herself seen."

"Least we know she's real. But what does that mean?"

"You can't just create a new person like that, without being born, without substance. For one thing the laws of physics don't allow it. You can't make something from nothing. Whatever she is, she must have come from somewhere else. Which is making me wonder if my machine might have done more than malfunction."

"You think it might have worked?"

Jason nodded and a smile spread across his face.

A load seemed to have been lifted from Jason for the remainder of that day. The problem had hardly gone away, of course, and there were still a million questions to ask. But he knew that he wasn't going crazy. That obviously counted for a lot, and put the whole situation in the context of a potential scientific discovery instead of a mental health problem. He was so excited, writing down so many things and talking about various theories. That night we actually made love for the first time in weeks, and that's when things took a turn for the strange.

I was straddled over Jason, my hands on his chest. We'd only just started really, getting past the slight awkwardness of it having been so long. There was a sudden charge through my body at his touch and I almost orgasmed right there. I wasn't even sure what he'd done, but his skin against mine was breathtaking. His hands were on my hips, but then I felt them move across my breasts, toying with my nipples. Except I could still feel his hands on my waist…

Looking down I saw there were hands caressing me, having reached around from behind whilst I remained atop Jason. They were pale, feminine, with black varnish on the perfect nails. I froze and glanced over my shoulder, to see a beautiful girl pressed against me. She was naked, her long black hair loose and partly covering her face, but not enough to hide her perfect lips, and deep dark eyes. I gasped and went to move but she traced her fingers over my flesh again and once again I almost fainted from the sheer pleasure of her touch.

"It's OK, Melissa," she said in the softest whisper. "I told you three can be fun."

I won't detail the next hour's events, sorry but this isn't that kind of story. Suffice it to say it was filled with more physical pleasure than any other night I recall. Jason looked freaked when he saw Kayla behind me, but she assured him it was nothing to be scared of, and he believed her. We'd asked her to show herself, and she did. I won't lie and say that's the full reasoning of our decision to not completely freak out. The truth is her touch did something to both of us that, frankly, neither could bear to stop.

After the night's activities, I cleaned up and then returned to the bedroom to find something else unexpected; Kayla was still there. She was sat on the edge of the bed, just silently smiling. She was stunning. Her body was perfect. But then, of course it was. This was a girl who'd been dreamed up to be perfect, how could she be anything else? In my head I'd always pictured her as a slightly awkward looking fifteen-year-old, but the girl before me was about twenty years of age. That would put her at the age Jason was when he met me, which would also be about the time he stopped thinking of her. She'd somehow grown along with him and then stopped when she was no longer in his thoughts.

"That was fun," she said as I cautiously kept my eye on her and walked round to my side of the bed. "I love you, you know. Both of you. I'll see you soon."

There was a crackle in the air, that eerie blue light again, and then she was gone. There was a slight smell of ozone, like you get during a storm, and the sheets were crumpled from where she'd had them wrapped around her naked body.

"Melissa?" said Jason, both of us staring at the ceiling.

"Yes?"

"I think we need to get some answers."

Professor Malcolm Albright had been Jason's tutor at University, and they'd remained in touch, on and off, in the years since. I think Jason had always hoped that the Professor would join him in the lab; that they could work together on exploring the theories they'd spent so many hours discussing. Sadly it wasn't to be, as Albright had left the University under 'scandalous circumstances' and become increasingly elusive ever since. One rumour had it he was sleeping with several students; others said it was drug use. Quite possibly it was a combination of both. In any case, Jason had only ever managed to get the occasional email back from him, but when he wrote to Albright and gave him the gist of our current situation, the response came fast. He even sent a phone number and an address where we could find him.

"Tell me everything, don't hold it back," Albright enthused as we joined him in his living room. Albright himself was a short man, balding with thick glasses. He was thin; his shirt hung from him in a way that made me assume he was one of those brainy-types that often forgot to feed themselves.

"My emails gave you most of it already," Jason reminded him as we shifted some books to make room on the couch hidden beneath them.

"She was physically manifest, you said? Physically, not just visually."

"Yeah she was definitely corporeal."

"And you both felt comfortable having sex with her?"

"You told him that??" I exclaimed.

"With scientific analysis you never know what piece of data is relevant and what isn't, so yeah I told him."

"I'm not interested in your private life anyway, I'm just fascinated that you felt comfortable with it," said the Professor. "Were you fully aware that she wasn't a human being?"

"Little hard not to be," Jason shrugged. "But things were so passionate, the way she touched us, it just overrode our desire to panic about it all. I mean, in retrospect it's kind of weird."

"She's your fantasy girl, the perfect woman your mind could dream up. All she is is everything you wanted her to be. So much so that she isn't even threatened by your current lover, and is happy to share you with her."

"She's an adolescent fantasy alright," I agreed. "I'm not even into girls, or at least I haven't met one before where I've thought I might be. But something about her…"

"It's everything about her. Everything. She's perfect, for what she was dreamed up to be. The perfect lover to a young mind. Loving, sexy, protective, but not possessive."

"How can she be real, professor?" asked Jason.

"I'm going to go out on a limb and say that your machine worked. It was designed to send a signal out into the ether, into every conceivable plane of existence. You got a power surge one day and assumed this was a malfunction, but perhaps it was actually a reply. You had no way of knowing how a reply might come through. You couldn't possibly calibrate the machine for it, could you? I think Kayla is that response."

"How can a girl I dreamed up as a teenager be the response to a message to other realities?"

"You're assuming she was already Kayla when the response was sent. I'm hypothesising that she wasn't. But that's what she became as soon as you received the message."

"My head hurts," I said aloud.

"I apologise, my thoughts are going a mile a minute, and it makes my words unclear. My students would often complain about that," said Albright. "Put it this way, what if the dimension closest to our own is without form and function? What if the things that live there, if you can even call it life, have no mind, no thoughts, no being, but they just exist? The basic essence of life without the individuality of substance that we give to it here in our universe. If one of them came here, they would have to take a form, have to have some sort of consciousness, however rudimentary. They'd just have to; our world doesn't allow existence without form and thought. Even if that thought is just instinct, hunger, sex drive, thirst, everything has to have some form of nature. But of course, a thing without imagination or even the most basic of thoughts can't possibly come up with a form and thought pattern for itself, so somebody else has to do it for them. You were the first person that touched the reply, so it took something from your brain. And thus the traveller became the very thought that it took."

"I wasn't thinking about Kayla when that happened."

"You wouldn't need to be. It picked a random thought, but one that didn't already exist. The universe doesn't allow two of the exact same person, so it couldn't just choose to become your mother, or a celebrity you had in your mind, for example. It had to take something from your thoughts that didn't already have a physical presence in this world."

"So it needed a form to take, even though it wasn't even physical to start with, so it chose Kayla?" I asked.

"Not exactly. I don't think 'chose' is the right word. That suggests an existing consciousness which I'm not convinced even existed."

"Have you ever seen Ghostbusters?" Jason asked the professor.

"Everyone's seen Ghostbusters."

"Right, well remember near the end? That demon god Gozer needs a physical form to use to destroy the Earth, so he takes a thought from Ray's mind and becomes the Staypuft Marshmallow Man. Is this like that; is that what we're saying? I mean, without the part about destroying the earth. Hopefully."

"Yes and no. Kayla took the choice of her form from your mind, it's true. But it's more than that. Gozer was conscious of who he was before; he didn't really become the Stay Puft Marshmallow Man. He knew the entire time that it wasn't who he really was, it was just the body he chose to walk around in. If I'm right about this, then Kayla isn't aware that she was ever anything else. She's not pretending to be your adolescent fantasy girl…she actually is. Body and soul. With no knowledge that she was ever anything else."

"So there's no malice here, no deception?"

"Not if my theory is right, no. I'm also curious about the electrical activity around her. I think that might be how she arrived, through electrical current. Maybe that's similar to properties in her own world; perhaps she needs it to exist here. Like taking a fish out of the sea and putting it in a bowl of saltwater, I suppose. It's not quite the same as where it came from, but close enough that it can survive."

"Why isn't she always here? She blinks in and out.

"I don't think our reality allows for something else to come here and just join in like they're one of the gang. It's probably difficult for her to maintain a hold here. But she's trying, because of her connection to you. If she lost that, I think she'd just dissipate."

"We don't want to kill her," I said.

"No, no we do not," Albright agreed. "I'd like to try and meet her, if I may. But I want to continue working through some of the theories I have. Could you meet me back here in a few days, perhaps? And bring her?"

"I'll try." Said Jason.

We saw Kayla a few times in the following days. I was in the kitchen one morning and she was sat on the counter, swinging her legs. She was wearing all black, as you'd expect for an adolescent Goth girl fantasy, but she looked happy. I talked to her, and it was like talking to anyone else. She knew about films and music, politics, the best brands of hair dye. Which just gave further weight to everything Albright had been saying; she wasn't just pretending to be anything, she was Kayla.

"Wait a moment," I said suddenly, interrupting our conversation. "You're, um, 'linked' to Jason, right? But he's not even here, he's at work."

"Not just Jason. Not anymore. I take strength from you too. I don't mean 'take' as in steal it; I just mean that I'm linked to you in the same way that I am to Jason. I wasn't, but after we made love, I felt your compassion and understanding, how much of Jason was in you, and it allowed me to move around more freely to have connections to both of you. I hope that's alright."

"Of course it is, I just don't fully understand all this so forgive me if I sometimes seem a little freaked."

"I don't understand it either," said Kayla, drawing her knees up to her chest and wrapping her arms around them. "I know who I am, but I don't know what I am. I'm not like you, or Jason, or any of the other people I see walking around when I'm with you. They don't have these rules governing their movements; they don't come and go as I do."

"Does it scare you, not knowing?"

"Sometimes. If I think about it too much. But when I'm around Jason, or you, then I just feel happy."

"That's sweet, but there's a whole world out there. I feel bad that you have to be attached to us."

"You guys are my whole world, and that's fine with me." She hopped off the counter and brushed a strand of black hair from her face.

I put my arms around her waist and stepped closer to her, looking into those perfect eyes.

"We'll look after you. You might be different to other people, but you don't need to worry about that."

"I trust you," Kayla replied with a whisper, leaning closer so her forehead was pressed against mine.

Jason had been emailing Professor Albright back and forth but the professor hadn't wanted to meet again just yet. He wanted us to return with Kayla, but he said he wanted to prepare first. In the meantime Jason had continued working at the lab, tinkering with the machine. His intent was to make it deliberately suffer an electrical surge by creating a fault that he could then fix, allowing the continued use of it to resume. He now knew that there never had been a fault, and the electrical surge that had burned his hand had been caused by Kayla's arrival. But since neither of us wanted to share Kayla's existence with folk who may choose to experiment on her, Jason couldn't reveal this information. So artificial sabotage seemed the way to go. Create a problem, blame that for the previous 'fault', and then fix the problem.

This had meant him working long hours at the university, and Kayla would alternate her time between the two of us. The night when things took a turn for the worse, he was heading home late and took a shortcut through an area of the town that he'd usually avoid.

"Money and phone. Now," said the hooded man who'd stepped from the shadows. Jason described him as having his face covered by a bandana and he was holding a knife.

"Alright, just hold on," Jason had replied.

"Don't fucking tell me to hold on. Money and phone, now."

There was a surge of blue light in the alleyway, and Jason was no longer alone. Kayla stood next to him, her hands and eyes crackling with electrical energy.

"What the fuck..."

"You won't hurt him," she said.

Jason told me how the mugger had lunged at Kayla with the knife, only for the weapon, and the hand holding it, to be burned away to ash the moment it touched her. He'd screamed and Kayla had clamped her hand across his face, his entire body then burning up and crumbling to ash in seconds. She and Jason then walked home and told me the story.

"I'm sorry," said Kayla, sat on the armchair staring at the floor like a child who was about to be yelled at.

"It's not her fault, Jason. She was protecting you. How could she know that she could do that? She doesn't even understand what she is."

"I'm not mad at her, honestly, there's no blame here," said Jason, crouching down and looking up to meet Kayla's gaze, giving her a reassuring smile. "I've just never seen anything like that before. I've never seen anyone die before either. I didn't know you could do that."

"You're scared of me," said Kayla, a tear running down her face and leaving a black streak from her eyeliner.

"No. I'm scared, yes. But not of you."

"I just wanted to protect you."

"And you did," he said, holding her hand. "I'm safe now, because of you. I'm just a little shook up, OK?"

Kayla went back to wherever she goes when she's not here, and Jason and I went to bed.

"Why did you lie to her?" I asked.

"I didn't lie."

"I know when you're lying, Jason. You said you weren't scared of her, but I could see it in your face."

"Alright, yes, she scared me. Happy?"

"It's Kayla, she would never…"

"Since when did you get so comfortable with this? We don't know anywhere near enough about her to be as trusting as you seem to be."

"OK so she can do some stuff we didn't know about. That doesn't change anything."

"It changes everything, Melissa," said Jason, raising his voice. "We thought we'd got a physical manifestation of something plucked from my memories. That was weird, but fair enough, I could deal with that. What we actually have is a monster from another dimension that's capable of disintegrating people at a touch."

"Don't call her that!" I yelled back. "So we don't fully understand what she is, but it doesn't change who she is. That's what matters."

"And when she decides she doesn't just want to be our little sex toy anymore, what then?"

"That's how you think of her? Why would you say that?"

"Because I thought I understood what she is, and now I'm terrified, Melissa."

"I'm not."

"Of course not, but then I don't spend the day making out with her do I?"

"What are you...?"

"Don't think I don't know. I can smell her on you every time I get home."

"Alright so we fool around, that doesn't change anything I just said."

"It does. Because we both saw, that first night, what her touch can do. How it can affect your thoughts, your judgement."

"In the middle of sex, Jason! Jesus, haven't you ever been so into something that you'd give anything to keep it going a little longer? But that doesn't change your thought process afterwards."

"Tomorrow, I'm going to speak with the professor. Try and figure out some more about her."

"Fine. And you can sleep on the couch tonight."

Jason visited Professor Albright the next day. I didn't go, but he told me how the visit went. When he arrived, the professor's house seemed even more in disarray than it had before. Not just the house, either. Albright himself looked exhausted, on edge. Jason said he thought back to those old drug-binge rumours and wondered what he might have been doing since we'd last seen him.

"You shouldn't have come," said Albright, reluctantly stepping aside to let Jason in.

"Why not?"

"It's dangerous." "That's why I'm here."

They went into the living room, Jason taking a seat but Albright remaining standing so he could keep pacing the floor.

"Kayla killed someone," said Jason, cutting straight to the point.

"She killed someone?"

"It was a mugger, she was defending me."

"So she was defending you. I mean, it's still awful, but the way you started that story made it sound like she'd gone insane or something."

"No, no she's still her. It's just the way she did it. She has these powers; she just burned him to nothing with a single touch."

"That's the electricity. That's their life, you see. I think electrical energy is the thing which connects our reality to theirs, the only common factor to be found in both. It's probably how they come here, too."

"What do you mean 'they'? There's only been one."

"Oh no. No, no, no," said Albright, almost bursting into nervous laughter. "No there hasn't."

"What have you done?"

"Me? Oh nothing. You're worried I've snuck into your place of work and used the machine? I haven't."

"Then what do you mean?"

"I mean that 'they' have been coming here, to our reality, for a very long time. Kayla is the first to be quite so strong, to be able to hold her form and manifest physically. Probably due to your machine. The others have never had that ability, never been able to hold on quite the same. Like a message only partially transmitted."

"Why on earth would you think there had been others?"

"Electricity. It's a thread, between our world and theirs. Even before we properly learned to tap into it, we had lightning strikes, natural current flowing through things. It's always been there, dangling in the water waiting for a fish. If you think your Kayla is the first to ever take that bait, then let me ask you this: what about angels? Ghosts, demons, children's imaginary friends? All the times people see things that can't possibly have been there, plucked straight from their mind, only to then disappear without a trace? Except maybe atmospheric changes like temperature fluctuations, a smell of burning, the hairs on your neck standing up. No, Kayla isn't the first visitor we've had, Jason. Not even the millionth, by my reckoning. She's just the first to come for such a long stay."

"But there's still no evidence of malice, right? No evidence they're invading or..."

"Not unless we give it to them," Albright interrupted. "Remember, these beings have no personality, no thoughts, and no real consciousness until we give it to them. They become whatever they take from us. So for you, a sexy Goth girl that likes three-ways and is protective of you. But what if the thought that they latched on wasn't quite so pleasant? What if someone decided to intentionally bring these things...these powerful, possibly un-killable things...and make them whatever they envisioned? Soldiers, terrorists, just think about that."

"Fuck."

"Alarming isn't it? And the problem with a thought like that, is once it's out there, people with less ethics take it on board."

"What did you do, Professor?"

"I made a mistake. I made a terrible, terrible error. And now I need to leave, before they come."

"Before who does?"

"Whoever they send."

"You're not making sense."

"I telephoned a friend of mine. A former colleague, actually. I wanted a second opinion. I know him, trust him. His insight would be invaluable. Except I didn't realise that he now works for the military."

"Oh Jesus, Albright."

"Even if he himself is trustworthy, that line will have been tapped. They'll know about this by now, and I'm not waiting around for the men in black suits to turn up and force me to help them weaponise this."

"Did you tell them about me?"

"No, I made it sound as though this was my discovery alone, nobody will be looking for you. But they know there's a machine, and they know where it is."

Jason phoned me as he left the professor's. He was frantic. He said he needed to destroy the machine, that it wasn't safe. He had to make sure that it couldn't be used. With that in mind he stopped at the workshop on the way home. I don't know exactly what he did, but I can't imagine he just hit the thing with something heavy. He needed it to be unusable, impossible to duplicate. He'll have burned his notes, wiped computer files, and destroyed everything that might let it be built again. He must have interfered with the machine in a way that caused a severe problem. Because it exploded before he could even leave the laboratory.

I was worried they might ask me to identify Jason's corpse. I don't think I could stand that, staring down at what was once the man I loved and knowing it was no longer him. As it happens they never asked. The explosion was so great that there wasn't enough of him left to be identified. I did get interviewed by the police. They wanted to know if Jason had been showing any signs of getting involved with extremist groups, if he had suicidal tendencies, if he might have gotten drunk and then gone to the lab. Anything to try and explain why this might have happened. After hours of questions something snapped and I told them. I just told them all of it. And that's how I ended up in here. The only person that could possibly corroborate what I was saying was the professor, but of course he couldn't be found by then. Either he'd gone into hiding or he'd been taken against his will. Either way, he was well out of reach. Kayla offered to manifest and prove the truth of my story, but I decided against it. The danger to her seemed too great, the possibility they might find some way to take her. I couldn't risk it.

I won't be staying here, though. Kayla is sat behind me right now, stroking my hair. She says she can get me out, that she'll do whatever it takes. I assume that might mean the deaths of some orderlies, but perhaps not if she can hold back a little. Either way, she's getting me out of here, and not just for my sake. Whatever Jason did to hide the work he'd done, it wasn't enough. Kayla told me that the signal she responded to has been activated again. Somewhere, someone has rebuilt that machine. And not just one, either. She can hear multiple signals, all at once. Someone has industrialised this now, and I can't imagine it's for anything good.

The lightbulb above me flickers and Kayla rises to her feet, her hands and eyes crackling with electrical energy.

"Are you ready?" she asks.

SPARKS

POWER CUT
CHRISTOPHER LAW

It took me a few minutes after waking to realise where I was, my mind still muddled by sleep and the drugs in my system. Then I became aware of the antiseptic smell and the soft hum of the machines, the distant sound of people talking quietly beyond the curtains and the crisp feel of the sheets and blankets, the unmistakable firmness of a hospital bed. I might have realised quicker if I could see but I was born blind; my world is one of touch and sound. I wasn't alarmed, although that might have been the drugs. My entire life before that moment was jumbled and distant, as if I had slept for years. I wasn't in pain and, so far as I could tell, I was physically intact. I thought about calling for help but it seemed like something that could wait and I drifted back into sleep, certain everything would be explained in due course, my drowsy mind dismissing the whole experience as a vivid dream, strange but benign.

The second time I woke my wife was sitting beside me, her perfume cutting through the hospital smell. My thoughts were much clearer and I tried to say hello, belatedly realising that whatever had happened to me might have involved her as well. The guilt I felt at not thinking of the risk to her sooner was washed away by the simultaneous relief that she was okay.

That was when I realised there was a tube running down my throat, working my lungs without any involvement from me. The alarm I hadn't felt the first time I woke arrived, hysterically focusing on the tube, the plastic taste and feel of it. Physically, I still felt perfectly fine, but if I was on a ventilator that clearly wasn't correct. I tried again, hoping to make some kind of noise to alert my wife, since talk was impossible. No sound emerged, my lips and tongue immobile. I'm a solicitor by trade, my days spent in the intricacies of inheritance laws in Britain and beyond. I get paid to sit and think, trusted to find the best way around the tax regimes and idiosyncratic laws of a dozen countries. I pushed my panic down, forced the fear into a corner and tried to raise my hand, reaching for my wife. I couldn't move my hand, couldn't even twitch a finger. I felt the command leave my mind, travel down my arm, but nothing happened at the far end. My emotions harder to control now, I thrashed and screamed within the confines of my mind, trying to wake myself from the dream. I lay motionless, able to feel the blankets over my body and the IV tubes in my arms, the bunged-up sensation from the catheters dealing with my waste. I could feel everything, I just couldn't move.

I was still trying when I heard the chair scrape as my wife stood up, felt her kiss me.

"I know you are in there, sweetheart. I'll be back later, I love you."

After she left me alone with my thoughts I continued to try until I was worn out and drifted back into sleep, my dreams dominated by increasingly clear and coherent memories of my life before this bed. On the verge of sleep I thought I could sense someone come to my bedside; if so, they were silent and left before I woke again.

The day when everything changed was almost like any other – the first day of the three weeks annual leave I'd taken for our silver wedding anniversary. The actual date wasn't until ten days later, by which time we'd be in the Seychelles, and my wife still had a full week before her own leave started. I'd taken the extra week to take care of the last few bits and bobs before our flight on Saturday, as well as devote a few days to working on my book. It's a collection of the quirkier cases that have come before British courts I've been working on since my post-grad days. I like to claim it would be finished by now if it didn't take so long to get Braille copies of the source material, or I had the money to pay a team of full-time transcribers. That's probably not true but procrastination and the written word are ancient bedfellows.

I allowed myself a lie-in that morning, waking long enough to kiss my wife goodbye as she left and then allowing myself to doze until almost eleven, Scrabble and the cat beside me on the bed. Scrabble is my guide-dog and the cat is a stray that chose us a few years ago, an elderly queen that likes to groom Scrabble, my wife and sometimes me. My wife says the three of us look adorable when we're all asleep, Scrabble by my feet and the cat on my chest.

It was a glorious day in mid-April, full of the promise of a glorious summer when spring's riot was done. After a lazy, indulgent morning I listened to the one o'clock news on BBC One, unable to ignore the interminable wars in the Middle East and the fallout of Trump's election. It would have broken my father's heart to see what has become of his home country. He always thought it probable after the incompetence of Bush-Clinton-Bush. It's a blessing he died in two-thousand-nine. After the news I left, as much because Scrabble needed to do her business as the errands I had to run. We went the long route into town, through the park and then along the seafront. It was half-term and the park was noisy with children, the swings and skate park bustling. I sat on a bench for an hour or so, my fingers running over the patterned dots of my book – a so-so police procedural. If it had been quieter I might have paid more attention to the insults sent my way by the group of thuggish malcontents but not by much. I'm disabled and I look more like my Arabic father than my English mother. I'm used to the abuse.

When we finally reached town we went to the bank first. I got the foreign currency needed for our holiday and double-checked that our travel insurance was adequate. It took the kid who served me almost fifteen minutes to find a Braille copy of the terms and conditions but he was so mortified that I had to let him off. I expect things to take a little longer, be a little more difficult, because I experience the world a little differently to most. The delay gave me time, as an afterthought, to get some Travellers Cheques. We weren't travelling anywhere unstable or dangerous but I like to have a few cheques with me just in case.

After the bank I ran a few more errands – the chemist for the collection of pills my ageing wife and I require, then the dry-cleaners. The night before our flight we were throwing a party for our friends and families. It was going to be a big affair, all the money we might have spent on university fees for our children just sitting in our account earning more interest a year than we tended to spend.

We'd both have rather had the children. We tried for years before we had to give-up, both of us scoring badly on the fertility front. Another round of IVF was financially possible but we'd failed so many times neither of us could face it again, even if the doctors hadn't advised against it. After that we looked at adoption but the agencies and government never liked my blindness. They couldn't explain why it was a problem, it just was.

The situation couldn't be changed, not without going to lengths neither of us was willing to contemplate. So, with more money than we've ever known what to do with, our gaggle of nephews and nieces have tidy sums waiting for them when they hit eighteen and more in store when my wife and I die. We update our wills every couple of years, if nothing requires it sooner. No-one will be left never needing to work again but, if they're wise, they'll live a whole better life than they would have. Finally, feeling good, I went to The Leg for a pint and cigar. I'm not really a smoker or a drinker, my father was the one with the problem, but occasionally I like to indulge.

"I don't care what the tests say," my wife is speaking in the low, controlled way she does when she's truly angry. She's holding my hand as she speaks, her perfume not as strong as usual. I can tell from the way she's squeezing my hand that she's upset. I'm doing my best to make my fingers move, to squeeze her hand in return. "He's still in there. I know it. I'm not going to let you. I won't."

It has been months, almost a year, since I first woke and I'm in a different hospital bed – a private room where the flowers and air-fresheners are almost enough to overpower the bleach and phenol. I was moved here when the NHS couldn't afford to keep pursuing a lost cause and, unless I've forgotten how to count and analyse since I became trapped, I know the private health insurance has also declared me gone. Everything keeping me alive is being paid for from our savings. No matter how she juggles, the money must be almost gone. Everything I've suffered, trapped in my own mind, screaming and begging before gods and demons I've never believed in, can be no worse than what she is going through, left alone in the world.

"I understand," the doctor is on the other side of my bed. His English is good but there's a trace of somewhere Eastern European in his accent. His voice comes from above me, my wife's from one side. The doctor is a tall man, barrel chested from the depth of his voice. "He seems like he's just sleeping, like he might wake at any moment, but he isn't. I hate to say it, but he is gone and all any of us – me and you – can do is prolong his suffering. We have to let him go. Honour his wishes. His living will."

I'm in here! Your tests are wrong! Your machines are wrong! I'm in here! I don't care what I signed!

I'd scream it if I could but I'm still unable to breathe for myself, my fingers and toes as immobile as they've been since the first time I woke. I can feel everything as well as I ever could, maybe even better, and my mind is as capable as it ever was – I calculate immense sums and list the facts I know to keep my mind from wandering. It sounds arrogant without verification, but I'm right most of the time and, with so much free time, I find the mistakes when I review my work. It'd be harder if I could see, I'm sure – if I needed visual markers rather than mental to keep track. Arrogant, maybe, but also true.

The bits of my brain that make me who I am, the elusive corners where the soul lies, are as healthy as they've been since I was born. It's the cruder parts, the animal control centres they can monitor, that have broken. They have wires and sensors all over my body, but none of them can register my thoughts. They can only monitor the electrical impulses that make muscles twitch, keep our lungs pumping and our hearts beating.

I read an article about this a while back, there's a name for what I'm living through. All those coma patients, the ones in persistent vegetative states, who suddenly recover and rejoin the world, their waiting loved ones.

You know the story, a staple of melodramas and soap operas. I'm one of those coma patients, one of the shut ins. In the past we were the ones who were buried alive and somehow managed to break through our coffins, burrow through the dirt and be murdered as revenants and vampires. Now we are simply left to listen, trapped and unable to act, as we are abandoned, as our loved ones lose hope and the confines of our minds close in. My wife read the same article; we had a long conversation with some friends about the implications and the horror of finding ourselves in that situation. At the time, my flippant best coming out after a few too many, I said I'd rather be killed and my donor card obeyed – take everything and anything that might help someone still alive and leave the rest for the worms. Now that I'm here, listening to my wife do her best to keep her hope alive, trying to do right by me, I wish I'd said something else.

My silent visitor, the one who never leaves, is happy I didn't. I can't tell you how I know this, given that the visitor never makes a noise, not even a breath or a sigh. I just feel the presence by my bedside; know that someone's there, watching me die. The feeling has been growing stronger recently, feeding on my increasing fear as I know my wife's deadline approaches.

"Ain't it 'gainst yer religion to drink?"

There was a powerful stench of body-odour coming from the thug leaning against the bar next to me, far too strong to be masked by the cheap deodorant he had sprayed over his clothes. There was also a hint of cigarette smoke and lager in the stench. I can't say for sure if I recognised the thug's voice as one of the ones that had shouted at me in the park. In retrospect I have no doubt and can't help but wish that Scrabble – who did recognise him – had been able to overcome her training and attack him first. She only rose from where she had been lying by my feet and pushed her head into my hand. She was a guide-dog, one of the best. They never bite.

"I'm not religious," I said, working my thumb against the base of Scrabble's ear. I could feel her trembling. "Just having a drink."

They'd been working me for an hour, ever since I entered the pub. Perhaps I should have turned right around and taken the dry-cleaning home, cracked one of the Japanese beers in the fridge, but I've been drinking in The Leg since we bought our home. Our house is in my wife's hometown and she's been drinking in The Leg since she got her first fake ID. It's a good, mellow place most of the time, favoured by leftists and weirdos – the sort of people who don't get freaked by blind secular Arabs. I've been getting grief from bigots since I was born; I figured I'd just ride it out like I always had.

It started with the normal crap, the cheekier members of the group who'd drifted in putting bags and bottles in my way in the hope that I'd trip, probably pulling faces and making gestures – their kind always did. I didn't respond to any of it, Scrabble leading me around the obstacles she couldn't push aside with her nose. She was my third guide-dog and, much as I loved the previous two, she was the best by far.

I smoked my cigar, bought from the tin behind the counter, and drank my first pint in the beer-garden. I was feeling good and I knew my wife would be working late that day; I had plenty of time to nap away the effects of a second. I chose to drink it at the bar, chatting to the landlord. We've know each other for almost thirty years, in a casual way. I didn't stop to think that there might be a problem brewing. Maybe I was too trusting.

"Ain't religious?" the thug laughed. "All you Pakis are religious, it's in yer DNA."

"I'm not Pakistani. My dad was Syrian," I can't say for certain, having never been able to see, but I'm fairly sure Syrians and Pakistanis don't look that much alike, beyond not being European.

"Whatever. Yer all in the same game. Ain't they?"

The final comment was shouted out to his friends, who obediently cackled and howled, some of them calling me names and the others asking where I'd hidden my bomb. One of them started to sing Rule Britannia, but he didn't know the words and was too drunk to enunciate.

"It's time for you to leave," the landlord said, his voice thick with embarrassment and disgust. "Now."

"We ain't leavin'," the thug jeered. "I just got a fuckin' round in."

"Then drink 'em quick and get out. You aren't welcome here."

"Ain't welcome? You hear that, lads – we ain't welcome in our own country?"

My memories are still jumbled after that, I don't know exactly what happened or in what order. The thugs took exception to the request to leave, leapt on the opportunity for violence. From what my wife has said whilst she's been sat by my side, holding my hand, I know that they were a gang of English fascists, on the prowl for a scrap. They'd have taken on some of their own kind but they saw me in the park and then bad luck landed them in my local.

They're all doing time now, writing illiterate Tweets on the mobile phones they smuggled in up their arses and selling the drugs brought in by drone. They could be serving their time in a Siberian Gulag, breaking rocks in the nude, and it wouldn't be enough to compensate for everything I've lost. No amount of suffering could equal my inability to control my own body, let my wife know that all I want is to hold and kiss her again. My unfinished book, the labour of my life, and our luxury holiday are minor details when set against the knowledge that I will never feel her in my arms, never bury my face in her hair again.

At night, when I'm alone and the ward beyond my door is quiet, I amuse myself with the things I'd do to them if I ever could, the things I'd pay to have done if I couldn't do them myself. Those are the times when my silent visitors feel closest, the air tense as if the right cue to speak is due.

There was a lot of shouting and yelling after The Leg's landlord told them to go and then, delighted by the opportunity, the thugs threw me to the ground, stamped on my head and ribs. One of them pulled the landlord over the bar, his bloated heart failing halfway down so that they only battered his corpse. Glasses and bottles flew everywhere – I can hear the sound of them breaking whenever I want – and Scrabble forgot her placidity training and tried to bite and maul as she defended me. One of them attacked her with a broken bottle, lost a finger or two but still killed her. With a double murder on their hands (they thought they'd killed me too) and cocaine mingling with alcohol in their system, thrilled by the glory of violence, the thugs fled The Leg and did everything they could to spark a race-riot. They were brought down in less than twenty minutes, unable to find enough support for their brand of murderous hate. I was found with my skull cracked open and my lungs punctured, both of them. My arms and legs were broken and one of them had ground a jagged bottleneck into my groin before he ran into the street, screaming for the Pakis and Yids to come out and meet him. About a month ago my wife told me that, no longer fuelled by cocaine and booze; he hung himself in his cell, broken by the real hard men.

    I hope he suffered, I don't care that he was only eighteen. I hope he suffered. If my visitor chose to speak, I'm sure I'd hear that he did.

    "It's the right thing to do," the doctor is talking to my wife again, standing on the opposite side of the bed from her, like I'm not even here. "I'd choose a different outcome if I could, I really would, but…"

    "I understand," I've never heard her sound so small, so broken. She's still holding my hand, I'd give my soul to squeeze her fingers – I'd give it to twitch the tip of my pinky. "I can't believe he's gone," she hitches, strangles a sob. "I can't. This can't be real; please...it can't be real."

"You loved him, I can't ever know how deeply, but you have to do this. Let us honour what he wanted, who he was – let us donate his organs."

"I know it's what I should do, what he wants," her tears are falling now, I can feel them dripping on my cheeks as she bends down to kiss me. I want nothing more than to flex my fingers, arch my back, anything. "I know I must let him go."

"He's been gone for a long time. All you can do is remember him."

It isn't quick when they flip the switch. The hum of the machines and the static in the air fade quickly, but gradually – like slipping under the water in your bathtub. My attempts to refuse, make the machines keep me alive for just another day, all fail. My chest stops rising and falling, my heart stops beating. My visitor finally steps forward, lays a hand on my chest and says something I can't quite hear and for the first time in my life I can see.

The gates and walls of Heaven are more glorious than you can imagine. I'm new to colour so I am perhaps a little easier to impress than you but the gold tracery catching the sun, the pristine white of the marble look exactly how they feel, softer than kitten fur and smoother than silk. A man born with working eyes would be as incapable as I of describing what I see as I float, lighter than air, towards the gates. I will be with my wife again behind those walls, the years that I have to wait before she joins me a time of joyful anticipation. The children we never had will join us there, the violence and hate my life ended with all wiped away. My father will be there, ready to use action-figures so I can feel the fights between the good and bad guys, my eyes closed so I can remember that the blindness is a part of me, intrinsic to who I am. I know that, as I draw closer to the gates, I will be blind again behind those walls and I do not mind – these moments of sight are all the proof I need to believe. Then the path to the gates crumbles away and the walls become pockmarked. I feel hands and claws around my ankles, working up towards my knees. I see my wife above the crumpled gates, standing over the arch and framed by the ever higher walls that rise behind her. I almost hear her scream my name as my tongue tries to call hers.

It is a terrible fall, down towards the churning ocean of blood, flames licking the shores. All the way down the malformed eagles and vultures scream and hiss at me, delighting in the fact that I glimpsed Heaven and they are hunting me.

I land abruptly, my new bed made of rock and inset with upturned nails that pierce my ankles and wrists, make a scattered line along my spine.

"Welcome."

I'm blind again and cannot see the monster above me, only feel the acidic sting of its warm spittle. The feel of it in the air is the same as my silent visitor. "You saw Heaven, belonged there, but things have changed, my little love."

I hear the screams echoing all around me, feel a hundred tiny hands cutting and peeling my skin back. I try not to think of my wife, hope she never thinks of me – the connection will drag her down. I understand so much; see the futility of hope, now that I am in this place. I can't help but think of her, all the good things and the bad. The bad loom larger and larger as the pain increases until I can't remember what the good things were.

"Innocence burns now," my tormentor laughs, ripping my testicles away with one hand as the other digs into my midriff. "Hell is the fate waiting for us all. Heaven is no more."

I'd not be here if the machines were running, if my wife hadn't let the doctors flip the switch. As I lose the last of my purity and hope, I want her to come suffer with me.

I'M YOUR ELECTRIC MAN
DANI BROWN

James sat crossed-legged on the floor of the basement, his trinkets spread around him. He took the time to secure everything with some chewed gum. Nightly earthquakes were a thing. James assumed they happened everywhere, but only because he hadn't been anywhere else.

The day's scavenging brought more wires. He had to throw out the bulk of what he found. Somewhere along the line, the desert flooded and left behind a heap of rust. He couldn't part with all the broken wires. Some he used as decoration upstairs. Sun had bleached most of the books, rendering the text unreadable. Not that it made any difference to James. Much like the rest of the population, he didn't know how to read. He was learning how to decipher the old symbols, guessing at what they meant.

Without a rule of law, there weren't any to be broken. Reading, knowing anything, it was all frowned upon.

Children followed him around the streets, throwing rocks and insults. The only purpose in life was mere survival. His entire life, James had been haunted by visions of more. Even as a child, the town viewed him as an outcast. He raved on during the day of his nightmares, until no one wanted to know. If he could only get them to listen, to understand, they'd realise there was more to life than eating stewed weeds and burying the children.

He picked up an old book. He could still make out the letters. It looked like nothing more than patterned chicken scratches. If he could just work out what they meant, his life would be easier.

The room started to shake. All his treasures rattled on top of their chewing gum anchors. He counted down in his head, a skill still not lost. The shaking went on longer than ten seconds. The first of his trinkets broke out of its bounds and landed on the floor with a metallic shatter. He hoped it wasn't important. The candles flickered. The shaking didn't stop. Something was wrong somewhere. James felt it spreading from the pit of his stomach and coursing through his body.

The candles blew out with a final sigh. The dark had a chill to it, with the faint hint of wetness. Desert weather was reliable, if it was anything else. Nothing but clear blue skies for months on end. The rain didn't come with the quakes. It came when it wanted.

James picked himself off the floor. He knew his own basement better than he knew any other room in the house. The shaking continued as he went up the stairs. He could hear the screams of the townsfolk as he climbed up, grabbing the polished wooden banister for balance. The earth continued shaking, like it wanted to shake off its last remaining inhabitants and start again. James couldn't blame it. The world really was a rather shitty place outside of his dreams.

Rain pelted down. His roof, salvaged from relics of old, wouldn't be able to stand it. Thunder sounded. He ran for the kitchen to grab pots during the lightning strike. He couldn't risk a leak to the basement. Spikes connected with his foot. The swearing rivalled the thunder and hail pelting down on the roof. Each footstep brought more pain, like the slow drip of water finding its way in. A flash of light let James see the damage.

He doesn't know when they grew legs, but it happened as his dreams predicted. He didn't like those dreams. Visions of the future were nightmares yet to come. The dreams of the past offer the hope. The storm raging outside might be the one to set the world alight. James fixed a copper rod with wire to the roof two weeks ago. He couldn't make out the words in the remaining books, the ones kept out of the sun, but he understood the pictures better than most. He grabbed the pot and threw it under a drip during the flash, then sat on the kitchen floor, pulling spikes out of his foot. Walking cacti. It didn't make sense. Evolution was fast, but not that fast without an agent. The cactus howled. Being stepped on hurt, as did having its spikes caught in James' foot.

James threw another pot under another drip. Most of his trinkets lived in the basement. He didn't care that much for the kitchen floor, but it served as the basement's ceiling. The next flash of light revealed the cactus sulking in the corner. Another had joined it. James thought they'd be grateful for the rain. The door creaked open. James assumed it was another cactus seeking shelter. More lightning revealed something white with arms and legs. Where the head should have been sat a visor of black. James rubbed his eyes. The scene before him resembled his dreams too closely to be real.

Another flash of light and ticking started to come from the basement. James jumped to his feet, forgetting about mobile cacti until his foot came crashing down on another. The spikes sent fresh jolts of pain through his body. The ticking in the basement grew louder. He couldn't walk on his foot. He dragged himself along the floor, until he came to the candles and matches. A crash came from the direction of the group of cacti and the creature in white. It sounded like his last remaining oil lamp.

Light shone out of the kitchen floor. Something down there was working. Another flash of lightning and more light came out of the floor. He didn't even need the candles that had caused him so much pain. A buzzing made the little wooden house vibrate in competition with the thunder. But, it continued. The thunder only lasted a few seconds. James turned around to pull the fresh spikes out of his foot. He didn't get very far before a boot landed on the small of his back. James squinted his eyes shut and whispered, "Not there, not there, not there". It was the same reaction he'd give to the worst of his nightmares. Heavy breathing, as if through a filter, reached his ears.

"This isn't one of your dreams, James."

"Not there, not there, not there."

The buzzing was louder than his voice. Even through his squinted eyes, he could see the light coming the floorboards. But, loudest of all, was a fresh drip looking for a way into his trinkets. He squirmed beneath the boot. Somewhere, he imagined a struggle with his patchwork quilt. A bit of delusional thinking to ease the fact that the boot on his back was very real.

"Not there, not there, not there."

"Now, now James. Stop denying reality. We've been watching you very closely for years now."

"Not there, not there, not there."

His foot throbbed. One of the cactuses found a way into his bed. He didn't know why he was plagued so badly by them. The other townsfolk only had one or two per year enter their homes. Even his neighbour, living further from the actual town than himself, wouldn't see this many.

"My foot."

He drooled with the pain and tried to suck it back in before it could fall through the crack in the floor and into his trinkets.

"I have the perfect thing for your foot."

"Please don't chop it off."

It was the first thing to come to his mind. It sounded like the creature draped in white laughed, but it was cold, mechanical.

"What are you?"

"Now we're getting somewhere. If I move my boot, will you run?"

"How am I going to run with spikes in my foot?"

James heard movement around him and the sulks of pained cacti. The boot lifted off his back and James breathed a sigh of relief. With the buzzing, the storm and the spikes, he didn't register the pain until it was gone. A hand grabbed his ankle. James turned over.

"What are you doing?"

"Taking out the spikes."

"Are you human?"

After a few minutes of listening to the buzzing and another rattle of thunder, James asked again. The second time didn't provide an answer either.

"Hey, why do I get so many walkers?"

"Be quiet and hold still."

That wasn't the answer James was looking for. The spikes had little barbs to tear more skin as they came out. James yelped. He needed to stop walking around his house with bare feet. Even with the door and windows shut, the little fuckers found a way in. He looked over at the door, more entered. They shut it behind them. The light shining out of the floor boards lit up his entire house.

"What's going on in my basement?"

"Another few minutes and you can find out."

"When did the cacti grow arms?"

Something hit the bottom of the kitchen floor.

"Hey, what's happening? I need to go check on the stuff down there."

"It seems your lightning rod received a direct hit and powered everything up."

James was confused. He could get answers regarding his basement, but nothing else.

"That was the last one. Can you walk?"

James stood up. The foot that received the spike penetration, twice in one evening, was a bit tender. He could walk, but with a limp.

The white clad creature threw his shoes at him. James looked at his foot. It swelled. The holes where the spikes had been leaked clear liquid.

"Put them on. We've lost control over the cacti. They were programmed to gravitate to you."

James swallowed.

"What?"

"The cacti, there will be more. Put on your shoes."

"My foot won't fit."

"Do you want it to be three times its natural size before the storm is over?"

James squeezed his foot in. He could feel the liquid secretions gluing the fabric to his foot. That was going to hurt when it came off.

"Let's go check on your trinkets. We don't want the tumble weeds to catch fire."

James limped behind the creature in white. It wouldn't confirm its humanity, nor would it deny it. The last thing he saw before returning to the basement was an entire colony of walkers taking up residence by his bed and chewing on the extra wires he hung up around it.

The stairs seemed longer and steeper than any other time he went down them, reinforcing the idea that he was trapped in a nightmare. But he couldn't feel pain in his nightmares. James shielded his eyes against the light with his hand. The thunder rumbled on outside. Storms in the desert could last for hours. He stood on the bottom step, looking around. Damp patches appeared on the walls. Some of his trinkets let off steam. He tried to run for them, but an arm stopped him, along with the throbbing in his foot.

"There's nothing more you can do here."

The voice was hard to hear over the buzzing and sizzling. James looked around. The sizzle and steam went together as water fell into his trinkets. The parts were frying. He tried to move away from the arm, but it was a lot stronger than him.

"My life's work."

"It isn't important anymore."

Sweat broke out on his forehead as he became more distressed. He felt a spike in his arm and looked around. There wasn't a cactus in sight. He looked to the ceiling below his bed and saw their shadows cowering up there, away from the storm. Calmness washed over him.

"You know too much."

He heard the words, but didn't take them in.

"You tried to share this knowledge with others, but they wanted to keep their heads in the sand."

Green lights started to flash from the ceiling, but the lights of his scavenged bulbs shone brighter. A flash of lightning drowned them out. Sound came out of one of the trinkets. James didn't have the name for it, but it sounded like an electronic version of a music box.

With the lightning gone and the electronic music box playing some noise, he vaguely felt the sting of another spike. Only one. It wasn't like stepping on a cactus. He felt his body float to the floor. He could have watched, if he wanted. The house above him moved. The floorboards were pulled up by gloved hands as James watched, slumped on the stairs. He forgot to swallow. The drool formed a soggy mess across his shirt, before the rain reached the basement and soaked him through. His trinkets sent sparks flying into the water. He would drown down there if he didn't escape, but he didn't care. He didn't even try to move his arms and legs or kick off his shoes to swim away. Mobile cacti fell through and landed with howls and splashes. They didn't seem to like the water. James watched them, not bothering to move if one became too close. With the ceiling above him gone and the rain pelting in, everything appeared a blur.

Multicoloured lights flashed above him, reminding him of the string of painted bulbs he found. The parts were too rusted to try to make them work. As the lights grew closer, the rain stopped hitting him. He could hear it falling outside and see the rush of water into his basement. A little toy man, with chipped red paint, floated past with steam coming out of his ears. James started to cry. His entire life, he searched for relics of the past and saved them in his basement, even before he buried his parents beneath the vegetable garden when they succumbed to the coughing disease. His entire life floated past.

He reached out for the toy man. The creature in white did nothing to stop it. James grabbed its cold body and pulled it close. The lights stopped flashing. A large yellow orb, brighter than the sun shone overhead. James squinted his eyes shut.

"Not there, not there, not there."

The creature clad in white ignored him. A portal opened. The creature grabbed James. James held tight to the toy.

"Bring it with you, if it brings you comfort. We have to get going."

James was directed beneath the light. It felt hotter than the noon sun at the height of summer. The water from his clothes started to evaporate. It couldn't save his trinkets.

"My trinkets."

"Forget about them. You have one."

The creature didn't let go of James as they were beamed up. The portal slammed shut behind them. James could no longer hear the rain and felt a chill against his skin.

"Where am I?"

His question went unanswered. The toy in his hand flashed its eyes. It wasn't entirely broken.

The creature started to peel off the white. It was just clothing. James felt embarrassed watching, but he couldn't turn away. He wanted to know if it was human beneath the suit.

Long legs were first to appear. They were skinny, too skinny to belong to a person.

"What are you?"

His question went ignored, again. The toy clicked. Long fingers came next. They weren't quite grey, but they weren't green either. The creature's skin was smooth. His helmet came off. James stared into big black eyes, and then looked away, ashamed.

The floor teemed with mobile cacti. The first sweat of fear broke out on his skin. He hated the cacti. They left him nowhere to run. His toy buzzed in his hands. It wasn't the steady buzz of what happened in the basement during the storm. It sounded sick. A long-fingered hand took it away from him.

"We're just going to fix it; you can have it back in a few minutes."

"This way, James."

James had no choice but to follow through the sea of cacti. They moved to clear a path. It sounded like they hissed at him, the same way an angry snake hissed when the rock she slept under was moved to reveal the blistering sun.

The cacti weren't in the next room. He was led down another corridor. He wasn't sure if the purpose behind it was to disorientate him or if the place really was that big. After many twists and turns, a door opened. It didn't have any handles. It opened automatically.

He was led into a room. His toy waited for him.

"We gave it a new coat of paint; you're going to have to wait a few minutes before you can touch it."

"Sit down."

James didn't argue.

"Where am I?"

"We'll answer in our time."

The room around him lit up.

"Is all this run on electricity?"

"Yes."

James looked around. The lights created pictures that moved. The images formed into his dreams and nightmares. He couldn't look away.

"You are the electric man."

"What does that mean?"

"As you already know, a long time ago, Earth had electricity."

James wiped his eyes, convinced he dreamed.

"This isn't one of your dreams, James of Earth."

A creature waved its arms at the moving pictures.

"Those are your dreams, your nightmares, and your life story."

"You've been searching your entire life, but do you know why?"

He shook his head.

"You were chosen at birth to bring Earth back to a time of prosperity. A long time ago, war broke out on Earth. As punishment, all but the very basic of technology was taken away. But you already knew this."

One of the creatures stood up and put its long grey-green fingers on one of the screens.

"There, right there. Can you see? You had a vision, age five; as you watched the cacti fight over a tumble weed."

James stood up without thinking and went over.

"Even then, the cacti watched. You thought they might have been agents of a secret government living in the mountains. And they were secret agents of a sort, but you were only half right."

"What are they?"

"Normal cacti, with a few spliced genes. They have only the basic rudimentary thoughts. At first they had a lot of mechanical elements, but with the gene splicing, the next generation born were able to incorporate it into their makeup. But they can walk, follow you. If you left the desert, they would have been replaced with something else."

"Why me?"

"Your dreams, they set you apart. You could see the past and you could see the future."

His clothes dried with a slight breeze blowing in from above.

"We're going to give you the things you need to restore electricity to Earth. It'll be solar powered. Humanity proved they couldn't handle nuclear power or coal."

The screens around James filled with mushroom clouds and frames of men arguing and pressing buttons. Black clouds crossed over them. Buildings with smoke pouring out and sooty, into black streets.

"What about my trinkets?"

"Apart from Mister Robot there, they've all been destroyed."

James felt his heart hit his ankles. He sat down hard. His life work, washed away in a flood.

"We have better trinkets for you. And the knowledge of how to use it. Knowledge you can share."

James shook his head. The entire town thought he was crazy.

"They'll believe you this time."

He reached for his toy and then pulled his hand back, remembering the wet paint.

"Go ahead, it should be dry now."

He pulled it into his arms.

"This way please."

The creatures lead him to a different room. One with the softest looking bed he had ever seen.

"Just for you."

He went to it and noticed a helmet with wires stuck out above the headboard.

"What's that for?"

"To give you the knowledge as you sleep. It is powered by electricity, the same type you'll be spreading across the Earth."

James clutched his toy. He was tired. He didn't want to get into the bed.

"Will it hurt?"

"No."

A creature took him by the hand. Another pulled away the blankets so he could get into bed. They didn't put the helmet on; instead he was brought food and a drink.

"To help you sleep."

His toy was taken from him and put next to the bed, on a little table. When he was done eating, they took away the plate and cup.

"Lay down now."

They put the helmet on.

"Is it too tight?"

"No."

James closed his eyes. For the first time in his life, he had no dreams and woke up feeling refreshed. It took him a few moments to grasp he wasn't safe at home in his own bed. A creature came in.

"You're awake then?"

The helmet was pulled off. James grabbed his toy. He didn't feel any different.

"What happened?"

"You've been given what you've been searching for your entire life. We're bringing you home now. And stop stepping on the cacti, they don't like it."

Food was brought out for him. He sat in bed and ate. Feeling sleepy again, he laid his head on the pillow. He woke up in the desert. It wasn't his house. He could tell by looking around. Everything was new. His toy sat on the table next to a letter. This was when he discovered he could read.

"James," it read. "You have the knowledge. You have the lights. Flick the switches on the walls. You have the tools. Turn on your lights and let the neighbours come to you."

The toy next to him had eyes that suddenly lit up, making him jump.

"Good morning James. May it be cactus free."

He put his feet on the floor. It was more solid than the floor in his old house. He looked at the walls and saw the switch. He turned it on and waited for the neighbours. A cold breeze blew in from somewhere, but all the windows were shut. He noticed the buzzing. Even the walls seemed alive.

"James, put me on the floor."

He went back to the toy and placed it by his feet. It followed him around as he looked at everything in his new house.

The sun was setting outside. Soon, he would see the flicker of his neighbour's candles as his lights remained steady. He had one of the screens the creatures had. It switched on as he walked past. His brain recalled something about motion sensors.

The first knock came as night spread across the desert.

"Are you the electric man?"

"I think so, yes."

"We've had dreams about you, all last week. They said you can fix things."

James shook his head. He didn't recognise the person standing on his porch. He didn't realise he had a porch until he opened the door.

"Let me get my tool box."

The toy beeped by his ankles. James braced himself for an earthquake that never came as he set up basic wiring in the house of his first neighbour and gave the family a lamp.

"It won't work until the morning. The light needs to hit the panels on your roof and store up the energy."

SPARKS

POWER TRIP
DAVID COURT

The worst thing about it? Dan's perfect green eyes were the last to go.

The sensible part of Brigitte knew he'd have been dead way before then, more than likely a victim of ventricular fibrillation as the current passed through his heart. If that hadn't killed him, the shock from his flesh burning would surely have done the trick.

But even at the end, as Brigitte was forced to leave him, dragged away by her colleagues, she'd taken one last glance back. Perfect, undamaged white orbs glared back at her from a smoking and jerking husk, and Brigitte was convinced there was still life in those staring pupils.

The expression in those eyes.

Pleading for her help, or begging for death? Moments later, Dan's blackened shell had burst into flame, rendering both redundant. Brigitte was deaf to her colleagues' cries as eager hands grabbed her and pulled her away.

The lives of Brigitte and her office colleagues had been, temporarily at least, spared quite by chance. A networked game of Quake – one of the few games that would run on the underpowered office computers – had dragged on longer than expected. Ordinarily, this wouldn't have been an issue, but it had been determined that tea and coffee duties for the whole of the next month would be determined by who scored the least frags. With something of such importance on the line, it wasn't unexpected that Brigitte, Eric, Dan and Clive found themselves late and having to sneak into the meeting room, mingling with the assembled crowds at the edge of the room, as though they'd been there all along.

Eric had, as ever, beaten them all soundly. Clive had narrowly come last, managing to snatch defeat from the jaws of victory in an attempted sneak attack on Brigitte. It wasn't an ideal result, as Clive's tea and coffee-making skills were somewhat lacking. A good cup of tea, Dan had once insisted, should have the colour of the skin of He-man. Clive's were a closer match to Skeletor.

Dick Elswood, owner of Stimulus Laboratories and their top-level boss, was in full flow. All the department managers were standing behind him, pretending their level best to appear captivated by every eloquently annunciated word that spilled from his moustached lips.

A slideshow unfolded on a large monitor behind him, showing detailed animations of radar dishes swiveling into position and satellites in geosynchronous orbits neatly aligning themselves. Some bombastic and inspiring music was playing in the background, loud enough to hear but not loud enough that you could make out the tune or for it to drown out Dick.

"...and, of course, none of this would be possible without the boffins from Tesla Lab," Elswood smiled, gesturing to a group standing in front of the stage. "So, without further ado, let's switch it on."

Tesla lab. Always bloody Tesla lab. And nobody used the phrase 'boffins' any more. This was the twenty-first century, for frag's sake.

Stimulus Laboratories was, ultimately, a think-tank. A privately funded organization, it housed dozens of individual groups of scientists and technicians, all of whom were beavering away at any number of unconnected secret projects. Other than the odd rumour, many of them didn't even know who their colleagues were; let alone what they were working on.

So, having mostly ignored every part about the meeting email other than what time to attend, Brigitte and her small team had no idea what was going on.

Elswood, away from the microphone now, stood on the edge of the stage holding a champagne flute aloft. He began to gesture at the assembled crowds and the managers behind him to raise their glasses too.

"That's not fair!" moaned Clive, never usually one to miss out on a freebie. "They've all got glasses!"

"They were all here ten minutes ago, Clive," smirked Brigitte. "During which time, you'd been busy throwing yourself off the edge of the Quake map with a misplaced rocket jump."

Eric laughed, and it was only then they noticed he'd somehow managed to be holding a full glass of champagne in his hand. Clive was about to ask him where he got it from when Elswood began the countdown from three.

Brigitte and her team had no idea what everybody else in the room – themselves included – were counting down to. Sometimes, it's just easier to go along with the crowd. Right on cue, timed to match the over-exuberantly bellowed "Zero", the lights briefly flickered and dimmed.

There were a few moments of silence, followed by some murmurings from some of the assembled crowd. A shower of sparks exploded from the stage, and the room was plunged into sudden and complete darkness. The general vibe of anticipation quickly transformed into confusion and mild panic.

"Everybody stand still!" Elswood could be heard shouting above the general bewildered hubbub. "No need to panic – the emergency lighting should kick in at any mom-"

Brigitte clearly remembered two things happening at the same moment. The emergency lighting, as Elswood had reassured, did burst into illumination. So, however, did poor Dick. Jerking around on the stage like a marionette in a typhoon, violent blue flames exploded from his every orifice. Despite his fierce thrashing, his limbs violently twisting with enough force to snap bone, he staggered about in front of the crowd, somehow managing to remain upright.

Those who'd considered panicking whilst immersed in darkness had now decided, not unreasonably, to fully commit themselves to it. It was clear from the general shouting, screaming and hollering that a great deal of the assembled crowd was tempted to join them in blind terror as well.

Still Dick stumbled around on stage, his vacant sockets and open mouth glowing bright blue from an inner light. His blazer was appropriately beginning to catch fire, flickers of orange and yellow flame appearing around the collar and lapels. It was disappointing, but not unexpected that none of upper management were trying to help him. All they could do, it would appear, was attempt to stay out of the way of his flailing, flaming grip.

Sensing the mood of the room, Brigitte and the crew had begun to make their way towards the exit doors.

Dick's limbs suddenly jerked out straight, like a man crucified. White-hot bolts of lightning leapt from the fingertips of this electric messiah, arcing like phosphorous-bright wildfire through the assembled management. Like a poorly-rehearsed boy band, they jerked and writhed as the electricity coursed through them. What remained of Dick was finally engulfed in a brief inferno that sputtered and faded as his ashen corpse collapsed in on itself. Brigitte could feel the hairs of her neck and the backs of her hands stand up on end as unnatural energies surged around the room. Fingers of lightning shot from person to person, felling each as they hit, an ever-growing deadly radius approaching them from the direction of the stage.

They'd fallen through the doors, screaming survivors at their heels. The aroma of freshly painted and polished lecture theatre had been overridden by the acrid stench of charcoal and the sulphurous reek of smouldering keratin. Only a handful of them had escaped from the room, the remainder presumably electrocuted and draped over each other in a smoking pile of corpses.

Blindly, they ran. In any direction away from that hall, but somehow instinct and perhaps something more had kept them together and, as one, they found themselves back in their lab, puffing and gasping for breath as they collapsed against the walls.

This was a refuge of sorts. As Software and Hardware support, they were afforded a certain level of privacy. After all, nobody sane would dare venture down here, lest they be blindsided in a flurry of unintelligible jargon.

The usual identikit corporate posters found dotted throughout the remainder of Stimulus Labs weren't to be found down here. There wasn't a motivational one-sheet with some supposedly inspiring photograph of scenery (with an insipid empowering quote) in sight. The only posters down here were ones of vintage computer games or some in-joke you'd need a degree in computer science to comprehend, and a master's degree to get.

They stood there in silence for the longest time, heavy and labored breathing being replaced by gentle sobbing from all of them, except Eric. He simply stood there, calm and quiet, staring intently at his empty champagne glass, as though it held the answer to everything.

And then Dan, level-headed Dan, always calm in a crisis, suddenly rose to his feet. There was a look of determination in his face, that familiar expression that always appeared just as the rest of the team were panicking over whatever was the most recent and highest priority work-related crisis.

He strode over to his desk and picked up the phone, holding the receiver to his ear. After taking a deep breath, his index finger flashed towards the speed-dial button.

A jagged, witch's claw of white lightning leapt from the earpiece and engulfed Dan's head before spiraling around the rest of his shuddering form. The phone, reduced to a misshapen mass of molten juniper-green plastic, fell from his jerking grip.

And that was how they'd lost Dan. Ironic that the one amongst their number who'd made a career out of being management material, but never being promoted, had met their fate.

Even huddled in the confines of the IT store room with the door closed, they could still smell him – that sharp tinge of ozone and copper. It was Clive who broke the silence.

"Does anybody know what Tesla Labs were actually doing?"

"I'd heard from Janine in Reprographics that they were doing experiments in sustainable energy," muttered Brigitte, staring at the floor and refusing to make eye contact. "Harvesting the electricity present in humid air, something about the ions in charged water in the atmosphere. Hygroelectricity, she called it."

Clive looked at her, quizzically, somewhat annoyed that she couldn't see his expression.

"Janine from Reprographics? The woman who does our copying and faxing?"

"She's got a photographic memory," answered Brigitte, still concentrating on one patch of the floor. "She's wasted in that job."

Eric was still holding his wine glass, temporarily baffled by the concept that anybody still faxed anything these days. Something suddenly sprung into his cavernous impenetrable mind, joining the party of restless neurons.

"I think that was Faraday team," he proudly announced, placing the glass carefully down on one of sturdy metal racks that lined the wall of the room. "I play squash with Shaun from Franklin Labs, which is next door to Tesla. He said that they were building something to pick up alien radio signals, weird orbital power fluctuations or something."

Clive and Brigitte stared at him, incredulously.

"Shaun is mostly full of shit, though."

Tutting loudly in that unique way that only agitated Brits are capable of, Clive reached into his jeans pocket and pulled out his mobile phone. Brigitte's eyes widened in panic and in a single impressive move, she lunged towards him, striking his hand with enough force that the tiny device spiraled out of his grasp. It bounced twice against the metal shelving units and landed on the floor face down. Clive threw his arms up in the air.

"What did you do that for?"

"You saw what happened to Dan!"

"If it is the electricity that's screwed up, it's a mobile phone. It's not connected to anything. And I doubt there's enough power in a mobile phone battery to electrocute a grown man."

He shook his head and crouched down to pick up the device.

Eric piped up, his tone dry and emotionless.

"The desk phones in the room back there run off power provided from a USB-C cable. There's not enough power going through that to electrocute a grown man."

Clive's hand halted, his open trembling fingers hovering over the mobile phone.

Eric took the change from out of his pocket and began to arrange it on the metal shelf in front of him, piles of smallest coins to largest. He looked down at Clive, frozen there like a statue.

"But, you know. Tell Dan that. You be my guest."

Clive looked at Eric, and then back to the tiny, innocuous looking phone. Treating the tiny device with the reverence and fear one might give to an unexploded WWII bomb, he slowly stood up and backed away.

It suddenly rang, the synthesizer tones of the theme from Knight Rider filling the tiny store-room. Clive and Brigitte nearly leapt out of their skins, whereas Eric barely batted an eyelid, placing the last of his twenty-pence pieces onto his currency piles.

"You might want to answer that," he deadpanned.

Clive signalled to Brigitte to pick it up, a gesture that was countered by a less polite one from her reminding him that it was his phone. After a few moments of hesitation, he gritted his teeth and picked up the device. Tentative fingers swiped against the cracked screen to switch it to speaker phone, and he hurriedly placed it down on a nearby shelf, eager to be rid of it.

He leaned in as close as he dared.

"Hello?"

The faint sound of static could be heard through the mobile device's tinny speaker, white noise that rapidly fluctuated in volume. There were sounds behind the shifting frequencies, the distant murmur of voices straining to be heard.

Suddenly one sounded, as clear as day through the garbled crackles. The voice of Dick Elswood, barked and emotionless.

"Coming"

Even Eric joined the others in shrieking when the small device suddenly flipped itself into the air, the screen exploding in a shower of sparks. By the time the chunks of it had landed back on the shelf, every piece of it had melted into fused blobs of plastic and wire. Each tiny fragment momentarily arced with white crackles of power, before falling silent and fizzling away into ash.

Clive, his voice cracked, pointed a shaking finger at where the phone had sat.

"You heard that! You all heard that!"

Eric, ever the optimist, nodded.

"Yeah, somebody is coming to rescue us."

"No, whatever killed everybody out there is coming for us," countered Clive, the pessimist – The Yin to Eric's Yang. They were the same at work. Every bug was an insurmountable issue for the eternal worrier Clive, and merely a challenge to the infinitely more pragmatic Eric.

Brigitte felt compelled to speak.

"Look, something crazy is happening with the electricity, I'll grant you that. But what's out there that you're so scared of?"

"I... I think I know what's happening here," announced Clive, his tone suddenly serious and utterly sincere. "I've encountered it before. Vengeful ghosts, out to kill us. Matter can't be destroyed, right? Even when you're dead. They're controlling – no, they are the electricity. Come to wreak jealous retribution on the living."

Brigitte didn't know where to start. She raised a finger in the air as though to speak, but had to compose herself again. No, the words simply refused to form. Eventually, she managed to spit them out, hardly believing what she found herself saying.

"You've encountered this before, Clive?"

"Nineteen eighty-three. Advanced Dungeons and Dragons. Into the Necromancer's Necropolis."

Eric rolled his eyes skywards.

"This is ridiculous. We've shut ourselves inside a store cupboard. We have no idea what's going on out there, and we can't survive by eating..."

He gestured wildly at the few occupied shelves "...trackballs, 28.8k modems, acoustic couplers and dust."

Brigitte stepped over to him and placed a hand on his shoulder. She'd intended it to be reassuring, but it came across as more than a little clingy.

"You don't know what's out there."

"There's an old saying. Fortune favours the bold. I guess I'm about to find out."

"But, Eric..."

"That was Captain Benjamin Sisko, Deep Space Nine, Season six, episode six. Sacrifice of Angels. I don't care what's out there. Sentient alien energy, harnessed forces beyond mortal understanding, I can't just stop in here. If Dan was here, he'd have a plan. The least I can do is try to fetch help."

A confident hand pulled the door slightly ajar. The smell of Dan drifted languidly through the gap.

"...or it could be electrical ghosts, Eric."

"I'm not even entertaining that thought, Clive" were the last words he said before the door was closed and he was gone.

If there was a hypothetical list called "Colleagues you'd want to be stuck in a store cupboard with in the event of a potential apocalypse", Clive would be very low on said list. Possibly even behind Nigel from the front desk, whose hobbies seemed to mostly revolve around Live Roleplaying and smelling of slightly-off soup.

The ridiculous sentient electrical ghost hypothesis, poor as it was, was the best thing he'd brought to the table. Brigitte was trying to do the British thing of panicking in relative silence, but Clive was incapable of doing even that. The time he wasn't pacing around muttering to himself — doing that annoying thing where you weren't sure whether he was trying to get your attention or not – he was drumming his fingers irritatingly on the shelves. He'd learned that each shelf, dependent on its thickness and load, produced a slightly different sound when tapped.

Much to Brigitte's irritation, he seemed to be trying to compose a fingertip version of The Imperial March by trial and error.

Tap tap tap tap taptap tap taptap
Tap tap tap tap taptap tap taptap
Tap taptaptap tap taptaptaptap tap tap
She should have gone with Eric.

The sudden noise from outside roused her from a not-unpleasant daydream in which she was force-feeding Clive dismantled shelving rods. She sat upright and saw a similarly roused Clive sitting across from her, blinking his eyes wildly. They both hurriedly clambered to their feet, grabbing what was nearest to hand; Brigitte, a bulky toner cartridge and Clive, an old laptop.

"Eric?"

Brigitte received no reply, save the sound of wooden table legs squeaking against laminated flooring.

"What are you doing?!" whispered an incredulous Clive as Brigitte stepped towards the door, raising the toner cartridge like an unwieldy powder-filled club.

"It could be Eric!"

"If it is, he knows where we are!"

She realised her hand was trembling as she turned the door handle, pulling the door open a fraction to peer through. Clive, realizing his plaintive cries were being ignored, suddenly fell quiet and backed into the shadows behind one of the shelves.

She saw Dan first, a blackened corpse draped across the wall. His skin was desiccated and cracked, and it looked as though any contact with him would reduce what remained of him to a pile of ash. Eric stumbled into view in the office, his back to her. His scalp was mostly bare, his thick, auburn hair reduced to sparse clumps dotted across a scorched dome. His shirt was similarly blackened. Long, streaked marks traced across pinstripe blue lines. She went to call his name again, but something stopped her. He was standing between two desks, holding himself upright by holding onto each. He looked unsteady, as though he might fall at any moment.

Suddenly, he released his grip and stood, swaying and trying to retain his balance. It was like watching a child taking those first unaided steps. An unsure left leg moved forward and his body weight shifted to match it. Slowly he faltered forwards, feet dragging along the ground.

Brigitte had to remember to breathe again, watching him with a sense of growing unease. Eric stopped and began to slowly turn, jerky movements spinning him gradually on the spot.

Little by little, he turned to face her. His eyes were gone, replaced by charred, dark cavities. The burns across his back continued across his front, a patchwork of brown and black smears crudely dotting his stumbling form. The absence of eyes wasn't the worst thing – that would be the crooked grimace across his mouth. Eric looked inordinately pleased with himself.

He began to shuffle towards Brigitte, his grin widening with every awkward movement. His jaw began to shift awkwardly, his mouth opening and closing like a landed fish. Weird sounds were emerging, like those from a singer warming up by doing vocal training – drawn out guttural vowel noises and bizarre clicks contorted from his throat.

And then a word, a tentative "Hello", the word drawn out and more awkward than it had ever sounded. And then repeated, as though Eric were testing it, feeling how the word felt as it passed over his dried and scorched lips through his blackened soot-stained teeth.

Brigitte whimpered a mostly unintelligible response, fear freezing her to the spot. With a strength of will she hadn't exhibited since the last Laboratory Christmas party had had a free bar, she pulled the door closed and flicked the latch.

She staggered, jolting in fright as her back brushed against the wall. A gentle arrhythmic tapping sounded against the outside of the metal storeroom door, like water dripping onto tiles. Clive stepped out from the shadows and joined Brigitte, placing a reassuring hand on her shoulder.

"It's Eric," she stuttered in a half-sob, leaning into him. "But it's not Eric."

Brigitte would even have preferred Clive's awful rendition of his tapped Star Wars theme medley to the noises that came from beyond the room now. They both listened, paralysed, as Eric spoke to them through the door.

At first, he'd just repeated the word "Hello". Different volumes and with varying inflection – even different languages and accents. Not-Eric had posed it as a query, declared it as a greeting, even announced it as a fact.

There had been silence for a while, and Brigitte and Clive had half-considered opening the door and making a run for it, but Not-Eric had soon piped up again, this time with an enhanced repertoire. He stumbled over some of the words, repeating the odd one over and over to himself, but with every passing moment, he was becoming more verbose.

He'd started with an apology. Like a talking thesaurus, he'd said sorry in more ways with more words than Brigitte knew could be used to express remorse. At times, it felt as though he were talking to them, at others like he was addressing only himself.

After the first few hours, Clive had retreated to the seclusion of the dark shadows in the corner of the room. He'd placed his fingers firmly in his ears and was rocking back and forth, all the time murmuring to himself with his eyes tightly closed.

There'd been a string of random words then, as though Not-Eric were still trying to determine how they sounded, like a translator working out the rules behind the syntax. This was interrupted loudly by one word, clear as a bell – not in the atonal voice she'd listened to for the past few hours, but clearly that of Eric.

"Brigitte".

It was the voice of the Eric that she knew. He gave her name that French twang that made it sound way more exotic than it was. She'd always mocked him, but secretly adored it. Brigitte stood up and leant against the door, imagining Eric doing the same on the other side. She pressed her palms against the warm metal. She glanced over to Clive, whose rocking silhouette remained oblivious.

"Eric?"

"Accident – it was an accident. You are conductive skin-bags of water, and our earlier attempts at communication were... flawed etiquette."

Flawed etiquette was a bit of an understatement, thought Brigitte. Flawed is swearing when you didn't mean to. Flawed is picking up the wrong spoon for dessert. The phrase somehow didn't seem to adequately cover barbequing most of the upper, middle and lower management tier.

There was something Brigitte had to ask, despite knowing she wasn't keen on hearing the answer.

"What are you?"

"I...we ...don't know. That knowledge will return, in time."

At least he hadn't said electrical ghosts. That didn't mean that could be ruled out, but the options were still open.

"What do you plan on doing with us?"

"What do you plan on doing, Brigitte?"

"I don't want you to kill me, like you did with Eric."

"Our first contact was flawed, as were our later attempts. But we have improved. All of Eric is not lost – we don't want to harm you at all. We just want you to join us."

"So, it's an invasion?"

"It has taken more of your chronology than we would have liked, but we've mastered control of your energies now. The power that drives you all, the energies in the air itself, all bend to our whim. We could kill you both now, if we so wished. Electrify the oxygen in your lungs; boil the blood in your veins. You're really quite, quite vulnerable as a species. But enough energy has been lost today."

"That sounds like a threat."

"If you stay in there, you'll starve. Now that's not a threat, but an inherent weakness in your physiology. Come out."

Not-Eric was right. Even if they wanted to, they couldn't fight.

She took one last look at Clive, who seemed to have drifted off to sleep, his fingers still wedged firmly in his ears. Brigitte sighed and flicked the latch, slowly opening the door.

Not-Eric stood there facing her. He was no longer swaying but seemed to have mastered the act of standing up straight. His empty sockets glared at her, his head cocked at an angle. His straight lips raised into a smile.

She looked back to the store-room as Not-Eric placed his burnt hand on her shoulder.

"He'll come in his own time. Leave him."

She walked, guided, through the empty corridors of the laboratories. There was something in the air; she could feel it, some sense of anticipation. Or, as the scientist in her couldn't help but remind her, it could have just been down to the ionization of the air particles.

She glanced at the main meeting room as they walked past. The corpses had all been tidied away. The smell of burnt flesh remained, but even that was fading with every step. Whenever she slowed, Not-Eric would slow as well. She was being directed, but not rushed.

The first glimpse she got of outside was from the windows in the stairwell. The evening sky shifted between iridescent purples, oranges and blues, the clouds themselves burning with a fierce inner light. The air around her grew heavier with every floor she ascended, uncomfortably so as they arrived at the roof. She was forced to gulp in larger breaths of air each time and Not-Eric sensed her concern.

"That will pass," he reassured her.

There were others on the roof, standing on the edge of the balcony and staring at the heavens. Some were charred and damaged, like Not-Eric; others were like Brigitte, seemingly untouched. A few of them were seated in a circle on the slate-chip flooring and they smiled at Not-Eric and Brigitte as they stepped past.

"What happens now?" she asked, staring out at the blinking lights of the surrounding city.

"Whatever you like," replied Not-Eric. "You're part of us already, whether you want to be or not. And you'll never know – or care – whether you made the decision voluntarily. The thoughts in your head are just neurons firing over the surface of your brain. Just another form of energy that we can manipulate."

She looked back at him, not concerned.

"But you probably don't care," he said, before turning to look at the skies.

He was right. Here, surrounded by this beauty, she couldn't for the life of her work out what all the fuss was about. Everything – the clouds, the lights in the city, the thoughts in her head – it was just so much energy, after all. They were all just so insignificant in the scheme of things but, paradoxically, crucial. It was only fair that everybody should feel like this, hear this electrical sermon. The Power Stations would be their cathedrals, the pylons their churches. This word needed to be spread, and the growing masses in the building and soon, the city, all knew the good news.

It looked like it was going to rain. Or at least thunder, anyway.

IN LOVING MEMORY
MARK CASSELL

Patrick and I clambered up the tree, agile as monkeys. The tree we'd chosen to climb was one of what seemed like a thousand. Squinting through the woodland, I thought perhaps I saw the conservatory of his house. If his mum knew we were there, tempting gravity beyond rusted barbed wire, she would've killed us. A pair of eleven-year-olds, we didn't care. Freedom of the summer holidays was as much in front of us, as was the spread of English countryside behind us.

Feet balanced on a hefty limb, I stared up at Patrick – he'd clearly climbed this tree many times. A breeze ruffled his blond hair. I had one arm wrapped around the trunk, the bark jagged and rough; while the other hand gripped what I assumed was a safe branch.

It wasn't.

When it made a sharp crack, like an echoing rifle shot, my heart wriggled into my throat. When a jagged bolt of miniature lightning traced the splintered branch, I didn't understand what was happening. It appeared only for the fleetest of moments, but I saw it.

Gravity snatched my skinny arse.

Patrick's pale face shrank in a blur of green leaves and quivering daylight. His eyes grew wider. The stink of wet vegetation filled my lungs as I plunged into whipping branches. Why hadn't I hit the ground yet? Was I that far up? Twigs and leaves slapped the back of my head, and clawed my flailing arms. Patrick was so tiny.

Still falling, and—

I slammed into the ground.

Dirt and sticks and dead leaves exploded around me. Arms and legs vertical, suspended almost. The agony, the wind rushing from my lungs, the force much more than a punch to the stomach.

Help me! I silently yelled at my friend. Why was he not helping? Didn't he care?

Maybe Patrick laughed; maybe he shouted something as he lowered himself from limb to limb. I had no idea. I could not see nor hear anything through the waves of pain, the roaring agony between my ears.

I writhed in a flurry of crispy leaves, my spine and shoulders and skull burning, throbbing. Heat spread into my legs and feet, into my toes, raging through my arms to numb my fingers. Colours and dark spots dotted my vision. I squirmed in the dirt like a dying snake.

I don't remember Patrick's first words, and I sure as hell cannot remember the return walk. Back at his house, we somehow avoided his mum. My T-shirt was shredded from where twigs and sticks had stabbed my back. I'll give Patrick some credit; he made a good effort in patching me up, pulling twigs and leaves from my skin. He swabbed the ragged gashes with cotton wool pads.

His mum never knew, though I told mine the morning after. I actually thought it was funny; I'd survived without a single broken bone.

"Darren!" Mum yelled when I removed my pyjama top. "You could've broken your back!"

Before breakfast, she stood behind me while I sat hunched over the table. Sunlight bled through the window, reaching across the tablecloth. With the occasional wince, I watched her hand drop dirt and bits of leaves and wood onto a tissue. I even noticed the spiral curls of cotton wool Patrick had left in my flesh. Soon it was time for the disinfectant, its sharp odour burning my nostrils. I knew what was coming, my muscles tense.

While I groaned under Mum's attention, Patrick was again climbing the tree.

Though I didn't know that at the time, of course.

We lived over half an hour's drive from each other and even though it was a sunny morning in my town, I guess there was a thunder storm over his. Lightning struck the tree while he was up there.

They say he most likely died before he even hit the ground

Twenty years later, I'd all but forgotten my fall. I've never forgotten Patrick, though. Never will. He was the closest buddy I ever had. In fact, I married his sister, Sonja. But that's not part of my story, that's completely irrelevant to what happened yesterday. Yesterday marked the anniversary of the fateful lightning strike.

Yesterday...

Dressed in an ink-stained white smock, I stood in my laboratory, surrounded by colour charts and the smell of chemicals. I held a tiny pot of red ink in one hand and a thin spatula in the other, about to place both on the worktop when a chill clawed my spine. I ignored it. The temperature in that damned factory was always fluctuating. It was an old building.

I set the pot down beside a row of others that were already lidless: a black, a yellow, and a blue. I stabbed my spatula into the red. Adding a dollop to the rainbow swirls already on the mixing slab. These samples had to be finished by the end of the day, and it was Friday after all. I glanced at the clock. It was nearly ten. The guys in the factory had problems with the raw materials, these useless pigments adding to our workload.

Again, a chill tickled my neck. I turned, and—

"Patrick?" My voice came out as a whisper of breath that fogged between us.

He looked just the same as he did that day. Still an eleven year-old kid, unkempt hair and a toothy grin. Wisps of smoke curled from his blue jacket amid tiny sparks of what I can only describe as lightning. When the smoke cleared, he approached me.

"Hi, Darren," he said, looking up at me. Crackles of electricity sputtered across his forehead. "What happened to your face?"

A laugh simmered inside me. I don't know why, and I sure as hell don't know how I managed, but I rolled with it. Again, my words churned breath-fog before me.

"I got old."

"You did."

"I'm married now." Why was I even telling him this?

"Yes."

"To Sonja."

Tiny traces of lightning, a peculiar energy, rushed across his cheek. "I know."

"You do?"

He sank into the chair at my desk. "You look like a doctor."

I touched the pocket of my smock. "I'm technical manager."

"Sounds boring." His eyes darted around the lab. "What do you do in here?"

"I match ink colours."

"Boring."

"Once formulated, large batches are made in the factory. Then they're potted and sent to the printers for magazines, packaging, that sort of—"

"I miss the old days." His eyes widened.

I looked past him and focused on the workstation behind. A pile of swatch samples glared at me like an impatient rainbow, pushing through grey clouds. So much work.

Patrick said something. I couldn't quite make it out, perhaps it was "beckon," or maybe it was "beaker" (there was a beaker on the work surface after all). It could even have been the word "beacon."

When I looked back, my school friend – my dead best friend from twenty years ago – had vanished.

My breath no longer fogged the air, and a warmth returned to the lab. My heartbeat, however, banged loud between my ears. I turned, almost stumbled. I was overworked. Clearly I'd been hallucinating. Right?

The remainder of the day was slow, yet I hurried those ink samples. To hell with the outcome. If there were any repercussions, my rushed work could be dealt with on Monday.

The smoke came again this morning.

After kissing Sonja goodbye as she left for work, Patrick appeared in my lounge. Smoke drifted from his ruffled blond hair, and tiny traces of energy cascaded off his shoulders.

"This is not happening," I muttered, hugging my dressing gown tighter. That was often my Saturday morning uniform, unless I had somewhere important to go. As it had before, my breath sent fog to mix with the smoke that clouded the room.

"This is happening," he said. "I'm only sorry it's taken all this time."

Unlike yesterday, I could not accept this bullshit. "You're dead." I all but spat the words at him.

"I am."

"But—"

"See me as a reflection of what I once was."

I glared at him. "What does that even mean?"

"I saw the lightning when you fell," he explained. "Then when I returned to the tree the next day, I saw it again."

I thought back to when I'd seen it myself, when I'd stood on that dodgy branch and saw a spark of electricity right before I fell.

"And," Patrick added, "I heard the voices."

Again, I thought back to my fall. I hadn't heard any voices. Had I?

"They told me to return."

"I didn't hear any voices."

"You wouldn't have."

"Why not?"

"You lived too far away."

"You died," I shouted. "You were barbequed by a freak lightning strike!"

"Yes. But as I've already said, I'm now just a reflection of what I once was."

"Why are you here? Why are you doing this to me?" My voice echoed.

"I need your help."

Such was the hammering of my heartbeat; I found that I had leaned forward so I could hear his last words. The final drifts of smoke rolled off his shoulders bringing with it an odour like burnt cardboard.

"Darren, please, I really need your help."

I wandered over to the sofa and collapsed into it. My palms were clammy. "What can I do?"

When your dead school buddy from twenty years ago asks for help, you're not going to ignore him. No matter what, no matter how absurd it is, you're going to help the guy. After a strange journey to the town where Patrick once lived, to the woodland where Patrick lost his life, I now found myself alone and doubting my sanity.

This area had now become a country park, and I faced a bench that overlooked an expanse of lush greenery and proud trees. Of course, Patrick's lightning-struck tree had long been felled. In truth, I had no idea where it would've originally stood.

I stared at the words written on the bench:

IN LOVING MEMORY OF
PATRICK JENKINS
A GOOD SON & GOOD FRIEND
1986 – 1997

It had been too long since I'd been there.

On the far end of the clearing a row of willows and crooked fencing separated me from the spread of woodland that pushed out into the countryside. The smell of cut grass clung to the air, and although it was welcome, there was something else. A familiar smell of burnt paper.

"Patrick?" I asked the bench. What the fuck was I doing talking to a park bench? Seriously, what the actual fuck?

Patrick…when was he going to appear? I was there for him after all, to help free him. But I didn't understand. None of this made any sense.

I had to go home.

No, I had to book an appointment to see a doctor. I could not go on like this.

Something rustled in the trees a short distance away. A squirrel, nothing sinister. I was now looking for monsters in the trees. Great. I'd started to hallucinate, seeing my dead friend and having him speak to me…so…I guessed I was heading straight for a nervous breakdown.

From close by, someone whispered. I jerked my head and my neck clicked. I winced. No one was there, I was still alone. More whispers, louder this time. Voices, two or three rapidly speaking, yet I couldn't quite make out their words. More voices, louder, dozens, becoming a cacophony. A crowd in my head, talking fast, some shouting, others screaming.

I clamped my hands to my ears.

And the lightning came.

Jagged sparks of electricity darted about the plaque, tracing the screws that fixed it to the bench. Faint curls licked the etched words. Still with those voices filling my brain, I staggered back, squinting as the lightning intensified. White dots filled my vision and darkness crept inwards from my periphery.

Agony tore up my spine.

I screamed, hunched, and my knees smacked the ground, sending fire up my legs. I lurched forwards and smacked my head on the bench seat. Pain lanced across my forehead and I sprawled across the ground as a new sound rushed at me. Louder than the voices, electricity buzzed and fizzed. My arms flailed, my legs kicked. Dirt and dust plumed as I writhed on the ground. Charging, loud in my brain, the cacophony of voices changed in pitch but they were no longer voices...

Static.

Shrill, intense like a rush of waves storming my head, it smothered me. Warmth spread through me, soothing, and led me into a kind of tranquil silence. But only for a moment. Short and sharp heat flared, embraced by the deafening roar of white noise.

Then nothing.

I lay there, gulping air that tasted of grass, of singed paper. I stared up at the sky. Blue, just one cloud floating. And a plane. I wondered where it was heading. With shaking fingers, I gripped the bench. The wood somehow grounding me, snatching me back to the moment. With incredible effort, on legs that felt like they were made of cotton wool, I crouched, then stood. I swayed for a second or two, and I thought perhaps I'd fall again. I breathed out, long and loud. A hiss.

There, a short distance from me stood Patrick.

That familiar smoke obscured him, and electricity sputtered across his face. He smiled. Sparks zigzagged across his teeth.

My throat felt as though I'd swallowed sand. I wanted to say his name.

He nodded.

I straightened and walked towards him with surprisingly steady footfalls. The closer I got to him, the more the scent of freshly mown grass and burnt paper overwhelmed me. Finally, as I reached his side, he focused on something behind me. Tiny sparks skittered across his pupils.

I turned.

Smoke drifted between where we stood and the memorial bench.

My lips parted but nothing came out.

Beside Patrick's bench, in a blackened heap and amid curls of thick smoke, was my body. Faint lightning traced my charred limbs.

My body…

The darkness closed in. Not just smoke, but an oppressive darkness. It was as though black clouds fell from the sky, pressing me into the grass. I brought my hands up to my face. I was still here. How was it even possible?

I looked at my burnt body that now seemed so far away.

"You're a reflection," Patrick said from somewhere inside the cloying dark. "Just like me, you're a reflection for them to use."

My breath came short and sharp, painful like someone stabbing my chest. Still I could smell grass and…my fried body. Such a stink on the air. I choked.

With the agony in my lungs, burning as it was, I thought how it was actually possible I could be short of breath if I was a ghost.

Was that what I was, a ghost? A spirit?

"A reflection?" I asked my dead friend.

A sense of movement, of shifting sideways, snatched me into the fold of rainbow colours. Only thing was, there was so much black. Smoke. Gravity seemed to flip me upside down, turning me inside out. I didn't know which way was up, which way was down. All I saw were colours churning in a mix of what looked like oil and diesel and fruit cordial.

Up. Was I facing up?

My body spun, my mind whirling. Gravity snatched me downwards – definitely down. I slid, phased, down into the earth, lower than the grass, lower than tree roots. Darkness, all consuming...

I didn't know if I closed my eyes, even though technically I had no eyes. I had no body...

A roar of white noise, washed over me.

"Beacon." Patrick's voice was louder than the static. "We're inside."

"Inside?" I demanded. "Inside a beacon? For what?"

Faint shadows surrounded us. A light glowed from somewhere, yet still I couldn't make anything out. The occasional spark flitted across the shadows. Perhaps I felt the floor beneath my feet...Yes, yes, I stood upright, knowing that way up above, my charred corpse lay crumpled beside Patrick's bench.

I was dead. Yet somehow alive. Underground.

And alone.

Such was the soft glow; I saw that I stood in some kind of tunnel.

"Patrick?" My voice fell flat in the gloom. As before, my lungs were tight, constricted. Above me, so many tonnes of earth and rock pressed down on me, heavy on my body, this incorporeal body. My breath hissed from a tight throat.

More of the gloom subsided.

I was alone now.

Flanked by rusted metal walls, glistening with years of accumulated muck and mould, I peered along the tunnel. Corroded and dented conduits, and perished cables that drooped from the arched ceiling, trailed into the distance in both directions.

Here I was, dead, yet my mind was alive, buried deep underground. My heartbeat – my dead, lifeless heart – drummed in my chest, filling my head.

"Patrick?" I called. Like a dead echo, my friend's name bounced around me.

I chose a direction, and began walking.

My boots splashed in water and soon soaked my trousers, and the further I walked, the more the atmosphere dampened my skin and the more I hoped to find Patrick. I had no idea how far the tunnel had taken me by the time the lightning came. Faint at first, it traced the rusted panels that lined the tunnel walls. Sometimes it even cascaded from the conduits and sparked from the cables.

Still I walked.

Still I called my friend's name.

On and on I went, thinking of the world above. The country park, the trees, the houses, the neighbourhood, and the town further away. Everyone above, right then, going about their business and there I was, dead, yet wandering around in some intangible state. All the while my earthly body was fried to a fucking crisp beside a memorial bench.

Up ahead, heavier lightning filled the tunnel. An archway of energy crackled and fell like a beaded fly-screen, sizzling as it hit the puddled floor.

Without hesitation, I passed through it. I felt nothing as that energy bounced from my shoulders.

Beyond... into the room beyond, a white light blinded me.

I cried out and squinted into the glare.

Past the threshold and I stood in a room no larger than a typical garage. Only there were no doors, no more conduits or cables, and no sign of a light source. It was as though the metal panels that covered every inch of the walls and floor and ceiling emitted the very light that blinded me.

There was Patrick.

He stood beside one of two metal rods that protruded seamlessly from the floor. Both were chest-height to his eleven-year-old body – his reflection – and he had a hand placed on the top. Jagged sparks traced every contour of his face to reveal the skull, glowing beneath his skin.

So bright.

I knew what to do.

One foot in front of the other, I strolled over to the conductor pole adjacent to him. My boots squelched. When my fingers curled around the warm metal, a buzz roared. Vibrations tingled, charged up my forearm, into my shoulder, humming through my torso, filling my entire body. Energy rushed across every pore.

I knew I experienced the same as Patrick, charging, expanding. It grew from outside of me, strengthening my existence in this ethereal state. Lightning raged around me.

I saw my bones through my hand, the pink and red glow of skin, the warmth flowing through me. And through those bones, the flesh of myself, I saw the expanse of space, of a nothingness, spreading outwards, taking me beyond.

The reflective surface of the room broke away in a flash of jagged white light, and weightlessness snatched me. Floating.

No longer could I see my hands, no longer did I see myself. I drifted on a wave of hot starlight. Up and outwards, one intense pulse, a shockwave blowing out, splaying in a web of energy, released. And I rose with that energy, bursting up through mud, the earth, the grass, upwards, from the Earth, rising higher and higher, into the sky.

And below me...

The memorial bench. My blackened and shrivelled corpse with smoke still drifting off those stick-like limbs.

Fire.

So many flames riding on a surge of energy created the moment Patrick and I connected, conducted. Fiery energy leapt through the woodland and tore down trees, burning, crashing. The blast raced through the neighbourhood. I had a glimpse of Patrick's old house, where windows exploded, scattering a million shards of reflected sunlight. Walls collapsed, cars flipped and exploded in balls of fire, and those that didn't burn simply quivered with flashing lights and shrill alarms.

Great chasms tore through the tarmac, heaving open the ground and cleaving wide, brimming with fire and lightning and smoke. And still I rose higher. Finally, I'd left my body behind and it was simply my consciousness shooting upwards.

What was once Patrick's neighbourhood burned bright as I shot higher, higher.

I was a part of the beacon, the pulse. So, too, was Patrick.

As we stretched with that beam, somewhere there will be a response. Somewhere, someone, something, will receive the transmission.

WOLPERTINGER
G. H. FINN

It was a patchwork of madness – an anti-scientific monstrosity so blasphemous that it mocked both a belief in a divine creator and the theory of evolution.

I stared at the thing snarling silently in front of me. It had huge, vicious claws. Eyes like saucers. Gnarled antlers sprung menacingly from its grizzled head. Old mould and cobwebs hung from its shaggy fur and rancid feathers. It's massive, jutting, jagged teeth had a time-worn yellow patina. Its nightmarish fangs and tusks were cracked. It leered at me. It was ancient. It looked…hungry.

"What the flaming fuck is that thing?" asked Bruce, my painfully Australian boyfriend who constantly did his best to depict himself as a walking cliché. I'm sure he only did it to seem cute. It worked. Most of the time.

"That's the genuine article," replied the balding, silver-haired antique dealer, Herman Glum, pointing with professional pride at the stuffed curiosity in front of us.

"Genuine?" spluttered Bruce, "Genuine my barbecued bollocks! That thing's about as genuine as a Roman didgeridoo marked 'Carved by me, Abraham Lincoln, in 55BC'"

Herman shook his head and rolled his eyes at me.

I'd known Herman Glum for years, since before I did my Ph.D. in Esoteric Anthropology, when I was just another graduate researcher, prowling through second-hand bookshops and antique emporiums, in search of the rum and uncanny. I found plenty of both. Herman and I had got on straight away, probably because we recognised each other as kindred souls. Both of us were in search of mysteries, long lost to history yet perhaps still tantalisingly discoverable in obscure manuscripts, weird artefacts and the enigmatic curios of ages past. Herman was getting on a bit, even when I first met him. Back when I was still a girl, a little naïve, but proud of my oddly mixed heritage – my maternal-grandmother was a Romani gypsy, one of the Kàlo people from Finland. She'd married a Jamaican man, one of the Maroons who claimed descent from a wild blend of runaway slaves, desperate pirates, heretic European Christians, and the indigenous Taíno tribes. Their daughter, my mother, moved to Scotland and married my father – who was the youngest son of the hereditary Laird of the Clan MacCrom. You could use me as the very definition of 'mixed-race'. Mum and Dad named me Miranda after the character in Shakespeare's The Tempest, because she says the line, "How beauteous mankind is! O brave new world, That has such people in it!

Bruce interrupted my reminiscing with another outburst.

"That thing is as unbelievable as a politician's promise and by the smell of it, it's nearly as corrupt. You could shave a koala, claim it was the baby Jesus and it still wouldn't be as fake as that."

I smiled, "What Mr Glum means is, this is a genuine original example of a Wolpertinger. It's genuinely antique. It isn't a modern reproduction. Not a knock-off. But of course, yes, biologically speaking it's a fake."

"Hang on, you're losing me," said Bruce, "What the hell is a Wolpertinger?"

Subconsciously I slipped into lecture-mode as I answered, "The Wolpertinger is the European ancestor of the American Jackalope. There are several regional variations on the name, including Wolperdinger, Woipertinger, and Volpertinger. Wolpertingers are found in the legends and folklore of Bavaria."

The old antique dealer interrupted, adding enthusiastically, "The Wolpertinger is pretty much the same creature as the Austrian Raurackl and is closely related to the Thuringian Rasselbock, the Palatinate Elwetritsch and the little-known Swedish Skvader. It's also a cousin to the Hessian Dilldapp".

Bruce looked blankly at him then turned his curly blonde head to me in the hope I would use words he might understand.

I smiled and took pity on him, "Wolpertingers are composite creatures made by taxidermists from bits and pieces taken from the bodies of a mixture of animals.

"Wolpertingers come in several broad types. This one is exceptionally big and more complex than most. Generally, they're contrived to appear as small mammals with mismatched heads and torsos taken from rabbits, hares, squirrels, stoats and occasionally foxes or badgers, but they also have antlers, fangs, claws, wings and, more rarely, some have horns, beaks or bills. They often have the hind-legs of birds such as pheasants. Sometimes they even have webbed feet, like a duck."

Bruce stared at me. "You're kidding, right?"

Glum adjusted his pince-nez spectacles and pointed at the moth-eaten Wolpertinger. It somehow managed to appear comic and yet also subtly menacing.

"Seeing is believing," he said.

I looked more closely at the chimerical creation that stood on the shop-counter. It was around four-and-a-half-feet tall, which was unusually large for a Wolpertinger. As near as I could tell, this specimen had the body of a beaver, the tail – or technically the 'brush' – of a fox, the forelegs of a badger (which terminated in claws surely taken from a bear) and the hind-legs of a massive bird of prey, complete with vicious talons. Giant wings sprouted from its furry back, so large I wondered if they came from an albatross, while the head was that of a huge eagle-owl, fitted with wolf's teeth, adder-fangs and boar tusks. Antlers sprouted from its head, evidently removed from a prized stag, each baring nine barbed tines. On either side of the antlers, sharp horns jutted upwards. A forked-tongue hung from its sabre-toothed, razor-sharp beak. The whole thing was such a misshapen mishmash that the effect should have been hilarious. But somehow it didn't seem funny at all.

Bruce wasn't impressed. "Were people meant to take this seriously? Or was it a joke?"

I shrugged. "A little bit of both perhaps. Maybe I better give you some background." I took a deep breath and began, "Wolpertingers do seem to have genuinely once been a part of the folklore of Germanic countries. Images of creatures resembling Wolpertingers appear in engravings and woodcuts dating back to the 17th century. The exact origins of the legends are very much open to interpretation but some of the more reasonable guesses might be sightings of things like diseased rabbits, animals born with disfiguring birth defects and, of course, short-sighted hunters wandering about in the woods at night after a few too many drinks."

Bruce smiled. I carried on, "Sooner or later some bright spark had the idea of sewing together the remains of various animals to produce what would look like the corpse of a Wolpertinger and thus seemingly provide evidence for any tall-tales told about his hunting exploits."

I pointed at the Wolpertinger. "Unveiling something like that in the local tavern would be bound to earn him a few drinks, if nothing else.

"Then it'd only be a small step for a professional taxidermist to make one, perhaps innocently, to display it in his shop as a curiosity and talking-point, or more likely to sell for an extravagant fee to some credulous tourist."

Bruce nodded. Making money was a timeless motive, universally understood. I nodded toward the stuffed monstrosity perched in front of us and added, "Bavarian inns frequently have Wolpertingers on display, mainly to attract customers. And for well over a hundred years there's been a thriving souvenir industry manufacturing Wolpertingers to sell to gullible holiday-makers."

I stared at the not-at-all timorous beastie on the shop counter. I frowned, and added softly, "But this one is a lot older…"

The antique dealer nodded and beamed. "It's over three-hundred years old." he said, smugly.

I raised an eyebrow, not bothering to hide my suspicion.

"Early 18th Century." he continued, "I think circa 1712, although I'll admit that's only an educated guess. But it is undoubtedly prior to 1734."

I was puzzled. "Why undoubtedly?"

He gestured at the Wolpertinger, "Because that was the year in which the creature's maker shuffled off this mortal coil. However, I'm convinced this was made earlier in his career, probably around the time he tried to buy Castle Frankenstein."

The shop became suddenly silent as both Bruce and I stared at Herman, albeit for different reasons. Eventually the silence was broken.

"You are so shitting me," said Bruce, "Frankenstein isn't real. He was invented by that Mary Shelley sheila back in the dark ages."

I pretended Bruce hadn't said that. He had many fine qualities, but a grasp of history wasn't among them. Nor literature. Nor the fact that few women like to be called a 'sheila'. Bless him, he wasn't good at anything that required much thinking. I sometimes wondered if he'd been hit on the head by a falling dropbear. But overall Bruce was nice, meant well, and, while I don't think good looks are everything, he was given such an unreasonably large helping that I tended to overlook his lack of either education or intelligence. But I did so wish he'd at least learn to keep quiet now and again.

    I tutted at Bruce and muttered, "Obviously the novel Frankenstein is a work of fiction, just like this Wolpertinger here, but Mary Shelley – who incidentally first published her novel in 1818, not during the 'Dark Ages' – didn't invent the name. There really is a Castle Frankenstein. It's built on top of a tall hill in the Odenwald, overlooking the city of Darmstadt, in Germany."

    Bruce looked amazed, "But there's no Baron Frankenstein, right?" he asked.

    Glum made a non-committal sound, answering, "Well...sometime before the year 1250, Lord Conrad II, Reiz of Breuberg, built Castle Frankenstein and created the imperial Barony of Frankenstein, which ruled the region for centuries, so technically the title Baron von Frankenstein is a genuinely historical one."

    "Wow," said Bruce. "But no Baron Frankenstein ever tried to make a monster though?"

    "Of course not!" I said in exasperation.

    Herman Glum paused, then nodded, confirming, "You are quite right. None of the Barons Frankenstein were interested in making monsters."

There was something a little odd about the way he said that, but I was too busy thinking about the Wolpertinger to spare it much consideration.

"So you know the name of whoever made this?" I asked, pointing a thumb at the weird and unnatural thing. It seemed to watch me from the ornate wooden stand upon which it was mounted.

The antique dealer's smile widened into a huge grin. "Oh yes. I have both the name and full proof of the provenance."

I could feel his excitement. And his expectation. I felt like I must have missed something. What had he said? The maker of the Wolpertinger had once tried to buy Castle Frankenstein? I almost gasped in surprise as the dreadful penny dropped.

Glum saw the look in my eyes and nodded, "That's right. This particular Wolpertinger is the work of none other than the infamous Johann Conrad Dippel."

Bruce looked at me, searchingly. "Is that name meant to mean something?" he asked.

I knew a little about Dippel, of course. In my line of work, I'd read about most of the world's great historical eccentrics, madmen, diabolists, charlatans, exorcists, forgers, pioneering scientists, magicians and all shades in between. But I wasn't really an expert on Dippel, so I invited Herman to explain further. He was delighted to do so.

"Dippel was born at Castle Frankenstein in 1673. He died in 1734. Dippel was a theologian, physician, natural-philosopher and alchemist.

"At school he was known, after the place of his birth, as Johann Conrad Dippel Franckensteinensis. He was a very gifted student.

"Dippel studied at the University of Giessen, earning a master's degree in 1693. Around 1700 his studies turned towards Hermetic subjects including alchemy, natural magic and what we would regard as... occult sciences.

"Dippel had both admirers and enemies. Swedenborg began as a disciple of Dippel, but ultimately dismissed him as a 'most vile devil... who attempted wicked things'. Dippel was eventually imprisoned for seven years on a charge of heresy.

"These days he is perhaps best remembered as the creator of Dippel's Oil which was once believed to be akin to the alchemical Elixir of Life. At one point, Dippel attempted to purchase Castle Frankenstein in exchange for his elixir formula. His offer was turned down, but nevertheless it was taken seriously."

Bruce looked surprisingly interested in the antique dealer's explanation – usually it was all I could do to get him to stay awake if I explained anything historical – but I remembered he was a bit of a fan of old Hammer Horror films, so probably the talk of Frankenstein had piqued his interest.

"So was this Dippel bloke a scientist or a wizard?" Bruce wondered aloud.

The antique dealer considered the question, then nodded, "He was both. In that period there was no clear line separating science and magic.

"Many claim that during his time at Castle Frankenstein, Dippel practised both alchemy and anatomical research. He allegedly invented a form of nitro-glycerine and in the process accidentally destroyed a tower at Castle Frankenstein.

"There are numerous stories about Johann Conrad Dippel," he paused, choosing his words carefully. "I am sure most are modern inventions or at least wild exaggerations, but it is said Dippel performed appallingly gruesome experiments on corpses.

"Legend has it he attempted to transfer souls from their original bodies into others. At the time, alchemists frequently experimented with soul-transference using cadavers. Dippel supported the theory that such transference of souls was possible and detailed this in his published writings – He claimed that souls could be transferred from one corpse to another.

"There is also a rumour that he was driven out of the region when word of his activities reached the ears of the locals."

Bruce sniggered, "What, by a mob with pitchforks and burning torches?"

Herman inclined his head, smiling, "Perhaps. It is however a definite matter of historical record that he was banned from entering both Sweden and Russia because of his very, em, controversial theological opinions."

Bruce was intrigued. "But he didn't, you know, make a bloody Frankenstein's Monster? Did he?"

Glum paused as though considering his next words carefully, before stating, "Dippel frequently experimented with dead animals. He was described as an 'avid dissector'.

"Dippel wrote and published a dissertation entitled 'Maladies and Remedies of the Life of the Flesh'. In this work, Dippel claimed to have discovered both the Elixir of Life and a method to exorcise demons via the use of specific potions he concocted from boiled animal bones, flesh and possibly other.... unnamed.... ingredients.

"Dippel turned his back on his earlier Christian beliefs, losing his faith and calling Christ 'an indifferent being'. Casting aside theology, he employed all his energy on alchemical experiments. At this point in his life historical records become vague and Dippel's activities become rather folkloric in nature."

I was intrigued by this cryptic comment and asked Herman what he meant. Glum seemed slightly reluctant but continued, "At least one local priest accused Dippel of grave robbing, mutilating corpses, experimenting on cadavers, and... keeping company with the Devil."

Bruce was fascinated. "How much of that is true and how much just fairy-stories?"

"Who knows?" said the antique dealer. "Dippel mainly kept himself to himself, concentrated on his work, and ensured most of his experiments and discoveries remained private. Whatever he was working on, he wouldn't have wanted anyone to steal his secrets. He might even have actively encouraged any rumours that he had sold his soul to the Devil in exchange for secret knowledge, either to keep away nosey busy-bodies and rival researchers or to enhance his reputation as a sorcerer and alchemist, which in turn might have made it easier for him to gain audiences with nobles who were willing to pay for his knowledge of the Philosopher's Stone and the Elixir of Life."

Bruce considered this for a few moments, before announcing, "Sounds like a complete load of kangaroo-feathers. It's all just bunyip-shit if you ask me."

"We didn't." I pointed out, firmly.

It took Bruce quite a while to get his brain started, let alone into gear, but once he had, he wasn't easily put off. "So how and where does this, eh, Voldermortinger? No, Wolperdingerlinger-thingy fit in?" he asked.

Herman smiled, "I'm glad you asked young man. It's quite a fascinating story. I inherited this shop from my late father, and he from his father. The name on the door reads 'Glum Curiosities & Antiques' and Glum is my surname. It is the name my grandfather took when he moved, or should I say fled, to England in the 1930s,"

Herman's voice became quieter as he said, "My grandfather left Austria in 1936. He was one of the lucky ones who got out in time. Before...well, I'm sure you know the history. Our original family name was Gümpel, but as that sounded a little too Jewish for Oswald Mosley's Blackshirts and, during WWII, too German for the average Englishman to be comfortable with, my grandfather changed our surname to Glum. It sounded more acceptable, and also fitted his temperament rather well.

"My father died many years ago – my Grandfather outlived him. In fact my Grandfather had an exceptionally long life. Sadly he eventually succumbed to dementia and spent his last years in what is euphemistically called 'a home'.

"It was only when Grandfather's will was read that I discovered he still owned a large lock-up located, as the old song goes, 'underneath the arches' of a nearby railway-bridge. When I finally managed to open the myriad of locks the old man had installed, I found a veritable Aladdin's cave of hidden treasures. Including this very Wolpertinger."

"You've got a bleeding funny idea of treasure, mate." Bruce opined. I shushed him so that Herman could continue his story.

"My grandfather had imported some of the choicer items of his stock with him when he came to England – back in Vienna he had owned a very high-class pawn-brokers. One of the items he brought was this Wolpertinger, along with the receipt he obtained when purchasing it – from a man whose family had for generations worked as servants at Castle Frankenstein. The Wolpertinger had been kept in an old cellar for decades and was finally given to his uncle, a trusted servant. Or at least, so the seller claimed. I suspect he may have been more light-fingered than he admitted, but my grandfather was able to obtain proof the Wolpertinger had indeed originated at Castle Frankenstein. And if you care to examine the plinth the creature stands upon..."

I produced the magnifying glass I always carried when considering buying an exhibit and did so. On the left of the Wolpertinger, carved next to its foot, chiselled in an ornate script, was the name 'Johann Conrad Dippel'.

I was convinced. Herman Glum's reputation in the antiques trade was unimpeachable, and we'd been good friends for years. If he said this was Dippel's work, I believed him. And I would certainly want to buy the Wolpertinger for the 'special collection' of the Midwynter Museum.

Bruce was still unable to stop staring at the man-made monster. He gave it a cautious poke with one finger, then asked, "Why?"

"Why what?" queried Glum, his eyebrows raised behind his glasses.

"Why did Dippy Dippel make this thing?"

I had to admit, it was a good question.

The antique dealer spread his hands in a gesture which clearly said "Who knows?" but he offered some suggestions,

"Dippel may have made it as some kind of an anatomical experiment, to further his understanding of how muscles, bones, nerves, tendons and ligaments are joined and function.

"Or, maybe he was simply short on funds and created a Wolperdinger to sell, to make some quick cash. Who can say?"

Bruce nodded, apparently satisfied. But the question did still niggle at me.

Why did Dippel make the Wolpertinger?

I'd spent a good hour haggling over the price with Herman. Mostly because it was traditional – he'd have been shocked if I had agreed to the figure he first suggested – and also because it gave us both a chance to chat and catch-up. There was never any doubt whether I'd buy the Wolpertinger. It was exactly the type of exhibit I was looking for.

It was a Sunday afternoon. There would be no-one working in the acquisitions department of the museum, so there was no point going in before Monday morning. Bruce had manfully loaded the ancient monstrosity into the back of my Land Rover and then man-handled it up to my flat. In the process (and amid my loud protestations and cries of distress) Bruce had clumsily banged the unique antique against one wall, nearly dropped it down a flight of stairs and finally got it caught in a door. He started sulking because I shouted at him and went off to the kitchen to drain the fridge of beer, leaving me to deal with the Wolpertinger.

That was how the thing came to be sitting on my coffee table. The ancient monster looked out of place on top of the gleaming stainless steel and glass table. But it wouldn't be there long. It belonged in the museum, I'd just got Bruce to put it there while I inspected it. I held a small table-lamp up and shone it on the Wolpertinger like a torch, looking for any signs of damage to the artefact from Bruce's carelessness. The lamp had a long flex so I was able to check everywhere, using the lamp's bulb like a spotlight. Luckily there was no real damage, a few ruffled feathers but nothing worse, although part of the base now seemed to be a little loose. I examined the wooden mounting more closely, pressing it with my fingers to see if it had cracked. I felt something move beneath my fingertips. There was a sudden click. In amazement I watched as part of the wooden base swung open, revealing a cavity hidden within. I felt inside and my fingers closed on something – a small glass vial, stoppered and sealed with wax. The vial was filled with a viscous, tar-like liquid. Even though it was sealed in the bottle it still somehow stank. My guess was this was a sample of Dippel's famous oil, which he apparently invented by means of 'a destructive distillation of bones'. Though why he would hide it beneath a Wolpertinger was beyond me. I felt further inside the hidden compartment and found a folded sheet of parchment. I opened it delicately and saw it was covered with handwritten Gothic blackletter-script. German minuscules were never my favourite, but I could read them when I had to. I carefully began to translate the document. It was a letter addressed to the nobleman who owned Castle Frankenstein, and signed by Johann Conrad Dippel.

"What's that say?" asked Bruce, appearing from the kitchen and no-longer sulking as he drained another can of lager.

I re-read it to be sure, then paraphrased the German for Bruce's benefit. "Well, the gist of it is that Dippel was obviously pissed-off when his offer to buy Castle

Frankenstein in return for the secret of his Elixir was turned down, but he thought he'd have another go at it. He says that the oil he famously invented, while valuable, was not the real alchemical Elixir of Life, only a useful yet inferior substance, but that he had however discovered the true Elixir of Vitality after years of research. He claimed that this true 'Vital Oil' was so powerful it could resurrect the dead and animate the unliving. At least, that's what I think he says, my 18th century German is rather rusty. He goes on to claim that if coupled with a process he has developed which allowed the transplantation of a soul from its original host into another fresh body, then a person could effectively achieve immortality by animating and possessing one body after another, for all eternity. He offers a sample of his Oil of Vitality and this Wolpertinger as proof of his discoveries and invited the recipient of the letter to test this for himself. Then he gets a bit cryptic and goes on at length about 'Donner und Blitzen' but I think he's using the terms in some alchemical sense."

"Donner and Blitzen?" asked Bruce, "You mean Santa's reindeer?"

I rolled my eyes. "No. Of course not. Donner is the German word for Thunder. Blitzen means Lightning."

"Did it work?" Bruce asked.

I smiled at his foolishness. "Obviously no such test was ever carried out. I assume the then Baron Frankenstein dismissed Dippel as a raving lunatic. Or perhaps he never even read the note. If this was delivered to the castle about the same time Dippel was imprisoned for heresy, it may have just been shoved in a storeroom and forgotten."

"Shall we give it a go?" asked Bruce.

"What?" I wondered, genuinely puzzled.

"Shall we test Dippel's Oil of Vitality? See if it really can give life to the Wolpertinger?"

"Fuck off," I replied. I don't usually swear but under the circumstances it seemed justified. "Firstly, Dippel was clearly deranged and the Elixir of Life is a myth. Secondly, both the Wolpertinger and the vial of oil are valuable antiques now owned by the Midwynter Museum, not toys for you to play with. And thirdly, and this is quite an important point so do pay attention, even if by some unholy miracle the whole story was true, why the fuck would we want to bring to life a three-hundred-year-old patchwork monster that used to belong to Castle Frankenstein? You, my love, are about eighteen prawns short of a barbie even to think of such a thing!"

Bruce smiled and had the decency to look sheepish. I thought that would be the end of it.

I should have known better.

By the middle of the evening, Bruce had finished all the beer and was drunk.

By midnight, he'd finished off my wine, Bailey's, Malibu and the single-malt Scotch I was keeping for my birthday.

I'd given up and gone to bed, expecting he would fall into a comatose heap on the sofa, or at worse vomit in my geraniums. Again.

It was the crash from the living room that woke me. I was more annoyed than surprised. Bruce was probably so paralytic by now that he'd tripped over a chair or something.

Then I heard the sound of breaking glass. Worried that Bruce had hurt himself I stumbled from the bedroom, calling his name.

I hurried into the living room. The main lights were off but I could see Bruce outlined as a shadow. He was standing next to the Wolpertinger, swearing under his breath. I flicked the light switch on the wall and he spun round guiltily. He was so drunk it was amazing he could stand upright but even so he made a futile attempt to hide what he'd been doing. In one hand he held the small table lamp. In the other he had the bottle of Dippel's elixir. It was half empty.

"What the hell do you think you are doing?" I shouted.

Bruce drunkenly tried to feign innocence. "I, er, was looking for another drink..." he slurred, "Didn't want to wake you so didn't put the big lights on. Was using the lamp but I dropped it and the bulb broke... No worries though. You go back to bed love."

I was furious. "Bullshit. You're still holding the bottle of Dippel's oil. You've got it all over your hands. Idiot. Put it down before you spill the rest. Were you trying to use it? You fuckwit. What got into you? You know how much that cost. And it's the museum's money, not mine."

Bruce shrugged, "Just wanted to see if it'd work..." he said, shamefaced, shrugging and drunkenly waving his arms about.

I saw the broken bulb of the lamp as he carelessly flailed around, hardly able to stand up straight.

"Careful with that you moron. The lamp is still plugged in. Put it down before you hurt yourself. We'll talk about this when you're sober. We'll talk about it a lot."

Bruce smiled an apology and reached to put the lamp down on the gleaming metal coffee table, next to the Wolpertinger. But he was so drunk he missed. He tried to grab the falling lamp but stumbled into the table instead. The lamp tipped over, leaning against the Wolpertinger, resting against its fur and feathers, all of which were now coated with Dippel's elixir.

The broken bulb sparked. Foolishly, Bruce grabbed for it and was hit by an electric shock. It flung him backwards violently. I saw His head hit the wall and I heard an awful thud of bone on brick. He fell forwards, back toward the table where the broken bulb was still sparking.

I gasped in shock. How volatile was that oil? If it was flammable...

I half expected to see the prized antique burst into flame before my eyes. But no. The oil didn't burn. It did however seem to conduct the electricity. I let out a sigh of relief that the artefact wasn't about to disappear in fire and smoke after all, then stared in amazement as actinic blue bolts of electricity arced up and down the

Wolpertinger. The current from the broken table lamp lit up the monstrous thing with an eerie, unnatural glow. Sparks shot away from its body as the electricity tried to earth itself. As I watched, the Wolpertinger seemed to absorb the flow of the electric charge. It almost shone now. Lit up from within and with jagged electric discharges skittering across its horrible body. It looked like it had been struck by lightning. I tore my gaze away from the Wolpertinger to check on Bruce. I nearly screamed. He was resting against the stainless-steel of the table and the electricity was coursing through him too. His body was spasming wildly. I knew better than to touch him.

I dragged my eyes away and had enough sense to cross to the wall and pull out the plug of the table lamp.

The electricity cut off. Thank god for that. I caught a twitch of movement in my peripheral vision and looked back at the coffee table, fearfully wondering if the Wolpertinger had been badly damaged. The museum could sack me.

That's when I saw it move. Just for a moment I could have sworn the thing had twitched. A small, jerky, unnatural motion. But I'd only seen it out of the corner of my eye, and now the antique was still.

Of course it was. It was just a thing. Not an animal. It wasn't real, and never had been. But, I supposed, electrical currents could make dead muscles contract. Like frog's legs in a dissection class. ...

My mind raced back to Bruce, afraid that the electric shock might have really hurt him, but I didn't actually believe it. They had safety cut-outs on modern fuse boxes, didn't they? The mains switch would trip before a lethal charge could happen, wouldn't it? I looked at Bruce and my mouth fell open, but I couldn't say anything. He was dead. I knew he was dead.

I'd seen him hit his head on the wall after the first shock got him, but I hadn't realised he'd smashed his skull against the stainless steel rim of the coffee table when he fell forward again. I don't know if the electric shock would have killed him. Maybe, maybe not. But the front of his silly, handsome face was caved in. He'd hit the corner of the metal table and it had punctured his skull like a blow from a pickaxe. I could see blood around the wound, but worse, I saw pieces of ruptured brain tissue poking out of the deep, hollow red cavity that used to be his forehead. I swallowed bile, trying not to throw up. I felt my knees buckle and I slid to the floor, half squatting, half kneeling.

Bruce had always been an idiot. But he'd been my idiot. He was funny. And kind. And never really meant any harm. I hadn't ever considered him marriage material, but I did love him.

I thought I was going to burst into tears, but I didn't. I was in too much shock. I didn't really believe this was happening. It was just a mistake. A dream. A misunderstanding. I tried to make myself take deep breaths and figure out what to do. Phone an ambulance? It was too late for that, but it was what you did anyway, wasn't it?

I wondered where I'd left my phone and was just about to look for it when I saw the Wolpertinger. It's unnaturally huge eyes were staring at me. Watching me. I told myself not to be stupid. Not to get hysterical. But then the thing's paws twitched, its pupils dilated and its beaklike jaw widened, revealing the mass of teeth within.

    I scrabbled backwards, screaming, not trying to stand, just to get away from the Wolpertinger that was jerkily moving on the table before me. Its feathers fluttered, its fur bristled, its claws and talons seemed to stretch and grow, the horns and antlers and tusks that stuck out from its misshapen form thrashed from side to side as it shook its head. It looked as though it was trying to wake up, or to clear its vision. The beak of a mouth twitched open. I expected it to roar or screech but instead it coughed up a cloud of dust – the accumulated filth of centuries, expelled from ancient lungs stitched into a body that had never before drawn a breath.

    I reached around looking for a weapon and found a pair of shoes I'd absent mindedly kicked off earlier. I grabbed one and threw it at the Wolpertinger, missing its head but catching it a glancing blow on one wing. I held on to the other shoe, narrow heel pointing outward, ready to strike. The shoe felt like a silly, useless defence, especially when I saw the array of natural weapons attached to the Wolpertinger. Claws to rip, tusks to gore, a beak to bite, talons to slash and slice and snake fangs filled with poison.

    I didn't stand a chance, and I knew it.

    The Wolpertinger shuffled around on the table, stretching and shambling almost drunkenly, as though it was trying to come to terms with its bizarre patchwork body and the weird combination of limbs that it was moving for the first time. But, to my horror, it seemed to be coping all too well.

It leapt into the air, flapped its wings and gently almost floated to the ground. It peered at me with glowing eyes. They were lit with an unnatural, almost electric luminance. The thing seemed to sniff as though trying to catch my scent. Half on two legs, half on four, it shambled, judderingly toward me. The forked tongue flicked out of the beak, between the rows of adder fangs and wolf teeth. It's gaze fixed upon me and it coughed out more dust, and then, my stomach churned in terror as it spoke.

"Jeez, me mouth's as dry as King Tut's jockstrap. I could murder a beer. We got any tinnies left?"

My relationship with Bruce changed a lot after that.

I'd like to think we're still good friends. Of a sort. But it's hard. We're not exactly physically compatible anymore. And technically he's the property of the museum. Luckily I've managed to avoid him being put on public display, so he just has to keep very still if anyone else is in my office. Getting rid of Bruce's original body was easier than you might think. The Midwynter Museum now has one extra mummy in its storage vaults.

I've been wondering if there might be some way to use the rest of Dippel's elixir to transfer Bruce's soul out of the Wolpertinger and into... well... let's just say a more suitable body. I haven't worked out how. Or who. Yet. But I'm working on it.

I keep wondering if Dippel ever made any other Wolpertingers? And I can't help but speculate about even darker things.

Dippel really had found a way to transfer a soul from one body to another. Or perhaps not a soul but a consciousness, I'm still pondering the metaphysical implications of this. But how often had he repeated the process?

Officially, Dippel had died in 1734. But...

If he had a working method of soul-transference, had Dippel really died?

Or had he secretly taken possession of another body? Might he not have jumped from cadaver to cadaver, again and again, down the centuries?

Was it possible that, even now, his mind and soul still lived on inside a stolen body?

But I haven't really got the time to worry about that right now. I have other, more pressing problems. I suppose I'd have to admit that Dippel's anatomical and surgical skills were at the level of genius, albeit that special kind of genius found only on the far side of madness. But he didn't give any thought to practicality. I mean, a beak edged with tusks and filled with canine teeth and adder fangs? Terrifying, yes. But how was the creature meant to actually eat anything? I cautiously locked the office door

Luckily Bruce was perfectly happy to survive on a liquid diet. Possibly forever. He was laying back happily on his fur and feathers, waiting for me with his mouth wide open and his long forked tongue sticking out eagerly.

With a sigh, I opened another can of Fosters and began to pour.

THE REEL TOO REAL
SAMANTHA HILL

Julie watched from the kitchen window, amused if somewhat frustrated. Nigel lifted what she expected to be another piece of ancient audio equipment from the back of the van. His most tender moments were reserved for these noisy old acquisitions of his, and yet, it was still with an affectionate heart that she watched him fumble for the keys in his pocket whilst holding steadfastly on to his new toy.

Heading towards the front door, Julie prepared herself to make all the right noises and ask all the right questions. Though it was true that a lot of the machines he brought home held little interest for her, she was aware that projecting just the right amount of interest was the key to harmonious living. Too little and he'd sulk, too much and she'd be there all day. She had begun to prepare a little script in her head when Nigel came in with a tape machine, and lovingly stood the old girl on the living room carpet. Julie was surprised to find herself strangely drawn to the thing. It was an old reel to reel from the 1970s. With its two big spindles for eyes, and what he delighted in informing her was called the capstan for a nose, it had a rather comical little face.

Seizing on her interest with a vigour, Arthur went back out to the van to fetch the 'piece de resistance' and came back with a dusty old box full of reels of tape.

"Fella chucked these in for free," he told her gleefully, as he placed them on the coffee table. Julie felt an unexpected thrill as they rifled through the boxes, setting aside the damaged and broken ones and picking out the playable ones to have a listen to later on.

After a slightly more amiable tea than usual, Julie and Nigel made their way through to the living room and opened a bottle of scotch. Julie couldn't help but think that the funny little machine was a bit of a godsend. They hadn't spent an evening together like this in such a long while, although she couldn't quite put her finger on why that was.

They warmed their bellies with whisky and their hearts with a rekindled companionship. They switched on the reel to reel and worked their way through the old tapes, admiring some of the better ones and laughing at the more hideous offerings such as one which sounded like a bunch of Chinese business men doing terrible Elvis covers in a karaoke bar.

Then, out of nowhere, they found a real treasure, or a reel treasure as Nigel put it, pleased as punch with his pun. Julie was enjoying herself so much that she even laughed at his appalling joke instead of cringing. The recording appeared to be of the family who'd previously owned the machine. The first voice they heard was that of a little boy, whispering into the microphone.

"It's 1974 and we're having a party….."

"Tommy, I've told you before about recording us with Daddy's equipment,' said a female voice followed by the sound of the machine being turned off. There was a momentary silence before the recording resumed with the sounds of guests arriving, laughing and joking, glasses clinking. Julie and Nigel sipped their whiskies silently and listened enthralled, as more faceless guests arrived to join the revelry.

Before they knew it, the party spirit began to ebb. Fewer voices could be heard and the music was turned down. The familiar sounds of a post party clean up could now be heard, and Julie thought sadly of how long it had been since they had thrown a party themselves.

"You know, this is really quite something," she said. "If you have the chap's number you should give him a call. He may not even know that this recording exists. Do you think that it's him and his family? He'll probably want it back."

After debating for a while as to whether or not 9.45pm was too late to telephone somebody, and deciding on no, he went to the hallway to make the call.

"The bloke was really grateful. It turns out that he used to record his family on this thing all the time and didn't realise that he'd left any of the personal tapes in the box. He thinks it's probably him, his wife, their son and some friends on the tape. He remembers that party very well. His wife has since passed away, the son, too, so I guess something like this is a real treasure. Poor chap. I offered to drop it off to him later on in the week but he seemed in a hurry to get it back. He was very insistent on coming over to get it now so I gave him our address. I hope you don't mind, love?"

"Of course not," Julie said, giving his arm a squeeze as he sat back down.

"Poor man, I'm really glad you called him. Shall we have a little listen to the rest of the tape while we wait?"

They each poured a fresh whisky and cuddled up on the sofa together to hear the final instalment. The tape resumed with a man and a woman chatting and the soft, almost eerie, sound of the little boy singing 'Three Blind Mice' near the microphone.

Then, the adult voices increased in volume, becoming more heated. It was hard to make out what was being said, or shouted, especially as plates and glasses were now being smashed. Julie's body tensed and she leaned in towards Nigel. The sounds from the reel to reel were becoming more and more uncomfortable. There was a scream, and footsteps growing louder as they moved away from the now silent woman and closer to the microphone. The steps came to a halt and for a moment all Julie and Nigel could make out was the frightened whimpering of the small boy, "No, Dad, please......"

There was a click. And then silence.

They looked at each other, both confused and yet clear about what they had just heard.

Then the lights went out and the machine turned off completely. Julie fumbled for the light switch, but the room remained dark.

They stared at the murky outlines of one another in a shocked silence. The telephone in the hallway seemed much farther away than usual, and the fact that the detached house they lived in had no close neighbours no longer seemed like a blessing.

The next sound they heard was the kitchen window breaking, and although they didn't want to admit it, they both knew who it was that had come calling.

After all, they had invited him.

THE CONVERSION OF ANDREW CURRANT

C. H. BAUM

The corruption of innocents is delicious and euphoric. This one was almost orgasmic. The more pristine the innocent, the more complete the corruption, the better the reward in Infernum. Lucifer would be pleased with this one.

"Andy, I dare you to doorbell ditch old lady Cavin." Micky prodded like his future depended on it.

"No way, Micky. You do it. She creeps me out." Andy's twelve year old mind conjured up images of an old lady cackling and laughing when she caught him, leaving remnants of rotten spittle on his cheeks and lips. In truth, none of the neighborhood kids had ever really seen old lady Cavin with any clarity, just quick glimpses behind leaded glass windows.

"You're chicken Andy. If you don't do it, I'm going to tell everyone in Mrs. Campbell's class that you're a coward. Even Dana will laugh at you, because she will know it's true."

Andy wrung his small hands, and wiped the clammy sweat on his jeans. "I'm not a coward, Micky. It's just that it's daylight. That ol' bat will see me for sure."

"That's what a coward would say. A coward would make a list of excuses because a coward is scared." Micky pushed the dare like a used car salesman pushes a lemon.

"Okay. Just once. I'll run up there, ring the doorbell, and then run over behind that old van. She's the devil's sister, you know. No one can call me a coward if I doorbell ditch the devil's sister."

Micky smiled his immature smile, deliciously anticipating the naughtiness of the act and ran over behind the van to watch from a safe distance. He didn't want the devil's sister to see him when Andy rang the doorbell.

Andy crept up the front lawn. The house was old; it looked like it was built in the neighborhood fifty years before there was a neighborhood. Peeling paint created claws that reached out silently to scratch at unsuspecting victims. The house didn't even smell like the rest of the neighborhood. The mold and mustiness made Andy imagine ancient, crocheted Afghans thrown over plastic covered couches, old nylon socks with no elastic draped over lamps, and an open can of cold baked beans on the floor next to a recliner. The porch moaned in protest at

Andy's size three Converse; heralding his approach to the ancient doorway.

Andy thought, it's only a few feet away now. No turning back. I can do this, while extending his arm and pointing his finger in anticipation and accusation at the chipped doorbell. This close, he could see the black veins that crawled through the pristine ivory of the old bell, like a sun bleached tortoise shell, barely poking through the surrounding sand.

He sucked in a breath and held it there, dreading the actual act of pushing the ringer, frozen in fear. The petrification was broken as Micky made clucking sounds from behind the van. Andy steeled his resolve and committed to depressing the alabaster ringer.

He expected an ominous ding, followed by a booming dong, but got the uninterrupted ring of an old telephone instead. He was pondering the oddity of the ring when the door flashed open; a slender old hand closed like a vice on his slim wrist, and yanked him inside. It all happened so fast, his reaction was not to scream, cry, or twist his arm against the grasp; he just whimpered as he expelled the breath he had been holding while being transported wholly into the foyer of the old house, and hearing the door slam shut behind him.

The devil's sister was actually very attractive for her age. Her black hair, shot with gray streaks, was pulled back in a severe bun, with an errant wisp that had escaped and was caressing her slim chin. She had striking purple, almond shaped eyes. Andy had never seen someone with eyes the color of ripe eggplant. Her smile revealed perfect rows of bright, straight, clean teeth. Then the devil's sister spoke in a smooth and pleasant voice, "I'm sorry I had to yank you in here so suddenly, but there's a giant hornet's nest next to the ringer on the porch, and they go mad at the noise. I need to call an exterminator before someone gets stung."

The buzz of the irritated hornets broke into Andy's thoughts and he turned to see an angry swarm attempting to sting the window and the doorway where he stood moments before. Andy stammered, "Miss Cavin?"

"Yes child....you look shaken. Would you like some milk? We need to wait for the hornets' fury to die down. I just happened to be baking some cookies too. That's always a pleasant way to pass a few minutes." She waved him forward, towards the kitchen and said, "Come, come."

Andy followed the perfectly creased skirt into the kitchen, too ashamed to raise his eyes further while sinking deeper and deeper into the wonderful aroma of baking cookies. She placed three cookies from the cooling trays on a plate, and stretched over to open an ancient icebox with General Electric scrolled in cursive across the front of the door. She pulled out a pitcher of milk and poured him a tall, cool glass to accompany the cookies.

"Sit, my child, sit," she invited, while pointing at one of the two dining room chairs.

Andy plopped down in the wrought iron chair and Miss Cavin sat down across from him, pushing the plate of cookies and glass of milk over to him. She also grabbed a cookie for herself and left them in a moment of silence while they both chewed the still warm deliciousness.

"Mmmmmmmm. These are really good cookies, Miss Cavin. Better than the ones my mom makes. She always burns them."

Miss Cavin laughed and he let the pleasant sound of her humor roll over him. "Burnt offerings are discouraged young man; they do not taste as good."

He smiled, even though he had no idea what she meant.

She smiled back and asked, "You rang my bell child. Did you need something?"

He decided honesty was the best policy. "Well Miss Cavin, I'm Andy and I was going to doorbell ditch you on a dare. I....I'm sorry."

"Please child, call me Day. I admire your honesty, and your bravery. But there's nothing to forgive, and I'm not in that business anyway. I'm a harmless, old lady, and nothing would have come from it other than tragedy if I hadn't heard you coming. Had I been upstairs when you rang the bell, you might be a pincushion for a bunch of angry hornets." She smiled and then bit into another cookie.

Andy was relieved, and the cookies were fantastic. "Miss Cavin, you treated me nice, even though you knew I was going to trick you. My mom wouldn't do that. She would have punished me. Do you have any children?"

"Day, call me Day, child. And, I do have children, but not in the way you think. I have Daemonium."

Andy had never heard that word before. He rolled it around in his head before he repeated it, "Day Moan Eeum. What's that?"

Day stood and smiled right at him, her big smile was delightful, and her violet eyes sparkled in the light of the kitchen. "Come. I will show you."

Andy found himself following her into the ancient living room, where he expected an old couch, with a couple of sitting chairs, but met with something quite different. There was a large, hulking table that occupied the entire space of the living room. The table was accompanied by a mix of mismatched chairs, placed at strategic points around the edge, and the table was covered with the biggest mess of wires, electronics, speakers, and coils that Andy had ever seen. It was like all the old appliances in town had dragged themselves to her living room and then exploded.

"What is this stuff?" Andy asked earnestly.

Day lightly caressed the base of his neck and said, "I fix these electronics. When they are done, they contain my daemonium and I care for them like children. These are my passion and my calling. Would you like to help me fix one?"

Andy immediately answered, "Of course." He jumped at the chance to please Miss Day and to help her with her work. After he had been so mean to her, he really wanted to make it up to her; make her proud that she had let him into her home.

He made his way over to a large china cabinet, lit from inside, containing shelf after shelf of antique, yet pristine, small appliances. "These are already fixed, Miss Cavin, I mean, Miss Day."

"We don't want to touch those. Their daemonium have already been claimed by others; they are hibernating until their time is ripe." She nudged him over towards the table, pushing him with a delicate hand in the small of his back.

She resumed their conversation after turning him away from the china cabinet. "Ok, this is the carcass of an old telephone. It was made long before cell phones, even long before rotary phones." Miss Day gestured for him to sit in one of the chairs at the corner of the table, and sat down ninety degrees to him. She pushed some of the other wires and electronics out of the way, and pulled an old oak box over the table so that it separated them. It had a black cone growing from the top plate and a black crank on the side that looked like it belonged to a giant pencil sharpener. Another black cone was attached to a braided cord and bumped along the table behind the box as she slid it over for inspection.

Andy's curiosity was certainly piqued and he asked, "Miss Day, is this telephone older than you are?"

Miss Day giggled and said, "No my child. I am much older than this phone. I was already a grown woman when they made it."

Andy couldn't image her age. She must have been born when the dinosaurs were still roaming around.

Day grabbed a pair of pliers and a screwdriver and extricated the black cone on the front of the telephone. Then she pulled away the oak top plate and removed the sides. They were left with an oak plank with a bunch of wires, and with a coil connected to the old crank. She reattached the crank and spun it around, but nothing happened.

"What's wrong with it, Miss Day?" Andy asked as he peered over the carcass of the old telephone.

"See that metal coil at the top? The one that attaches to the crank? That's called a magneto and it creates electricity when you crank it." She used the screwdriver to identify some of the wires and continued, "Then the electricity flows down these wires, and is stored in the big black battery at the bottom. My guess is that the battery unit is dead, but that the magneto still works and generates electricity. In order to fix this, I need to test the magneto coil. You think you could help me with that, child?"

Andy nodded excitedly, ready to help in any way needed.

"Ok child, I'll need you to hold this wire with your right hand, and this one with your left hand. While I'm testing it, you might feel a little shock, but you can't let go. If you let go, the daemonium may be lost forever. Do you understand child?" She was very serious and intense while she implored, "If you let go, it could stay broken forever."

Andy again nodded excitedly. "I'll hold it as long as you need me to, Miss Day." To show his eagerness, he grabbed the appropriate wires in each hand, pinched them between his thumb and index finger, and then crushed down with all his immature strength. "I'm ready."

Day stood up from her chair to get a good hold on the crank and winked at Andy before she started. She began slow grinding the magneto and watching Andy carefully. She knew he was getting shocked, but he doggedly held onto the wires. "Fantastic, child. You're doing an amazing job." Then she cranked the magneto faster, a blurry whir of electrical production.

Andy groaned against the shock, but he didn't let go. When she cranked even faster, like a possessed whirlwind, he couldn't have let go if he wanted to. The electricity paralyzed the muscles in his hands, and shook his forearms uncontrollably in short, seizure like convulsions. "Ngnnnnnnnnnnnnn."

It was over quickly, and Day smiled over at him. "You did wonderfully my child. This will certainly return to its former glory. You are responsible for the life of this daemonium." Then she shocked him even more by grabbing each side of his face, and kissing him deeply. He felt her tongue graze his and she sloppily sucked his bottom lip, letting it slip back while staring him in the eyes and panting with hot, wet breath on his face.

Andy stammered, "I, I.........Miss Cavin............I never kissed a girl before."

From very, very close, she whispered, "I am not a girl, Andy. You will understand when you're a man."

Andy slipped out the front door, studiously avoiding any noise that might irritate the large hornets' nest. He glanced back over his shoulder to see Day wink at him through the leaded glass, and disappear into the fog of the house as she backed away. As soon as he was off the porch, he sprinted across the front lawn, and rounded behind the old van where Mickey sat, crying.

"Mickey, I did it. I rang the bell."

Mickey looked up, completely taken by surprise that Andy had escaped alive. "You were in there for thirty minutes. It seemed like forever. I thought you were dead."

Andy smiled, a changed boy since he accepted the dare. "I helped her fix an old telephone. She is beautiful, and isn't like anyone I've ever met before."

Mickey hadn't seen Andy talk about anyone like that. Not even Dana. He snickered as he pronounced, "You love her!"

Andy glanced down and saw a dark urine stain in the crotch of Mikey's Wranglers. "You peed yourself. I was the one that did the scariest thing ever and you peed your pants. If you tell anyone that I love her, I will tell everyone you pissed your pants. If I even hear a rumour of it, everyone in school will know you wet yourself."

Mickey nodded. He didn't want anyone to know that he was so scared when his friend got yanked inside ol' bat Cavin's house that he'd peed down his leg. In his fright, he hadn't even noticed the pee until it was warmly running down his leg; too late to consciously cut the flow.

Mickey ran up to Andy on the playground, completely out of breath. "Did you hear, Andy? Did you hear?"

Andy turned from telling Dana he didn't like her anymore, and asked, "What? Did I hear what?"

"Ol' bat Cavin died. They are going to mettle her mistake tomorrow night. They already sold the house to someone that's going to gut it and remodel the whole thing."

Andy's heart broke, but still caught the absurdity of Mickey's statement. Through unbidden tears, Andy corrected, "You mean settling her estate?" He immediately followed with a gasp that ripped at his lungs, burning as he exhaled, and fell to his knees. "No, it……it can't be. I was going to help her fix more of her daemonium."

"Yeah, someone said they found her naked in the tub. Josh and Lucas heard the cops say that her corpse was floating in there, all pasty, wrinkly and saggy."

Andy stood up and punched Mickey straight in the face. "You son of a bitch. She was not wrinkly and saggy, and NO ONE CALLS HER AN OL' BAT!" Andy sniveled, uncontrollably shuddering, while standing over his friend with clenched fists. Mickey crab walked away, turned and ran for the safety of the recess supervisor.

"Go, Mickey! GO! Go tell on me you bastard!"

Dana sidled away, not wanting to be anywhere near Andy's fury. He turned on her now that Mickey was out of reach, screaming through the snot and drool of his grief. "Go tattle on me too, you bitch! GO!" He screamed out to no one in particular, but the whole playground heard him, "I HATE YOU ALL!"

Finally. It was his birthday. Eighteen years old. Andrew made plans with Mick to celebrate appropriately because you only become an adult once in your life. "Hey, Mick, Dana says we can come over to her house. Her mom has a ton of whiskey in the basement and works nights at the hospital. We can get drunk and maybe she'll let me make out with her."

Mick dragged his feet, "I don't know, Andrew. Her mom will notice we drank a bunch of the whiskey."

"There's no way she could count it all. We'll take a little bit from each of the open bottles. There's like twenty down there. Plus, her mom doesn't care about the collection. It was her dad's before he left. Dude, we can't go wrong."

Mick smiled and nodded his agreement. "Let's go! Andrew becomin' a MAN."

When they arrived, Dana held Andrew's hand and led them down to the musty basement. The old wood of the stairs moaned and complained from beneath orange shag carpet, as they descended. Dana and Andrew plopped down on a brown sofa that had a deer hunting scene stitched into the cushions. Mick sat in the recliner that looked like it had been recycled from the dump, disturbing a tabby colored cat that yowled in protest. The surroundings didn't matter, as long as they were left to their own devices; he had whiskey and a woman waiting to help him usher in adulthood.

They drank small thimbles of whiskey from a multitude of different bottles, and before long they were snorting, laughing and whirling their shirts above their heads. Mick stated the obvious, "It sure burns goin' down, and it damn sure messes up my brain."

Andrew dreamed.

Miss Cavin visited his dreams for the first time since he was twelve. She was not the same elderly lady he met all those years ago. She appeared as a younger woman, before the years started to take their toll. Andrew saw her with the eyes of a man, drawn to her animal sexuality. She was stunningly beautiful, hair flowing around her face like she was under water, and dressed in a skin tight, red skirt that hugged the curves of her hips. Her black jacket was open to her navel and she wasn't wearing anything underneath. The audacious show of skin left just enough to the imagination, but the flaunting of her cleavage made her intent clear. She began by planting a hot, wet, kiss on his slightly open mouth, and caressing the side of his face. She followed by whispering, "daemonium" in his ear. Andrew expected more, but she sauntered away slowly, looking over her shoulder one last time before fading into the fog of his dream.

The dream shifted and he was in an unknown forest, hunting a lynx. He could sense the animal nearby, and knew he was getting close to the end of the stalk. The lynx bounded out in front of his trail, and he threw a javelin, spearing the animal and pinning it to the ground. He didn't want to harm the majestic animal, but the dream followed its own desires; Andrew was just along for the ride. He sliced opened the stomach and cleaned the organs so that it wouldn't spoil the meat. Andrew assumed he would take the meat with him, but his dream-self threw the carcass and gut pile around the forest, scattering the regal lynx with reckless abandon. Andrew felt glee at the slaughter of his dream, while knowing it was wrong and cruel. He just couldn't stop himself from acting out.

"Andrew, get up!" Dana kicked him awake. "We fell asleep. My mom will be home any minute from the hospital, and you and Mick have to get out of here!"

Andrew crawled around the shag carpet of the basement looking for his shirt and shoes while wincing from his hangover. Mick was already headed up the stairs.

Dana panicked, "Damnit Andrew, hurry up!"

"I'm going, I'm going." He pulled on his shirt and shoved his shoes under his armpit right before heading up the stairs. He stopped for a brief second and turned to kiss Dana. "Thank you, I had a wonderful night. I'll never forget it."

She smiled coyly and patted his rear end. "C'mon, get moving. I'll see you in a couple days."

Andrew dreamed.

This one was much more sinister, darker. He was hunting a wolf, and even though it was dangerous, he revelled in it. The wolf had doubled back on him a couple of times, and Andrew knew that on the third time, he would catch it unawares. Andrew salivated over the prospect of killing and gutting the lupine prey.

The vicious part of him was growing in strength. He was hungry for bigger, more challenging prey and the part of Andrew that was concerned about the progression was violently pushed to the back of his psyche. Andrew had no place in his own dreams.

He sat behind a tree, up wind from the wolf, and smelled the animal before he heard him coming. He sucked in the scent of the matted fur, the creature's sweat, and the mud on its paws. As the wolf bounded past, he stepped out and ran his spear through its ribcage. Andrew laughed at the popping sound as the spear split and broke the ribs. He fell on the limp corpse and tore at the stomach with his knife, hacking in a fury of stabbing and slashing, flinging gore around the forest floor. He sectioned the quarters and threw the limbs in all different directions. Soaked up to his elbows in blood, he yanked out the heart and took a large bite of the sinewy muscle. The warmth of the flesh went perfectly with the mineral aftertaste of the blood. He licked at the gore that ran down his chin. It was delicious.

Andrew woke up, sweating and trembling from the exertion in the dream, and concerned about his subconscious progression to bigger, more dangerous prey. He thought, Maybe I should see a psychiatrist, before climbing into the shower to start his day.

Andrew dreamed.

The choice of prey was progressing, and he was helpless to stop it. He watched the pulse of blood through the artery running up the side of the prostitute's neck. It fascinated him. He snickered as he vividly imagined slicing it and watching the blood spurt through her fingers. His mirth made her turn her head towards him, assuming he would make good on his promise. She quested after her addiction, "You bring it with you?"

"Bring what baby?" He teased her, knowing exactly what he had promised her.

"You know......the sugar you promised me. I give you a little sugar, and you give me a little sugar. That's how this deal works." She smiled and licked her lips seductively, running the tip of her tongue around her mouth. It was meant to be sexy, but she ruined it by opening her mouth wide enough to see her rotten teeth and then scratching uncontrollably at her shoulder.

"I've got it right here...." Andrew fumbled in his jeans pocket for his razor.

He was interrupted by a cop banging on the window with his flashlight. Moments away from slicing her throat and dissecting her corpse, his prey was abruptly stolen from him.

"Go away, Pig!" he yelled through the dream.

The pounding on the car window continued, unabated. The policeman would not be deterred once he saw a known prostitute in the car with Andrew. The dream grinned with the prospect of killing the policeman too. He'd strip them down naked, and put them in a compromising position in the park.

The policeman continued to bang on the window, unaware of the sinister evil on the other side of the glass, stubbornly rushing towards Andrew's razor.

Andrew woke up to someone banging on his door. It took him a moment to realize it wasn't a cop banging on the steamy window of his car. His head swam with a splitting headache, and he somehow knew it was related to the abrupt end of his dream; he hadn't released the dream to run free and kill.

He could hear a muffled Mick through the door, "C'mon, Andrew, OPEN THE DOOR!" right before the pounding started again.

He stumbled up from his couch and swirled back the dead bolt with a twist of his wrist. "What? I was sleeping...."

Mick was out of breath, and panted, "Dana's all broke up. She's crying her eyes out. Someone killed her cat."

Andrew was agitated, "It's sad and all, but cats get run over all the time. Why on earth does that make you run over here and bang on my door in the middle of the night?"

Mick shook his head, "No, you got it all wrong. Someone didn't run over her cat, someone BUTCHERED her cat. Her mom came home, and found the cat hanging in the bathroom, with its intestines pulled out. Her mom works at the hospital and she's seen a TON of gruesome stuff, but when she saw the cat, she puked all over the bathroom. Whoever did it, rammed the shower rod THROUGH the cat's head and rehung the shower rod over the tub!"

Andrew had flashes of disturbing hunting scenes and a lynx. "Who would do something like that?"

Mick shrugged. "Who knows.....some sick weirdo, a demon, the devil......whoever did it was just plain EVIL."

Andrew grabbed his jacket to head over to Dana's. "C'mon, Dana needs support of her friends."

Mick nodded, "Yeah, especially because whoever killed her cat, also killed a dog over on 3rd and Eastern. Had to be the same guy."

Andrew's disturbing flashes repeated for the wolf. "What happened to the dog?" he asked, even though he knew the answer.

"It was a pit bull, one they used for fighting on the bad side of town. Whoever killed it hated the dog something fierce. He speared it with a fence post. The post went clear through the torso. Then he butchered it and spread the guts and body parts all over the intersection. He wrapped the intestines around the light pole like a holiday garland."

Andrew felt sick to his stomach. "That's disgusting."

"That's not even the worst part," responded Mick. "He also ripped out the heart and there were bite marks on it! He ATE half the heart!"

"Stop, STOP! You're going to make me hurl. Let's go to Dana's and see if we can calm her nerves." Andrew stepped out into the hallway and turned to lock the door behind him, before shuffling down the hall with Mick. He knew the cop had been Mick. The prostitute had probably been Dana. He thought, that's the clear progression. I almost murdered my friends.

Dana was inconsolable, crying softly against Andrew's chest while they sat huddled together on the old couch in her basement. Mick was oblivious, as he played the vintage video games while sitting cross legged on the floor. Andrew knew that if he fell asleep again, he would murder them in a possessed frenzy. He had to leave. He had to escape.

He kept to his own head while his friend grieved. Asking himself question after question. How did this happen? What is wrong with me? Why did this just start on my eighteenth birthday? The shock hit him like a wet slap in the face. Miss Cavin did this to him. She WAS the devil's sister. That old bitch had done something to him with the telephone, possessed his dreams somehow. She probably didn't even really die; she just moved onto another unsuspecting youth to corrupt. He got an idea and looked up daemonium on his phone. The first thing that popped up was, "Latin to English translation – Daemonium – Demon."

He whispered, "Holy shit."

His statement disturbed Dana and she looked up at him with red, puffy eyes. "What did you say?"

"Nothing baby. But I need to leave. I'm really tired and I have to work early tomorrow. I'm sorry about your cat. That's just not right."

Dana nodded and hugged him as thanks for the support. "Ok, Andrew. Come back tomorrow afternoon, after my mom leaves for work. I don't want to be in the house alone."

"Yeah, I'll be here." He pressed his lips on her forehead and shuffled out of the basement.

As soon as he got outside, he began talking to himself in hushed tones, "I DO understand now that I'm a man. You possessed me, you bitch........you psychotic old hag. But I won't sleep until I find a cure for the demon haunting my dreams."

It occurred to him that the demon took up residence in his adolescent body through the flow of electricity. So electricity would have to kick it out too. He remembered her saying that the daemonium could be lost forever, and he was determined to make sure her warning came true. There was an electrical substation near Dana's house, and he headed that way, following his intuition. The massive electrical towers tracked through the miles in single file, standing like sentinels with their high voltage wires only dipping to the ground over the substation fence.

Andrew grabbed a fist sized rock and slammed it against the padlock on the chain link fence until it shattered the shackle. He slipped inside and walked confidently up to one of the transformers. Two giant, porcelain wrapped antenna stood out from the head of the transformer, like some huge insect buried up to its neck in the soft soil.

As he got near enough to touch the antenna, he could feel the energy raise the hair on his arms and neck, and hear the droning hum of the massive charges flowing through the substation. He gave no heed to the warning signs with their angry red lightning bolts and grabbed both antenna at the top, where the high voltage wires connected to the substation. The instant he made the circuit, the electricity flowed. It was a massive rush of power that seized his muscles, and slapped his heart around in his chest. Burns crawled up his hands into his arms, blackening the skin. The mix of smells were intoxicating; crisp ozone carrying a hint of roasting flesh.

In an explosion of sparks, the safety equipment took charge and blew the transformer, shutting off the flow of electricity. Andrew's body stiffened, tipping over backwards and falling with his arms extended out; a perfect impersonation of a zombie from the old black and white movies. He glanced up at his paralyzed arms, ending in nothing more than claws, and made the comparison of hot dogs left too long on the grill; blackened skin crisscrossed with angry red cracks where the flesh had split open. He laughed as he remembered Miss Cavin saying, "Burnt offerings are discouraged young man; they do not taste as good." The memory chased him into unconsciousness as the chuckle died in his throat.

Andrew dreamed BIG.

SPARKS

PURKINJE FIBERS
ASH HARTWELL

Eric woke to the sound of birdsong, sunlight streaming through the gap in his curtains and a crushing pain in the centre of his chest. Had Eric not been gasping for breath, sweating profusely and clutching his chest while his legs scrabbled against the constraining weight of the duvet, he would have reasoned it was the fine spring morning causing his early rising and not a heart attack.

However, Eric gave little consideration to the cause of his waking as his head was full of thoughts of his long, and unproductive, life. He saw his childhood home, his parents as a young couple and the primary school he had attended. Then his teenage years and his mother's funeral, the secondary school he had occasionally attended and the backstreets where he completed his education. Next came the failed relationships, so many faces flashing before his eyes, the prison time and the long list of short-term, dead-end jobs. His curriculum vitae of despair gave way to his hopeless existence in a rundown flat living off government handouts and charity food banks.

Then he saw his own body sprawled on the bed below him as he floated near the patches of damp on the ceiling of his shabby bedroom. Then even that image faded to black like the end of an old romantic black and white movie. But there were no credits to run; nobody would put their name to the deadbeat life Eric had lived.

The white light Eric experienced wasn't the accepting love of The Almighty or the light at the end of his mother's birth canal out of which his reincarnated soul was thrust. The light hit Eric with a powerful jolt that lifted his body from the sweat stained sheets and slammed it down hard into the mattress. The light was blinding and it came from within Eric's own head, like the worst migraine exploding across the back of his eyes. And the light burned; Eric's nose twitched in a subconscious response to the harsh smell of melting plastic and crackling ozone.

Eric's tired, fatty heart took a slow, hesitant beat as if it were unsure at returning him to the living. Then it took another beat, more positive this time. He gasped for air, coughed then gasped again. The pain in his chest gradually receded, only to be replaced by a prickling tingle that also ran down his left arm. Confused at being back in his dreary flat and not standing at the Pearly Gates trying to convince St Peter he at least deserved a shot at an eternity in Heaven, Eric looked down at his left arm. The purple veins bulged over twitching muscle. Flashes of blue now arced through the light in his head like fireworks against a sky of brilliant white.

The smell of burning intensified, a thin wisp of smoke curled up from beside the bed. Eric struggled to roll over, his left arm still pulled awkwardly over the edge of the bed. He squinted, trying to see through the lightning storm crashing inside his head, and peeked over the side of the mattress. His arm stretched towards the electrical socket, his hand falling about eighteen inches short of the smoking plastic slots. A bundle of thin, almost translucent threads snaked their way out from the tips of his charred and blackened fingers bridged the gap.

The threads, individually too small for the eye to see, twisted together forming thicker strings, one protruding from each fingertip. They formed swirls and arcs in the air, crisscrossing one another on their way to meld with the socket. They glowed like fibre optic Christmas decorations, a visible pulse flowing from the mains outlet up to Eric's hand, causing his fingers to burn where voltage met soft, fleshy tissue.

As Eric watched, the cable-like threads detached from the socket and swiftly retracted up into his hand, leaving his fingers blackened but unharmed. The socket's warped plastic case fizzed and smoked, spitting the occasional spark spinning through the air to burn tiny holes in Eric's cheap carpet. As soon as he disconnected from the power, Eric's pain vanished. He felt hungry, he hadn't eaten since a dodgy kebab the night before, but apart from that he was literally buzzing. He could feel the electricity surging around his body and hear its persistent humming in his ears. It sounded like he was stood under one of those overhead power lines, suspended from giant pylons that bestrode the countryside like monstrous insects.

Holding his head, trying to stop the humming, Eric sat up. His tiny bedroom span on an invisible axis as his disorientated senses tried to adjust, leaving Eric feeling like the doner meat from the night before may be revisiting him at any moment. He took a few slow deep breaths and the vertigo gradually receded, although the humming continued.

Eric carefully inspected his fingertips and discovered the burns were superficial and amounted to no more than a discolouring of his skin. There was no sign of the pulsing fibres that had connected him to the socket. He tentatively placed the fingers of his right hand on his own left wrist, searching for his pulse. It felt strong and regular.

Despite his earlier visit to the other side it appeared today was not his day to die. Still, Eric thought it wise to get the burns checked out and let the doctor at least listen to his heart. If nothing else, today had served as a sobering reminder that he needed to re-evaluate his dietary and lifestyle choices. Although anyone suggesting he switch masala and naan for vegetables and crispbread would meet a swift and violent end. He looked at the red digital display of his alarm clock, deliberately placed on the other side of the room so he physically had to get out of bed to silence it. It proudly, and with annoying brightness, told him it was eighty-eight minutes past eight.

With a sigh, Eric began to dress. He would have to check the time on his phone when he rang the doctor's surgery, if there were no appointments available he would jump on a bus and head for the hospital. Not that he felt any lasting effects from either his heart attack or his electrocution. Eric was sure it was a heart attack he'd experienced; he made a mental note to check with Google to confirm his diagnosis. Although, if Eric was being honest he had never felt better.

That feeling didn't last long. By the time he had dressed and walked through to his small kitchenette his breath was coming in short, sharp gulps and he had a sweaty sheen on his brow and a warm glow to his cheeks. He spent a moment leaning with his hands on the edge of the work surface taking, slow deep breaths trying to drive away the darkness that lurked at the edge of his vision. It threatened to overwhelm his senses and send him crashing to the cracked and bubbled linoleum.

His heart was racing again, hammering against his sternum so hard, Eric half expected an alien to burst from his torso and scurry behind the fridge. He felt invisible hands constricting his lungs, the long thin fingers wrapping around each organ and gently squeezing the air out like a child coaxing the last of a tasty yogurt from a tube. Then the fingers slid away. Eric gasped for air, each breath stabbing down into his chest as his shrivelled lungs filled with the precious gas.

Eric's chest screamed with pain. He fought the urge to cough; choking on the very air he needed to survive. Each faltering inhalation whistling with the constrictive wheeze normally associated with a severe asthma attack. The urge to vomit swept over Eric and he pulled himself along the kitchen counter until he leant over the tea bag stained stainless steel sink. Eric's mind raced, the panic of oxygen deprivation momentarily replaced by the overwhelming fear of inhaling his own vomit and dying in a pool of puke in his neglected kitchenette.

Gradually the nausea passed and Eric got his breathing under control. His heart still thumped out a rhythmic beat on his chest wall and he felt crippled by the pain searing through his heart. In had started to spread through his shoulders and down his arms, a tingling itch he couldn't scratch. He pushed himself away from the sink and stood upright. The last thing his galloping heart rate needed was an injection of caffeine, but all Eric wanted was a coffee. If he was going to die then at least it would be on his own terms.

He shuffled over to the kettle and flicked the switch. As soon as the blue light flared into life indicating the kettle was on, the ends of his fingers sprouted a series of thin wires constructed of the same substance as before. The threads twisted together growing thicker and stronger, sprouting from the fingers of his left hand and snaking around the kettle, while those from the fingers of his right hand shot towards the socket. The outlet quickly became enveloped by the web of translucent cable, it sparked and crackled a few times then the fibrous material began to glow and pulsate, like a vampire feeding of the lifeblood of the house.

The water in the kettle began to bubble, steam spewing from the spout. Eric felt the surge of the electricity flowing up his right arm and passing through his heart, from right atrium to left ventricle, before pulsing down his left arm and into the kettle. As the charge surged through his heart it began to settle, the rate and ferociousness of the beats declined until he felt them no more. He remained upright, standing in his small kitchen suspended between the mains socket and the kettle, and yet he felt no pain.

The fibre thickened, intensifying its hold on both the socket and kettle, a spider web engulfing the appliance, mummifying it where it sat. This time there was no burning of his fingers. The fibres surrounded them and acted as insulation, as if they had learnt from their first attempt in the bedroom. Eric caught sight of his reflection in the smooth polished surface of his toaster and, despite his predicament, almost laughed out loud. His sparse, greying hair, now no more than dry straw, stood on end, making him look like an insane scientist.

The fibrous material glowed as it spread through his body, no longer constrained to his chest and arms. It had discovered his nervous system, attracted by the electrical impulses, and was following the messages to their source. He felt a brief but severe surge of pain which started in the base of his neck and seared through the centre of his brain with a blinding flash of bluey-white light. Images from his life scrolled before his eyes but not as some final death sequence but more like something was searching his memories and evaluating their worth. His lifetime of experiences and knowledge assessed and categorised for easy retrieval.

Outside Eric's twitching body, power humming through his nervous system, the fibres were beginning to spread too. From the open socket they had started to search along the wall just above the cracked tile splash backs, a few hair thin fibres at first. They probed, felt and sensing out a path which thicker, stronger cables followed. Instinctively, Eric knew they were searching out the route of the electrical mains. Thin tendrils had also started to grow from the web coiled around the kettle. Like new shoots of climbing ivy the almost invisible threads crept across the countertop, inexplicably drawn towards the nearest power source.

Finding the toaster, the translucent substance began to envelop it. More and more branches stretched out across the counter, lifting the small appliance an inch above the surface and swallowing it. Throngs curled down into the inner workings while others twisted round the flex, working their way up towards the wall socket in a smooth, almost fluid motion. Once there the fibres mingled with those spreading across the splash backs forming an iridescent living blanket that fizzed and sparked as it consumed each socket and appliance. Within minutes, thick branches of the material had zigzagged across the small kitchen connecting Eric with every electrical outlet and appliance in the room.

Eric hummed with electricity, a living substation diverting power from the house and storing it within the millions of tiny threads tightly coiled inside his body. He had become a giant electromagnet just waiting to channel its destructive power.

The fibres had almost engulfed his body. They suspended him in a cocoon that hung in mid-air halfway between the floor and the kitchen's single light fixing. A pocket of human tissue suspended in neon rope lights.

Not that Eric was aware of his plight. Where his physical form hung in his drab and lifeless flat the parasitic fibre scrolled through his long-forgotten memories, discarding the mundane. The fibre covered his face obscuring his vision and muffling any sound that wasn't the constant vibrating hum, but in his mind, he travelled through time. He saw his mother's face, still a young woman, smiling down at him but then she lay in a hospital bed her body riddled with the cancer that took her before her time, then his memories of her were gone. The memories of his father went the same way as did his early years and his misspent youth.

Then the images changed. They were no longer his personal memories and experiences but the pictures, diagrams and phrases that brought his entire knowledge to life. All Eric had learnt, his readings, the hours spent watching documentaries and those occasional snippets picked up from who knows where, flashed into view in the bluey-white light of his mind.

Eric no longer thought of himself as a person. He had become a component. A living media hub, live streaming his thoughts and memories for the benefit of the fibres that now connected him to the outside world. His five traditional human senses no longer gave him his information and he had no ability to process it if they did. He downloaded, streamed and scrolled, he tweeted, posted and hash tagged, liked, shared and requested. The fibres had reached his Internet hub connecting him to the giant hive mind of the World Wide Web and he had come alive.

Eric's mind toured the web at the speed of light, travelling through 186 thousand miles of electric cabling every second processing the random thoughts and images of the entire human race. He saw dancing dogs, singing cats and cycling budgies. He watched vile, twisted pornography and barbaric public executions. He read whole libraries, listened to the most beautiful music and absorbed the artistic works of the great masters. He knew who killed Kennedy, where NASA filmed the moon landings, and the truth of what happened to Princess Diana's car in that Parisian underpass.

He didn't control what he saw, where the information came from or how it was obtained but he understood the fibre, a harmonious understanding of their shared history. Neither could exist without the other. The fibre came from within him; it was part of him, part of his heart. It was the fibre that carried the electrical pulse around that most vital of organs ensuring it beat correctly. Their name was Purkinje, after the scientist who discovered them, but where Jan Purkyne believed them to be a vital component of the heart itself, it turned out he was wrong. They were a parasite.

An ancient species of parasite that had evolved with its host so effectively it had become an integral part of its host's survival. It lay dormant for two million years, biding its time, waiting for a chance to spread its powerful tentacles beyond its host into the outside world. A chance which now presented itself to the parasite through civilization's rapid development and reliance on electricity and interconnectivity. The Purkinje's ability to conduct and channel electricity and the messages that piggybacked the current made it the ideal time for it to breakout.

Eric's lonely existence, suspended within his run down flat acting as a viewing screen for the Purkinje, was just the start of mankind's downfall. All around the world people were cocooned in the Purkinje's fibre, the parasite spreading its influence through the medium that made life on earth so easy for humans. It consumed all the electricity mankind could produce, feeding of the grid and connecting through the cables, becoming one entity. It kept its hosts alive long enough to manipulate their bodies for its own needs then fried their carcasses when they died. Those parasites that had lain dormant in people who lived without electricity, or in remote villages in developing nations, died with their hosts, unable to find electrical sustenance.

The Purkinje understood the threat from weapons of mass destruction and disarmed man's ineffective missiles in their silos while revelling in the electrical decadence of cities like Las Vegas and Tokyo. They spread rapidly across the globe like bacteria, growing fast in the cities and spreading out along power lines until they covered most of the planet's landmass.

Their end was just as swift as humanity's. Without people to maintain the power stations the supply of electricity gradually failed, starving the Purkinje. The final entry on their Facebook page, which gave them hours of human entertainment, before humanity's last light flickered out, was short and to the point. It simply read:

Battery low ☹.

AUTHOR BIOGRAPHIES

CALUM CHALMERS

Calum Chalmers hates anything nice, in particular he loathes happiness; so writing horror kinda works out for him.
If his darkness excites you then check out his story 'The Change' featured in Thirteen Tales of Therianthropy and 'Cosmic Unicorn Thunderfuck' featured in Unicornado; to just name a few (he has more, I promise)

PIPPA BAILEY

Pippa Bailey lives in rural Shropshire, England. Principally a horror writer, independent reviewer, and YouTube personality, her supernatural and sci-fi stories have featured in several anthologies, and zines. Her debut nove LUX is due for release summer 2018.

EM DEHANEY

Em Dehaney is a mother of two, a writer of fantasy and a drinker of tea. Born in Gravesend, England, her writing is inspired by the dark and decadent history of her home town. She is made of tea, cake, blood and magic. By night she is The Black Nun, editor and whip-cracker at Burdizzo Books. By day you can always find her at http://www.emdehaney.com/ or lurking about on Facebook posting pictures of witches.
https://www.facebook.com/emdehaney/

Her story 'For Those in Peril on The Sea' can be found in The Reverend Burdizzo's Hymn Book anthology and she recently had her short story 'The Mermaid's Purse' published in the Fossil Lake anthology Sharkasaurus. Available on Amazon https://www.amazon.co.uk/-/e/B01MRXV1WR

Her debut novel 'The Golden Virginian', a tale of weed, water, magic and murder, is coming soon...

BETTY BREEN

Betty Breen is still a newbie to the world of writing, but it's in her blood and she loves doing it. This is the second anthology she has appeared in and hopes to continue this trend. A full time mummy and part time university student she spends as much time as possible exercising her creative muscles. Find her on twitter @just_betty5 or you can check out her blog runningonanxietyblog@wordpress.com where she tackles issues surrounding mental health and exercise.

PETER GERMANY

Peter Germany is a writer of Science Fiction and Horror from Gravesend in Kent who intends to finish a novel, one day.

He is influenced by writers like Dan Abnett, Scott Sigler, CL Raven and Joe Haldeman.

When not pretending to be normal at a day job, he is writing or dealing with a supreme being (a cat), an energetic puppy, and trying to wrangle a small flock of chickens. He also spends an unhealthy amount of time watching good and bad TV and movies.

You can find him at his blog: petergermany.com

LEX H JONES

Lex H Jones is a British cross genre author, horror fan and rock music enthusiast who lives in Sheffield, North England.

He has written articles for websites the Gingernuts of Horror and the Horrifically Horrifying Horror Blog on various subjects covering books, films, videogames and music. Lex's first published novel is titled "Nick and Abe", and he also has several short horror stories published in anthologies. When not working on his own writing Lex also contributes to the proofing and editing process for other authors. His official Facebook page is: www.facebook.com/LexHJones

Amazon author page:

https://www.amazon.co.uk/Lex-H-Jones/e/B008HSH9BA

Twitter: @LexHJones

CHRISTOPHER LAW

Christopher Law is the author of Chaos Tales, Chaos Tales II: Hell TV and the soon to be released Chaos Tales III: Infodump, plus a gaggle of other shorts and a clutch of novels he will get published. You can find him on Facebook as Christopher Law Horror Writer and at evilscribbles.wordpress.com. Other than that he's rather dull and middle-aged, still has a great view of the castle apart from the hill in the way and is thinking about getting some kittens.

DANI BROWN

Suitably labelled "The Queen of Filth", extremist author Dani Brown's style of dark and twisted writing and deeply disturbing stories has amassed a worrying sized cult following featuring horrifying tales such as "My Lovely Wife", "Toenails" and the hugely popular "Night of the Penguins". Merging eroticism with horror, torture and other areas that most authors wouldn't dare.

She isn't a one-trick pony. For less intense tales, the haunting "Welcome to New Edge Hill" and up-all-night-on-genetically-modified-coffee "Dark Roast" might be more up your street.

For more information visit her website http://danibrownqueenoffilth.weebly.com/

Or visit her on Facebook www.facebook.com/danibrownbooks

DAVID COURT

David Court is a short story author and novelist, whose works have appeared in over a dozen venues including Tales to Terrify, Strangely Funny, Fears Accomplice and The Voices Within. Whilst primarily a horror writer, he also writes science fiction, poetry and satire.

His writing style has been described as "Darkly cynical" and "Quirky and highly readable" and David can't bring himself to disagree with either of those statements.

Growing up in the UK in the eighties, David's earliest influences were the books of Stephen King and Clive Barker, and the films of John Carpenter and George Romero. The first wave of Video Nasties may also have had a profound effect on his psyche.

As well as writing, David works as a Software Developer and lives in Coventry with his wife, three cats and an ever-growing beard. David's wife once asked him if he'd write about how great she was. David replied that he would, because he specialized in short fiction. Despite that, they are still married.

You can find out more about David at www.davidjcourt.co.uk

MARK CASSELL

Mark Cassell lives in a rural part of the UK where he often dreams of dystopian futures, peculiar creatures, and flitting shadows. Primarily a horror writer, his steampunk, dark fantasy, and SF stories have featured in numerous anthologies and e-zines. His best-selling debut novel The Shadow Fabric is closely followed by the popular short story collection Sinister Stitches and are both only a fraction of an expanding mythos of demons, devices, and deceit. The novella Hell Cat of the Holt further explores the Shadow Fabric mythos with ghosts and black cat legends.

For Mark's FREE stories go to www.markcassell.com or visit the website www.theshadowfabric.co.uk.

G. H. FINN

G. H. Finn is the pen name of someone who keeps his real identity secret to escape the eternal wrath of several of the ever vengeful, trans-paradimensional, eldritchly squamous Elder Gods. And avoid parking fines.

Having written non-fiction for many years, Finn began writing short stories in 2015. He especially enjoys mixing genres (sometimes in a blender, after beating them insensible with a cursed rolling pin) including mystery, horror, steampunk, sword-and-sorcery, dark comedy, fantasy, detective, dieselpunk, weird, supernatural, sword-and-planet, speculative, folkloric, Cthulhu mythos, sci-fi, spy-fi, satire and urban fantasy.

G. H. Finn's links:

Website: http://ghfinn.orkneymagic.com/

Twitter: @GanferHaarFinn

Facebook: https://www.facebook.com/g.h.finn/

SAMANTHA HILL

Sam lives in Windsor in the UK with two teenagers, and actor, a four year old and his imaginary friend Toby. Her favorite things are horror films, The Marx Brothers, Fatty Arbuckle and William Goldman.

Sam has previously had work published by Crystal Lake Publishing and Siren's Call Publications. She is currently working on a project with the author Jasper Bark'

https://twitter.com/BurritoSister.

C. H. BAUM

C. H. Baum lives in Las Vegas, Nevada with two children and a freakishly gorgeous wife. He is a mortgage underwriter during the day, but spends his nights and weekends participating in the 3 R's: writing, reading, or riding his bicycle. If you see him pedaling around Las Vegas, please don't run him over.

ASH HARTWELL

Ash Hartwell was born in Maine, USA sometime during the hippie sixties. He now lives in Northamptonshire, England where he started writing around 2010. He has had around fifty short stories published in anthologies from Stitched Smile Publications, JEA, Static Movement, Horrified Press and Old Style Press to name a few. In 2015 he published his collection Zombies, Vamps and Fiends through JEA and will shortly see his debut novel - Tip of the Iceberg - which will be published by Stitched Smile Publications where he is a VIP author. He is still alive and therefore not yet famous.

https://www.facebook.com/ash.hartwell.31

http://www.ashhartwell.co.uk/

MATTHEW CASH

Matthew Cash, or Matty-Bob Cash as he is known to most, was born and raised in in Suffolk; which is the setting for his debut novel Pinprick. He is compiler and editor of Death By Chocolate, a chocoholic horror anthology, and the 12Days Anthology, and has numerous releases on Kindle and several collections in paperback.

In 2016 he started his own label Burdizzo Books, with the intention of compiling and releasing charity anthologies a few times a year. He is currently working on numerous projects, his second novel FUR will hopefully be launched at the convention.

He has always written stories since he first learnt to write and most, although not all tend to slip into the many layered murky depths of the Horror genre.
His influences ranged from when he first started reading to Present day are, to name but a small select few; Roald Dahl, James Herbert, Clive Barker, Stephen King, Stephen Laws, and more recently he enjoys Adam Nevill, F.R Tallis, Michael Bray, Gary Fry, William Meikle and Iain Rob Wright (who featured Matty-Bob in his famous A-Z of Horror title M is For Matty-Bob, plus Matthew wrote his own version of events which was included as a bonus).

He is a father of two, a husband of one and a zoo keeper of numerous fur babies.

You can find him here:
www.facebook.com/pinprickbymatthewcash

https://www.amazon.co.uk/-/e/B01oMQTWKK

Other Releases By Matthew Cash

Novels
Virgin And The Hunter
Pinprick
Fur [coming soon]

Novellas
Ankle Biters
KrackerJack
Illness
Hell And Sebastian
Waiting For Godfrey
Deadbeard
The Cat Came Back
Krackerjack 2

Short Stories
Why Can't I Be You?
Slugs And Snails And Puppydog Tails
OldTimers
Hunt The C*nt

Anthologies Compiled and Edited By Matthew Cash
Death By Chocolate
12 Days Anthology
The Reverend Burdizzo's Hymn Book (with Em Dehaney)

Anthologies Featuring Matthew Cash
Rejected For Content 3. Vicious Vengeance
JEApers Creepers
Full Moon Slaughter
Down The Rabbit Hole: Tales of Insanity

Collections
The Cash Compendium Volume 1 [coming soon]

Printed in Great Britain
by Amazon